TAKE

T J JOTT

My Boys.

My World.

CHAPTER 1

Mollie and Penny were in the staff toilets, it was 3.30pm on a Friday in May.

"Thank fuck it's Friday!" said Mollie. "It's been a very long week."

Penny was looking at herself in the mirror, deciding whether she would wash her hair before their girl's night out later. Penny laughed at Mollie and agreed,

"Yes, it's been a very long week, I wonder where Marie is?"

The two young women are both 24 years old. They work in an international school in Javea in Spain. Javea is a small coastal town on the Costa Blanca. Mollie and Penny both started work at the school two years earlier. They've become good friends and often had nights out together. They are waiting for Marie who is a teachers classroom assistant. Marie is 45 and is married to Sean. He is a black cab taxi driver back in the UK, together they have two teenage girls, Grace and Hannah.

Tonight, Marie is joining Mollie and Penny on the night out.

Mollie and Penny are studying their faces in the mirrors while waiting for Marie. Penny is a petite natural looking blonde with freckles, long hair and blue eyes, she's not one for wearing much makeup. Unlike Mollie, who likes to spread it on with a trowel. Mollie is pretty, with long dark hair and hazel eyes, she has a curvier figure than Penny. They are chalk and cheese. What with Mollie having false eyelashes, false nails, and tattooed eyebrows, she is the ultimate Essex girl and proud of it.

Penny's parents are both teachers. When Penny was young her parents travelled the world with her and her little brother, home teaching them along the way, whilst giving them both lifetime memories, before settling down in York where both parents took up teaching jobs in a private school. Penny and her brother were fortunate enough to attend the school for their education. Mollie had a very different upbringing. She grew up in a not so nice town in Essex, her Mum worked as a dinner lady at Mollies school, and her dad worked as a gardener for the local Council. Mollie and her sister attended the local council owned schools. Mollies Mums sister, and her husband live in Javea, running a local English Bakery in the town. Every summer, Mollie her sister and her parents would spend 3 weeks in Javea, staying with their Auntie Brenda and Uncle Ant in the under build of their villa.

Mollie looked forward to the holiday every year and would cry when they had to leave for the journey back home. As she got older Mollie started to plan her future and living in Javea was top of her list.

"Why don't you train to be a teacher Mollie," suggested Auntie Brenda one summer "all the teachers at The Elizabeth School here in Javea are English, apart from the Spanish teachers of course."

"Are they?" asked Mollie.

"Yes, I know most of them, they all pop into the bakery." replied Auntie Brenda.

"I'm going to be a teacher," decided Mollie "then I can move here and live in your under build, and I can work at The Elizabeth School." And that is what she did. She passed her GCSE exams, then her A levels and went on to Essex University and she became a primary school teacher. She worked for a few years in the UK until a post at The Elizabeth College became vacant.

Marie came rushing into the toilets looking hot and sweaty,

"I'm not sure I've got the energy to go out later I feel totally cream crackered and my feet are bloody killing me." she said. Mollie and Penny laughed at Marie. Mollie put her arm around her,

"You'll be ok Marie, go home put your feet up and meet us at Wozzies apartment at 8pm, the table is booked for 9pm so we can walk to the Arenal and have a pre-dinner cocktail or two."

Wozzie is Mr Rick Wozniak the school's headmaster, he is also their boss. Rick and Mollie are having a bit of a fling and she asked him if they could stay in his holiday apartment for the night. It's where she meets him in secret. Both Marie and Penny know about the affair, and they think Mollie is mad as she has a very fit Russian boyfriend named Artiom. He is 30 years old and a personal trainer with a lovely personality and clearly loves Mollie. Whereas Rick is a not so good looking 45-year-old, not so fit married father of three boys.

"Well, I might as well stay at the apartment with you two as my girls are both staying at friend's houses tonight, no point staying in on my own." said Marie.

"When's Sean back?" Penny asked Marie.

"He flies in on Tuesday. He is here for two weeks this time, so I've got some jobs lined up for him. The garden needs weeding and the car needs washing." replied Marie.

"Poor old Sean he will be going back to the UK for a rest." laughed Mollie. The three of them left the staff toilets and headed out to the school car park on their way passing by the school office, the schools secretary Laura Wozniak is the wife of the headmaster. She was tidying up the office.

"Bye Laura, see you on Monday." called out Penny. Laura looked up and saw Mollie, Penny and Marie.

"Bye, see you on Monday have a good weekend." replied Laura. She watched them head out of the door. She didn't like Mollie very much. She didn't like the way Mollie flirted with Rick in the school or the way she would see Mollie whispering to him in the playground like a 5-year-old. She certainly didn't trust Rick she was sure he had had affairs in the past. He always denies everything like a squirming little rat, but she was sure he was screwing Mollie the little slut. Only a week ago she had a call from Dolphins, the laundrette in Javea, telling her their holiday apartment laundry was ready for collection. But she didn't know the laundry had been dropped in, apparently Rick had dropped it in which was strange because they hadn't had anyone booked into the apartment. So, alarm bells were ringing in Laura's ears. She went straight down to the laundrette and collected the washing, there was a little envelope sitting on top of the freshly laundered sheets. Laura opened it and felt sick and angry when she saw what was inside. It was a large gold hoop earring. It appears it was found amongst the sheets. It wasn't Laura's she only wore studs. But a week earlier Mollie was hunting high and low all around the school for a gold hoop earring she had lost. Laura didn't believe in coincidences. She's kept the earring in her office drawer, looking at it inside the envelope every day since and disliking Mollie more and more.

Mollie, Marie and Penny say their goodbyes and head off home. Mollie drove to her under build apartment in nearby Tossalet. Marie drove home to her villa on the Montgo Mountain

and Penny went home to her little terraced town house in Javea old town. All of them were looking forward to getting dressed up and letting their hair down later.

CHAPTER 2

The three-woman met up at Mr Wozniak's holiday apartment. They had all driven there separately and left their cars parked close by each other. They left their overnight bags in the bedrooms ready for later and walked to the Arenal. They arrived at the Cava Cocktail Bar at 8-15 pm. It was getting busy. They went in and made their way to the bar.

"Ok, ladies what are you drinking?" asked Mollie.

"Oooo I've been fancying a Mojito all day." replied Penny.

"I'll have one of those too." said Marie.

"What are you having Mollie?" asked Penny.

"I've been fancying Sex on The Beach all day." laughed Mollie.

"Yes, but what do you want to drink?" replied Marie laughing. The young bar man came over to take their drink order and Mollie started to flirt with him outrageously.

"You're a bloody nightmare Mollie." said Penny "He might know Artiom."

"Artiom knows what I'm like, he knows I don't mean it, I'm just having a laugh," said Mollie.

"But I thought you really liked Artiom?" said Marie.

"I do really like Artiom. But I quite fancy this barman too." laughed Mollie still fluttering her false eyelashes at the young bar man. He was enjoying the attention he was getting from Mollie. She had decided to wear a noticeably short, and unbelievably tight white strapless dress. It could have been just a long top in Marie's eyes. But Mollie was wearing it as a dress. Her white and gold sparkly stiletto shoes were extremely high and had diamonds embellished on them. She could just about walk in them. She was also wearing her new gold hoop earrings. She was still looking for the one she lost. Marie looked at Mollie she hoped the strapless dress she was wearing would stay up all night. There wasn't too much fabric to it. Penny, on the other hand she thought looked lovely she was wearing a blue floral dress. Not too tight but not too loose it finished just above the knee and was belted at the waist with a white leather belt. She topped the look off with white wedged sandals. She looked fabulous. It is what Marie would like to wear if she was slimmer.

Mollie looked a bit tarty in Marie's opinion. But she can wear what she wants too. Marie herself was dressed for comfort in a lemon coloured long linen tunic top over loose fitting lemon trousers. Not very exciting, but that was Marie. Not very exciting. She teamed her comfortable outfit off with her sensible silver flat sandals.

Penny spotted people getting up from a table. The three women quickly got to it before someone else did and plonked themselves down in the chairs.

"Ahhhh this is so good." sighed Penny, drinking her mojito "I've been dreaming of this all day. "

"I've been dreaming of sex on the beach all week." laughed Mollie. This made the three friends laugh. The alcohol in their cocktails relaxed them and they began singing and dancing in their chairs, along to the live band that had started playing. Soon it was time for another round of drinks.

"I'll go." said Mollie standing up "Same again?" she asked.

"No let's have a goldfish bowl of ADV to share." said Penny excitedly.

"What's in that again?" asked Marie.

"It's orange juice, vodka, cava, gin and sugar." replied Penny.

"Go on Marie let's share the Agua de Valencia." said Mollie.

"Oh, go on then." laughed Marie.

Mollie slowly wiggled up to the bar. She took her time making sure everyone, especially the men noticed her, and they did. Once she was there, she then had to wiggle her way through a group of men that were standing drinking at the bar. Mollie recognised a couple of their faces they were probably the dads of children at the school. There weren't any women with then so it must be a boy only night out thought Mollie.

"Ooooh, Excuse me please." said Mollie as she squeezed her way in between them.

"Hello sweetheart." replied one of the men.

"Hello to you too." said Mollie, fluttering her false eyelashes and pouting her pumped up lips.

"What's your name beautiful?" asked the same man. He was about 40 with the brightest white teeth money could buy him in Javea. and very tanned skin resembling a well-worn brown leather shoe. He was wearing an expensive and smart, well ironed Ralph Lauren shirt, probably chosen and ironed by his wife. And the obligatory oversized and very expensive designer watch. He was also wearing a large quantity of Chanel cologne. Mollie looked at him and replied as sexily as she could.

"Mollie, what's your name?"

"Hi Mollie, I'm Neil. Are you here on your own?" replied Neil drooling.

"No, I'm on a girl's night out." said Mollie. The same young bar man from earlier came over to take Mollies order. She ordered the ADV and flirted again with the bar man. He told her he would bring the ADV over to the table. Mollie rubbed herself hard against Neil as she was leaving the bar area and wiggled her way back to Marie and Penny.

"Who was that you were talking to?" Marie asked Mollie.

"No idea. He said his name is Neil. I don't know him, but I do recognise a few of the others they are probably dads at the school gate." replied Mollie.

"What are you like?" laughed Penny. The young bar man brought the large glass bowl over to the girl's table. It was full of ADV and ice and had three long straws poking out of it. The bar man placed the bowl carefully in the centre of the table. "Enjoy." said the bar man.

"Oh, we will." laughed Mollie and pinched the bar man's bum. The young man blushed.

"Leave him alone Mollie." Laughed Marie "He is only about twelve."

"He loves it." said Mollie "And I'm sure he's older than twelve."

The three friends started drinking the cocktail from their straws

"It is very sweet." said Marie making a face.

"That will be the kilo of sugar in it." laughed Mollie.

"I like it." smiled Penny licking her lips.

"I'm not sure how much I'll be able to drink." said Marie.

"Don't worry Marie, we won't waste it." laughed Mollie.

They finished the cocktail without too much bother. Marie managed to drink her share after all.

 "Right, come on then girlies let's make our way to the Mexican for dinner." said Marie "I'm feeling peckish now. "

"Peckish, I'm bloody Hank Marvin." joked Mollie. Penny and Marie laughed at Mollie.

 "I think I need to eat to mop up all that alcohol." laughed Penny. They left the table and made their way towards the exit. It was busy now and they had to weave and squeeze their way through the crowded bar. Marie saw there were groups of young girls wearing dresses like Mollies with equally high killer heels. All of them looking tipsy. Trying to dance while drinking cocktails through straws. Marie recognised a couple of the girls; they were in Hannah's year group at school. She quickly scanned the group looking for Hannah. She wasn't there, she didn't think she would be. Hannah was a good girl. Marie wondered if the girl's parents knew they were here. Maybe they had dropped them off, she thought to herself. As they passed the group of men Mollie had to squeeze through earlier, Mollie saw that Neil had his arm around a teenage girl. His hand was on her bottom. Pervert thought Mollie. He is old enough to be her dad. They passed a few more people they all recognised, they all exchanged exaggerated waves, and blew kisses to them. Finally, they reached the exit and stepped outside. They half walked half danced the short distance to the Mexican restaurant. The air was warm, and the sea was whispering gently as the waves slowly caressed the golden sand. The sky was dark and clear and the strings of lights hanging outside the restaurants and bars were twinkling in the gentle breeze.

"We are so lucky to live here, it's our little Paradise." said Penny happily.

"Ahhh, I love living here." agreed Marie "Especially this time of year before all the bloody holiday makers arrive.'"

"Bloody holiday makers." said Mollie "They spoil it once they're here. You can't park the bloody car. You have to queue up in the supermarket. Queue for a bloody table in a restaurant. All the bloody shops run out of bloody ice. I mean it's frozen cubes of water for god's sake."

"I make my own ice." said Marie "Like you said it's only frozen bloody water."

"I can't be arsed to make them myself." said Mollie "Bad experience."

"Why what happened?" asked Penny.

"Well, I made some vodka ice cubes. Just vodka. They were in my freezer ready to go into my coke at the weekend. But Auntie Brenda had some of her friends' round for lunch and had forgotten to buy any ice for the sangria she had made. So, she borrowed my vodka ice cubes from my freezer while I was at work. She put all of them in to 2 jugs of sangria. A whole bottle of vodka. It was carnage. Her and her friends were slaughtered by 2-30 in the afternoon." laughed Mollie. Penny and Marie both thought Mollies story was hilarious." So now I buy ice cubes." laughed Mollie.

When they arrived at the Mexican Restaurant the large glass sliding doors were open. It looked busy inside and there were people sitting at the outside tables. There was music drifting out of the doors, but it wasn't as loud as the Cava Bar. A waitress met them at the entrance.

"Hola chichas." she said smiling.

"Hola. We have a table booked." replied Mollie.

"A table for 3?" asked the waitress.

"Yes." replied Mollie.

"Ok, follow me." replied the waitress and she went into the restaurant, they followed her through the busy restaurant until she stopped at a table set for 3 with a reservation sign on it.

"Here you are." said the waitress and she waited until they sat down before handing them the menus and taking their drink order.

"What can I get you to drink?" she asked them.

"Shall we share a bottle of white wine?" asked Mollie.

"Sounds like a good idea." replied Penny.

"Can we order a bottle of water as well?" asked Marie.

"Si, con gas?" asked the waitress.

"No, sin gas please." replied Marie.

"And a bottle of the house white wine please." said Mollie.

"Okay, Muchas Gracias." said the waitress.

"Wow, it's busy in here." said Penny.

"Friday night." replied Mollie.

"Who's that you're looking at Marie?" asked Penny, she had noticed that

Marie was looking at someone over at another table.

"It's one of my neighbours." whispered Marie.

"Why are you whispering?" laughed Mollie.

"I don't want them to see me." replied Marie.

"I don't think whispering will make you invisible." laughed Mollie.

"They are the ones that were letting their dogs' shit outside our house.

So, Sean put a sign outside saying, "PLEASE PICK UP YOUR DOG SHIT" on

our gate." whispered Marie.

"Did it work?" asked Penny.

"Yes, they let the dogs' shit outside the house the other side now." said Marie. Both Penny and Mollie shook their heads.

"That's bad." said Mollie. Just then the waitress came back with their bottle of white wine and the water and three wine glasses. She poured the wine in to the wine glasses, there was already glasses on the table for the water.

"Okay, are you ready to order?" asked the waitress. The girls had barely looked at the menu, but they knew what they wanted.

"Can I have the steak fajitas please?" asked Mollie.

"Yes." replied the waitress, she looked at Penny.

"I'd like the Prawn fajitas please." said Penny.

"And for you? "The waitress asked Marie.

"Can I order the chicken fajitas please?" replied Marie.

"Okay, fajitas all round." laughed the waitress.

"Yes." replied the girls laughing. The waitress rushed away with their food order.

"So, Mollie are you still you know what with Mr Wozniak then?" said Marie.

"Well, I am but it's getting boring, I thought I'd get the apartment for tonight then I'm going to finish it with him." replied Mollie.

"I'm glad to hear that Mollie. Artiom is so nice." said Penny.

"Well, it's only been a bit of fun with Rick, but the fun has died out now, it's just quick meet at the apartment, take your clothes off, quick shag, get dressed again and creep out without anyone seeing us." said Mollie "I've said to Rick, everyone that lives in the apartments have probably seen us, they will all know what we're doing."

"Have you ever been tempted to you know what at the school?" asked Marie.

"We did it in his office a couple of months ago, didn't I tell you?" replied Mollie.

"You told me." said Penny shaking her head.

"What happened?" asked Marie. Moving closer to Mollie with her eyes wide.

"We were in his office at school and things got a bit frisky, so he locked the door, then we were shagging on his desk when there was a knock on the door." said Mollie

"No! Who was it?" asked Marie with her hands over her face.

"It was Laura." replied Mollie.

"How do you know?" asked Marie.

"Because we stopped shagging. I sat back in the chair opposite his desk. He unlocked the door and about 30 seconds later she knocked again. Rick called out "come in" and Laura walked in." replied Mollie.

"What did she say? Did she suspect anything?" asked Marie.

"Definitely, she asked why the door was locked, Rick told her it wasn't, but she gave me a dirty look, threw some paperwork on his desk and walked out, she knew we was up to something in there." said Mollie.

"Oh my god, I feel sorry for Laura, you need to stop seeing him." said Marie If Sean ever cheated on me, I'd cut off his balls and post them to the bitch."

"I will." replied Mollie. The waitress came back with their plates and cutlery and a waiter followed her with the fajitas. He put the food down on the table.

"Is there anything else you need?" he asked.

"Your phone number?" replied Mollie. the waiter laughed and walked away.

"You are a bloody nightmare, Mollie." laughed Penny.

"He was nice looking, wasn't he?" said Mollie.

"Yes, but 5 minutes ago you said you were going to stop all this carrying on behind Artioms back." said Marie.

"I said I'm going to finish it with Rick. But yes, your right I'm lucky to have Artiom." said Mollie.

"Although if I was 10 years younger, I'd definitely be getting the waiters phone number." laughed Marie. Penny and Mollie laughed at this, and Mollie called the waiter over and ordered a second bottle of wine. They all enjoyed their chosen fajitas and drunk the second bottle of wine.

"That was lovely." said Marie.

"The food is always good here, it's definitely my favourite restaurant." said Mollie.

"Mine too, but I do feel like a pig now." agreed Penny.

"Its Fat Boy Friday so we can eat what we want." laughed Mollie.

"Water?" offered Marie, filling up her own glass and then filling both Mollies and Penny's, without waiting for them to answer. They all drank some water hoping it would dilute the amount of wine they'd drunk. The waitress came back and started to clear their plates.

"Postre, coffee?" she asked them.

"No thank you." they all replied.

"Maybe in 10 minutes." added Mollie. The waitress cleared the table, and the three women finished the water then ordered some coffees, after they'd drunk the coffees, they paid the bill and visited the toilets they made their way to the exit. It was busy outside.

"What's the time?" asked Mollie.

"Nearly 11 o'clock." replied Penny.

"Time for one more drink back in the Cava Bar then." said Mollie.

"Sounds good." replied Penny.

"Why not." agreed Marie.

The three women walked back to the Cava Bar laughing and joking. There were quite a few people about, some on their way home and some just arriving. The Arenal is always a busy place in the summer. With families, youngsters and retired people. Tonight, there was a mixture of everyone including skateboarders and skaters showing off their skill and tricks to anyone watching.

Marie noticed the groups of teenagers both girls and boys, drinking alcohol from bottles and cans and smoking weed, she looked for her girls faces, she couldn't see them.

When they reached the Cava Bar it was standing room only. The band sounded louder and the noise of everyone shouting over them was deafening, they managed to squeeze up to the bar. Mollie waved at the

young waiter from earlier on, he came over to serve them. A gin and tonic

for Marie, and Prosecco for both Mollie and Penny. They moved away

from the bar and stood swaying to the music, there was a few more

groups of people in the bar that they knew, and they all waved at each

other. Once they'd finished their drinks they decided to walk back to the

apartment.

"I've got a bottle of Prosecco in the fridge." said Mollie.

"Ooooo nice." replied Penny.

"Maybe a cup of tea for me." said Marie who was feeling very drunk. The

other two laughed at her. They made their way through the packed bar.

Standing outside with two of his friends was Artiom. All three men were

gym buddies at Rocky's Gym in Javea, and they looked it. They were

wearing tight fitting t shirts and skinny jeans. They were a good-looking

trio. Mollie saw Artiom waving at her, so she wiggled over to him.

"Hi Mollie." said Artiom as he bent down to kiss her Mollie kissed him

back and put her arms around his neck.

"Hi Artiom, was you inside at all? It's heaving in there." replied Mollie.

"Only to the bar, decided to stand out here far too busy inside." said

Aritom.

"We are on our home now don't stay out too late. Remember we're going shopping and lunch tomorrow." said Mollie to Artiom kissing him again.

"Get a room you two." laughed Penny.

"Ahhh, I think it's really sweet." said Marie.

"See you tomorrow." said Artiom to Mollie "Do you want me to walk you to your boss's apartment?" he asked Mollie.

"No, we will be ok it's only up the road, see you tomorrow. I'll message you in the morning. Love you." said Mollie then she waved at Artioms 2 friends "Bye you two, make sure my handsome boyfriend behaves himself." Artioms friends both laugh and wave goodbye to Mollie, Penny and Marie.

CHAPTER 3

The three tipsy women hold on to each other as they walk away from the Arenal towards the apartment. Most of the restaurants were closing. Some bars were still open, and groups of people were leaving the bars to go to the night club. There were people queuing at the taxi rank.

"It's handy having the keys to Ricks apartment, better than waiting for a taxi." said Mollie.

"No, you can give him his keys back Mollie, I'll drive us home in future." said Marie. They felt safe walking the short distance to the apartment. The further away from the beach they walked the quieter it became. Mollie stopped,

"Ok, stop, no one can see me I've got to change my shoes." she opened her bag up and took a folded-up pair of ballet slippers out. "These are the best Secret Santa gift I've ever received, thanks Marie." said Mollie. She took her killer heels off and put the ballet slippers on. The stilettos wouldn't fit in to her bag, so she hung them on her arm.

"How do you know it was me that bought you them?" asked Marie.

"You told me." replied Mollie "You had had a few drinks."

"I'm impressed you've kept those heels on all night." said Penny.

"So am I.," laughed Mollie.

They carried on walking along the road towards the apartment, there wasn't any other people about. A car drove passed them and beeped its horn, they all laughed, and Mollie stuck two fingers up. Less than a minute later another car slowly passed them, then it stopped just in front of them" Who's that?" asked Penny not recognising the car herself.

"No idea." replied Mollie. Marie looked behind them to see if there was another car or any people about, there wasn't anyone.

"Just ignore them." said Mollie "Come on." The 3 woman picked up their walking speed with the intent of quickly passing the strange car. But just as they got close to it the back door swung open. A very large man in his 40s jumped out.

"Get into the car." He shouted at Penny in a Russian accent.

"NO!" shouted Penny. The women were all very frightened. The big man grabbed Penny and forced her into car. Mollie started to scream at him to let Penny go and was hitting him with her high heeled shoes. Marie was frozen in fear, she looked all around but there was no one about. She was trying to open her bag to get her phone out, but she was shaking so much she couldn't undo the zip. Penny was trying to get back out of the car, but the man was very strong and then he pulled Mollie into the car and shut

the door. Marie managed to undo the zip of her bag and got her phone

out. She couldn't remember the police emergency number. She could see

both Penny and Mollie fighting with the man in the back of the car, she

decided to press the redial button for help. She knew who the last person

she had spoken to was she just hoped they would answer the call. Then

just as she pressed the re dial button the passenger door swung open, and

another big man stepped out of the car. He took a step towards Marie

and lifted his arm up, Marie saw the gleaming metal of a gun in the big

man's hand. She couldn't believe what was happening. Her two friends

had been abducted and now a gun was being pointed at her. She felt

frozen with fear. She was so scared, the most she has ever been in her

life. The faces of her daughters, her husband and her parents were in her

eyes. She heard the gun shot then fell to the floor instantly. Mollie and

Penny had just watched their friend be shot in the head at point blank

range. They both screamed, they couldn't believe what they had just

witnessed. The gun man climbed back into the car and the car sped off

leaving Marie lying on the pavement.

Penny and Mollie sat sobbing silently in shock in the back of the car, both

fearing for their own lives and both thinking Marie must be dead. The three men in the car with Mollie and Penny didn't speak for ten minutes.

Then the driver asked the gun man for directions. Mollie knew they was

speaking in Russian, and she understood what they were saying. Aritom

had been teaching her to speak Russian from the day they met. She knew

they were driving through Pedreguer from the road signs they had passed

and soon after leaving the town they turned down a narrow bumpy road.

It was very dark, but Mollie could hear the car driving over weeds and

rubble. The car stopped in front of a derelict house. The girls could see the

house was covered in graffiti and it looked half built without any windows

or doors. Mollie and Penny felt scared. What was going to happen to

them now?

CHAPTER 4

Sean was asleep when his mobile phone rang and felt about on the bedside table for it. He squinted his eyes to see who the caller was before answering,

"Hello, Marie?" he said into the phone, but what he heard next was screaming, a gunshot and what sounded like someone falling to the floor. Then a car door slamming and the car speeding away.

"Marie! Marie!" Sean was shouting Marie's name into the phone. He could hear someone moaning, was that Marie? He couldn't tell. He turned to look at the woman in bed with him.

"What's happened?" she asked propping herself up on the pillows.

"I don't know Tracey, It's Marie's phone but she's not there. I heard screaming and a gunshot, then a car driving away but I can hear someone moaning." replied Sean.

"Oh my God." said Tracey "Have you spoken to her today? Was she going out tonight? "

"Yes, I spoke to her earlier. She was going out with a couple of friends from work. I think I can hear people talking in the distance." said Sean

"Hello, hello can anyone hear me? Hello." he called out again down the phone, he could hear them talking.

"What the fuck has happened? call an ambulance Pete." He heard a lady's voice.

"Is she drunk?" replied a man's voice.

"I think she's been shot. I can see the hole in her fucking head." replied the woman.

"Fucking hell, I'm calling the police." replied the man. He called the police to say a woman was lying on the path with what looks like a gunshot wound to her head.

"There's so much blood, she will be lucky to survive this. Is that a phone?" The woman picked up Marie's phone from the pavement she could see it was on a call.

"Hello?" said the woman into the phone "Hello can you hear me?" replied Sean.

"Hello, yes I can hear you." answered the woman.

"Who are you? this is my wife's phone?" said Sean.

"My name is Claire. There's a woman injured on the pavement my husband has called the police." replied Claire.

"I think it's my wife." said Sean. Claire picked up Marie's bag.

"There's a bag here do you want me to look in it for you?" asked Claire.

"Yes, my wife's name is Marie Cole." said Sean. Claire opened Marie's bag and looked in Marie's purse at her driving license she could see the woman lying bleeding and injured on the pavement was Marie.

"I'm really sorry but yes this looks like it's your wife, she matches the photo on the driving license, I can hear sirens coming now stay on the phone." said Claire.

"Oh my god, what's happened?" said Sean in shock, "It's Marie, she's been shot I think, I can hear a siren, there's a couple there with her." Sean relayed it all to Tracey. There was a little cry from a cot next to their bed. Tracey leant over and picked up baby Ronnie. "You need to change your flight Sean, for today." said Tracey as she comforted baby Ronnie.

"Yes." replied Sean while he was trying to listen to what the couple who had found Marie were saying to the police. They had just found her. She's been shot in the head. There's a hole in head. There's so much blood. They didn't know if she was dead. Her husband is on the phone.

"Hello, who are you?" A man's voice came on to Sean's phone.

"I'm Sean Cole. I think it's my wife Marie who's been shot. I'm in the UK, she must have called me, is she ok?" asked Sean.

"I'm Officer Juan Garcia. I will keep you informed on your wife's condition we are waiting for the ambulance to arrive. You will need to get to Spain I think." replied Officer Garcia then the phone went dead. Sean got out of bed.

 "What's happening?" said Tracey.

"The police are there, and the ambulance has just arrived. I was talking to a police officer but then the line went dead. I don't know what's happening." replied Sean.

"Phone back." urged Tracey. Sean tried to call back, but Marie's phone was switched off.

"It's switched off. I need to get to Spain today." said Sean.

"Ok, go and see if you can book on the next flight out." said Tracey. "I'll settle Ronnie back down and pack your bag for you." Sean got dressed and went down to the kitchen he opened his laptop and started to look for the next available flight to Spain. He looked at the time it was 12-15 am, he rubbed his eyes, what has just happened? It felt like he was awake in a nightmare. He had gone to bed feeling happy, he had finished work early for a change and had helped Tracey to bath baby Ronnie before feeding him a bottle of milk and reading him a story while Tracey was cooking their evening meal. Baby Ronnie was sound asleep by the time dinner was ready. They had dinner tidied up and then settled down on the sofa to watch tv. Just like a married couple, only they weren't a married couple, well not married to each other, Sean was married to Marie, he had met Tracey 18 months ago, and had been living a double life ever since. Tracey knew that Sean was married with two teenage daughters. She was happy to share Sean with his other family for now. Hoping that one day he would divorce Marie and marry her. Sean met Tracey after picking her up in his taxi from Gatwick Airport. She was just a fare, a pickup in his taxi. Sean always makes conversation with his passengers. Some like to talk some prefer not to. He soon knows which passengers want a conversation. Tracey was one of those. She had just flown in from Javea where she had been living and working as an estate agent for a year, they didn't know each other but shared the knowledge of Javeas restaurants and bars etc. Tracey's mum was in the UK and without any warning suffered a stroke and was taken into hospital for tests. Tracey decided to fly back to visit her mum for a couple of weeks until she thought her mum would be back home. But unfortunately, her mum suffered a further 2 strokes and has sadly died Tracey was devastated. Her mum was only 55, it was only Tracey and her mum, Tracey's dad had died in a car accident when Tracey was a young child. She didn't have any real memories of him only vague images in her mind that had probably come from photo albums. Tracey was now an orphan at 33 years old. Sean was picking Tracey up each day from her mum's house and dropping her at the hospital so she could visit her mum then collecting Tracey again to drop her back home. It was on day 8 that Tracey's mum died, Sean was waiting outside the hospital for Tracey, he could see she was very upset when she got into the taxi.

"What's happened?" asked Sean.

"My Mums died." replied Tracey, sobbing into a tissue.

"Oh no, I'm so sorry Tracey, what happened?" asked Sean.

"She had a massive stroke she was only 55. I wished I'd come back earlier, I didn't realise she was so ill." Cried Tracey.

"Your mum didn't know herself, she wouldn't want you thinking like this Tracey." said Sean. They pulled up outside Tracey mum's house.

"Do you want me to come in with you and put the kettle on?" asked Sean.

"Yes please." replied Tracey. They went into Tracey's mum's house. Which as from today was Tracey house.

"I don't know what I'm supposed to do now." said Tracey sitting down at the kitchen table. Sean filled the kettle up and switched it on.

"What did the hospital say.?" asked Sean.

"I'm not sure really, they said something about finding an undertaker to use and that the doctor would have to sign the death certificate. I wasn't really listening." replied Tracey. She began crying again. Sean went to Tracey and put his arms around her.

"You're in shock. You weren't expecting your mum to go so suddenly. I'll phone the hospital for you and find out what you need to do." he said.

"Thank you, Sean, you've been such a good help to me already. I feel as though I've known you for a long time." said Tracey.

"I feel the same about you Tracey, I think about you all the time." Sean kissed Tracey on the cheek. Tracey looked into Sean's eyes and felt something she'd never experienced before. She kissed him on the lip and Sean returned the kiss.

"Kettles boiled." said Sean.

Sean helped Tracey arrange her mum's funeral and then the day after the funeral he moved into Tracey's home. It wasn't long before Tracey fell pregnant with baby Ronnie. Tracey and Sean were happy with the news and Sean loves Ronnie equally to his two daughters in Spain. The hardest part has been keeping Ronnie a secret from the girls he knows that they would love their baby brother. He felt torn between Marie and the girls whom he loved so much and Tracey and Ronnie. He knew one day he would have to tell Marie about Tracey and Ronnie. And one day he would have to choose between Marie and Tracey. But he loved them both, in different ways. He loves Marie but not in the same way as when they were young, he loves her now like a friend a best friend. He doesn't find Marie unattractive, but he doesn't feel anything sexual anymore when he looks at her. She prefers to wear comfortable loose clothes and flat sensible shoes, she doesn't bother wearing make-up anymore and her hair is always tied back from her face. She said it is her natural look, and she didn't feel like she needed to dress up anymore, unless it was a special occasion and then Marie would emerge from the bedroom looking like a different woman. On these occasions Sean would feel a sexual attraction to Marie and after lots of persuading from Sean they would have sex. But it was getting less and less. Sean didn't blame Marie for this, it was just the way their marriage was going. So, when he met Tracey who looks like a younger slimmer version of Marie, he couldn't help feeling sexually attracted to her and he was pleased the feeling was mutual. Tracey came into the kitchen and put the kettle on to boil.

"Have you found a flight?" she asked.

"I can actually change the flight I've already got Booked for Wednesday, to one at 6 am this morning." Replied Sean.

"That's good, tea coffee?" said Tracey.

"Coffee please. I don't know whether to contact the girls. They are staying at their friends' houses tonight." said Sean.

"I think once they know something is wrong, they will be messaging you. Hopefully, they are both asleep and unaware of what's happened to Marie, it's 2 am in the morning in Spain." replied Tracy.

"Yes, I think you're right. I wonder what happened ? Why would someone shoot Marie? Things like this just don't happen in real life, do they? I wonder why she was on her own. Where were her friends? None of it makes any sense." said Sean. Tracey gave him his mug of coffee.

"What time will you have to leave for the airport?" asked Tracey.

"About 3-30 am. I'll leave my Taxi in the airport car park." replied Sean.

"I hope Marie will be alright Sean. I really do. And the girls, they will need you. Take as long as you need over there. Me and Ronnie will be here waiting for you." said Tracey.

"If Marie survives this, I am going to tell her about us, about you and Ronnie." said Sean.

"Wait and see what happens Sean. She will need you there." replied Tracey.

"I love you, Tracey." said Sean.

"I love you too. We both do. Me and baby Ronnie." replied Tracey.

CHAPTER 5

The ambulance arrived 20 minutes after Marie was shot. It stopped next

to where she lay lifeless in a large puddle of blood. There was now a small

crowd of people watching the drama from the opposite side of the road

and people were looking out of their windows and leaning over their

balconies in the apartments around Marie. The ambulance crew rushed to

help Marie, Officer Garcia filled them in on what he knew. His colleague

Officer Alvaro Gomez was talking to the couple that found Marie and with

the crowd opposite trying to shed some light on what happened to Marie.

Unfortunately, no one saw the shooting, and no one saw the girls being

abducted. No one saw anything. People had heard the screaming and the

gun shot and the car speeding away, but by time they got to their

windows and balconies the crime had already taken place. The ambulance

crew assessed Marie's head wound.

"Wow. This is a bullet in the head 100%. She's been lucky. It looks like the

bullet is lodged in her skull. We need to get her to hospital quickly. I think

most of this blood isn't from her bullet wound but from the large open cut on her head. Probably caused when she fell down after being shot." The ambulance crew got Marie on to stretcher and into the ambulance. The ambulance didn't go anywhere for 10 minutes while the crew was stabilising Marie.

Officer Garcia taped off the crime scene ready for the forensic team. There was a lot of different bloody footsteps and smears all around where Marie had been laying, Officer Garcia didn't hold out a lot of hope for any remaining evidence. He waited there with Officer Gomez until the forensic team had finished their job. Then they took away the police tape and asked a neighbour for a bucket of water to wash away the blood at the crime scene. The two officers went back to the police station with Marie's bag and phone.

At the hospital the surgeons were waiting for Marie's arrival. They rushed her through to the operating theatre. Once the antitheists had Marie under an anaesthetic, the doctors shaved her head so they could see what they were dealing with. There was a bullet lodged into Marie's head. She was lucky, if it had entered her brain, she would be dead. The surgeon removed the bullet and asked one of the nurses to bag it up, ready to give to the police for evidence. Once he had stitched up the bullet hole, he started to stick up the gash on Marie's head, most likely caused by her falling and hitting her head on the pavement. It was a deep wound, and it needed a lot of stitches. Once this was finished Marie's head was bandaged up and she was moved into the intensive care ward.

CHAPTER 6

Mollie and Penny were pulled from the back of the car and pushed into

the run-down villa. There was graffiti on the walls inside the house and

piles of rubbish in the corners with lots of empty beer cans, and plastic

drink bottles strewn everywhere.

 "Bloody kids have been here again." said Sergei the gunman "Give me

your bags." he said to the girls, they both gave him their bags He looked

in the bags to check their phones were inside.

"Take them down below." he said to Vlad the driver of the car. Vlad

pushed the two girls towards some stairs. Mollie and Penny walked down

the stairs. It was dark and smelly and there was some rubbish on the

stairs. At the bottom there was a metal door. It was covered in graffiti and

had large bolts and a padlock on it. Vlad unlocked the padlock and opened

the door, he switched on a light and pushed the girls inside. The girls

squinted and covered their eyes, the light was very bright. When their

eyes had adjusted to the bright light, they were surprised at what they

could see. They were in a room, the walls and ceiling were painted bright white, and the floor was a very glossy dark grey marble. It was very clean, and it didn't smell like the upstairs of the house, there was two doors opposite each other in the room, Sergio pushed the girls towards one door, he opened it and pushed the girls in to it, inside was a bedroom, it had a double bed, made up with clean looking bedding. Penny started to cry.

 "Get some sleep. You are safe here for tonight." said Sergio and he left the room. The girls could hear him locking it on the outside.

"Oh my god, why are we here?" said Mollie.

"Do you think we are going to be raped?" cried Penny.

"He said we're safe for tonight." replied Mollie.

"Do you think Marie has been found yet? "cried Penny.

"Yes, I would have thought so. I can't believe that bastard shot her." said Mollie

"Why did he shoot her? "cried Penny.

"Because she could describe them to the police, if she wasn't with us, she would still be alive." said Mollie sadly. The girls could see a en suite bathroom, they walked over to it and had a look inside, it was clean, and it had towels, soap and toilet roll. They went back into the bedroom, there was some bottles of water on the floor.

"Well, they don't want us to dehydrate." said Mollie.

"I need to use the toilet." said Penny. she had stopped crying.

Mollie sat on the bed. She was trying not to think of what might happen to them, tonight or tomorrow. She knew it wasn't going to be enjoyable, she also realised that if they could shoot Marie like that in the street, then the chances were they could be shot too. Penny finished in the toilet and sat next to Mollie on the bed, Mollie put her arm around Penny.

"Look Penny, we've got to try to stay alive. Whatever happens to us, we can get through it. We need to stay alive so we can tell the police who shot Marie." said Mollie. The mention of Marie's name set Penny off crying again.

"I'm not sure I'm as brave as you are Mollie, "cried Penny.

"I'm not brave Penny. I'm really scared. But I'm going to try to stay alive. I can take whatever is going to happen to me and so can you." replied Mollie.

"Oh my god, I feel so sick, what do you think he meant about were safe tonight?" said Penny.

"I don't know. Maybe we're being kept here tonight, and then moved to somewhere else tomorrow." replied Mollie. "If that's the case we might be able to escape or get someone to help us."

"Or they are just going to keep us hostage here." sobbed Penny.

"I don't think so Penny. I think they are going to move us tomorrow." said Mollie.

"Where to?" asked Penny.

"No idea. Probably to Madrid or Barcelona." said Mollie "Or even out of Spain."

"Why would they do that? asked Penny.

"I'm thinking maybe we've been abducted for people trafficking." said Mollie.

"What?" cried Penny "What for?"

"Sex." replied Mollie. "I've read about girls and young woman being taken from the streets late at night and being forced into working in brothels and sex clubs."

"Really?" asked Penny. A bit surprised and shocked at this news. "And do you think that's what is going to happen to us?"

"Maybe. To be honest if that's what is going to happen it will be the better option. Once we get out of here, we need to get someone to help us. We've got to stay strong Penny, come on we're both strong women. We can beat these sick bastards. No matter what happens, we must stick together and get through it together. I'll look after you as much as I can." said Mollie giving Penny a tight hug.

"We will get through this Mollie, as long as we're together we will survive." replied Penny. The girls used the bathroom, washing their faces clean of makeup, dirt and tears, then climbed into the bed. Mollie switched off the lights and they both laid on their backs staring into the darkness.

"Do you think Marie felt anything?" asked Penny.

"I think it was all over so quick, she was dead before she hit the pavement, when we get out of here, I'm going to make sure that evil bastard goes to prison for a long fucking time, "said Mollie,

"Me too, we will do it together Mollie, "replied Penny, the girls laid in the bed staring up at the ceiling in silence. They could hear the men outside their room moving about and talking in Russian.

"They are speaking Russian." said Mollie.

"Do you know what they are saying?" asked Penny.

"Something about St Petersburg. I can't really hear properly." replied Mollie.

"Maybe that's where we are going to end up, in Russia." said Penny.

"Could be." said Mollie. Eventually all the crying they had both done

earlier helped them both to drift into a restless sleep.

The three men were in the other room opposite where Mollie and Penny

were being kept.

"Ok we need to go. We will back in the morning. 7am. Make sure they are

up and ready for the journey ahead." said Sergei to Pavel, the large man

who had grabbed the girls from the street.

"Ok, no worries. I'll see you both in the morning." replied Paval. Seigel and

Vlad, the driver, left the under build of the derelict villa. Paval locked the

steel door on the inside and the 2 men locked it on the outside. Paval

listened outside the door of the bedroom that the girls were in, he

couldn't hear any noise, so he went back into the other room sat on the

black leather sofa. He turned the 60-inch flat screen tv on and set his

alarm for 6.45am. He settled down he knew he would fall asleep in front

of the TV.

CHAPTER 7

Sean checked that he had his passport and boarding pass in his bag. He gave Tracey a long hug, she was holding baby Ronnie. He had woken up again and wouldn't settle back down, so Tracey had got him up. Sean took Ronnie from Tracey and cuddled him tight.

"See you soon Ronnie. Look after Mummy for me." He passed Ronnie back to Tracey "See you soon, I will let you know what's going on when I can." said Sean.

"Bye love. I hope Marie is ok, and the girls. Don't worry about us we will be ok. Take care." replied a tearful Tracey. She was used to Sean flying back to Spain once a month, but this was different she didn't know when he would be flying back to her.

Sean got into his black cab he reversed off the drive and drove to Gatwick Airport. Tracey waved at the taxi until it was out of sight. Then she closed the front door and went upstairs. She climbed back in bed and snuggled down with baby Ronnie.

"Daddy will be back soon Ronnie. He loves us so much. Let's go back to sleep." she said and cuddled the baby until he fell back to sleep. Tracey didn't get back to sleep, she just closed her eyes and prayed that Marie would be ok. And Sean would be back with her soon.

The airport was busy. It's always a busy airport and Saturday mornings are the busiest. Sean parked his cab in the carpark and made his way to the customs. He only ever travels with hand luggage, having a set of clothes and shoes at both his homes, he only needed to take the clothes he is wearing. Once he had got through security, he bought a newspaper from the newsagents and found a small table to sit at in one of the many coffee shops. He ordered a coffee and a bacon sandwich. Sean looked at his phone and saw he had a missed call from Grace, she had only just called. He must have missed it while going through the security. He rang her back and she answered straight away. "Dad I called you, where are you?" said Grace, Sean could tell she had been crying.

"I'm at the airport Grace." replied Sean.

"Mum's been shot. She's in Denia hospital she's ok. I'm at Katies house, we both are. Katies Mum phoned the hospital just now and they said Mum was lucky, but she's going to be ok she was shot in the head." said Grace talking faster than normal in a high pitch voice.

"Mum phoned me last night just before she was shot was, she was on her own. I thought she was going out with Penny and Mollie?" asked Sean.

"She was with them earlier in the night. If you look at Facebook Mollie has put photos of them together. She was with them at 11pm." said Grace.

"Has anyone heard from Penny or Mollie? They must have seen who shot mum." said Sean.

"I don't know. What time will you be here? asked Grace.

"My flight lands at 9-25. I'll be round to pick you and Hannah up before I go to the hospital. I'll message you when I'm in the hire car." replied Sean.

"Okay, bye dad." said Grace.

"Bye, see you soon." replied Sean. He hung up, he sat there just looking at his phone, how was he ever going to tell Marie and the girls about Tracey and Ronnie? He knew he should, and he wanted to. He knew once Marie knew then their marriage would be over. Did he want that? He couldn't imagine not being married to Marie, but he knew he couldn't be without Tracey and Ronnie. He loved Marie. But he was in love with Tracey.

A message popped up on his phone, it was from Grace, it said Katies dad will pick him up from the Airport if he wants. Sean messaged back saying that would be great, yes please and thank you.

Sean didn't have Facebook, but he knew Marie's password, so he logged on to Marie's Facebook. There were loads of messages to Marie, all wishing her well. He scrolled through them all, there wasn't anything from Penny or Mollie, that's really odd thought Sean, surely, they would have messaged her. He looked at their Facebook pages, they had both put photos on from last night as had Marie. Things weren't adding up. He looked at the time 5.30am so its 6.30am in Spain. He decided to send Mollie and Penny a PM each from Marie's Facebook page, he said it was being sent by him and not Marie, and asked them what had happened, and where were they. Were they both ok? His bacon sandwich and coffee arrived, he sat looking through all the comments on Facebook while eating his breakfast, a few people have said it was a robbery. But Marie's purse and phone were left there with her.

Sean finished his sandwich and coffee just as his call for boarding came up on his phone. He made his way to the boarding gate. He started to feel nervous, in a few hours' time he would be at the hospital visiting his wife, who for some unknown reason had been shot in the head.

Sean checked Marie's Facebook account while he was queuing up, there was more messages. Nothing from Mollie or Penny. The flight wasn't full, and Sean was lucky enough to only have one other passenger in his row.

They had an empty seat in between them, the passenger was an elderly

lady, she didn't want to engage in any conversation with Sean, much to

Sean's relief. She spent the whole flight reading a book, only stopping to

eat her packed lunch and order a cup of tea. Sean had a coffee and then

closed his eyes, he couldn't sleep, he had so much going on in his head.

The plane touched down in Alicante at 9.20am. Sean was in Katies dad's

car by 9.45am.

"Hi Gary, thanks for this mate." said Sean.

"No problem Sean. Have you heard anything else?" asked Gary.

"I'm going to check my messages now. I was straight off the plane and

through passport control, didn't even stop." said Sean.

"That's good, probably because its early." replied Gary.

Sean looked at his messages. There was one from Tracey wishing him a

safe flight, and one from Grace, telling him Gary was on his way to the

airport. He replied to them both then logged into Marie's Facebook

messages, there was a new message from Rick Wozniak, the headmaster

and Marie's boss, it read "Hi Marie, hope everything is ok with you. I'm

trying to contact Mollie. I'm at my apartment now. I thought you, Mollie

and Penny were staying here last night? I Can see you've all left an

overnight bag here. where are you? regards Rick." Sean sent a message back to Rick "Hi Rick. This is Sean Cole, Marie's husband. You obviously don't know what's happened to Marie. She is in Denia Hospital, she was shot in the head last night. It doesn't look like Mollie or Penny were with her. I've sent them a message from Marie's Facebook account, they haven't replied. I'm on my way to Javea now. I've just flown in from the UK." Sean told Gary about the message from Rick,

"I don't understand why Mollie and Penny weren't with Marie. Or where they are now? Why didn't they stay at the apartment? It's all a bit odd, don't you think?" he said.

"Yes, it sounds like the other two have disappeared. Has anyone heard from them?" asked Gary.

"I don't know Gary. Mollie has a boyfriend. I'm sure he will be wondering where she is." replied Sean.

Rick was in the apartment wondering what was going on, he had just read the message from Sean. He hadn't looked at Facebook before messaging Marie, he looked now. He couldn't believe Marie had been shot in the head and left for dead, he was shocked. But why wasn't Mollie and Penny with her, and where are they now? Why hadn't they replied to him. He tried phoning Mollie again, it went to voicemail. He went out on to the balcony, he had dropped one of his sons off at the tennis club for a lesson

10 minutes earlier and thought he would pop his head into the apartment to say hello, as he was only up the road. He wished he hadn't given Mollie the keys to the apartment. He hadn't told Laura, she will find out now. Shit, he said to himself. What am I supposed to do with their overnight bags?

He decided to walk up to the English Bakers. He knew it was owned by Mollies Aunt and Uncle. Maybe they could tell him where Mollie was. Maybe she went home last night.

Rick walked the 10 minutes journey to the bakery shop. He passed the spot where the shooting took place. You wouldn't have thought that less than 12 hours ago, someone had been shot in the head there. The shops, cafes and bars were all open as usual.

Rick entered the bakers, Mollies Auntie Brenda was behind the cake counter.

"Hi, I'm Rick Wozniak. The headmaster of The Elizabeth School, I'm looking for Mollie?" said Rick to Auntie Brenda.

"Oh, hello we haven't heard from Mollie today, I've sent her half a dozen messages. Wasn't she staying in your apartment last night with Penny and Marie? I'm actually really worried, we know Marie is in hospital, apparently she was shot last night." said Auntie Brenda.

"Yes. They were all going to stay in my apartment. I've just been there, they're not there. I know Marie is in Denia Hospital. They have left their overnight bags in the apartment, but they didn't stay there last night. I've sent Mollie and Penny messages, they've not replied." replied Rick.

Brenda looked at her phone again. Still no reply from Mollie.

"I think we need to phone the hospital to check that Mollie and Penny didn't get taken there last night." said Brenda.

"I'll do that now." said Rick. He went outside and phoned Denia Hospital. After the phone call he went back into the bakery.

"They're not in the hospital." said Rick.

"Right. That's it. I'm going to the police station to report them both missing. This isn't right, Mollie always replies to me, if she didn't stay at your apartment last night, there must be something wrong." said Brenda Taking her apron off. "Ant." she called for her husband, he came out from the kitchen "I'm going to the police station to report Mollie and Penny missing. This is the headmaster. He has just been to the apartment they were supposed to be staying in last night. Their bags are there but they didn't stay there. Something is wrong, I know it is."

"Ok love. You go I will be ok here." said a worried Ant. He knew this wasn't like Mollie. Something was wrong. Most of the customers in the café were listening to Brenda, the shooting was the conversation of the morning. One of the customers got up and went over to Brenda.

"Hi. My name is Sandy I'm a translator, I can come with you to the police station. I go there a lot they know me. I might be helpful." said Sandy.

"That would be good, thank you. Do you want to come with me in my car?" said Brenda.

"It's ok, I'll drive. I'm parked right outside. Shall we go now?" replied Sandy.

"See you in little while Ant. If you hear from Mollie let me know." said Brenda.

"Can I take your phone number Mr Wozniak. The police might want it." asked Brenda.

"Yes, of course. I'll write it down for you." replied Rick. He wrote his number down on a paper bag and gave it to Brenda, she put it in her bag. Brenda and Sandy left the bakery. The conversations in the bakery started up again. This sort of thing didn't happen in Javea. A shooting and now 2 missing teachers. What was going on?

It was time for Rick to collect his son from his tennis lesson, he walked back to the apartment block to collect his car and drove to the tennis club.

Jake is 14 and the eldest of Ricks 3 sons. He was waiting for Rick, he jumped into the car.

"Have you heard about Mrs Cole? She was shot in the head last night. She might never walk or talk again." said Jake excitedly.

"Who told you that?" asked Rick.

"Everyone is talking about it. It's all over Facebook." replied Jake.

"Well let's not spread rumours Jake. We don't actually know what condition Mrs Cole is in, or what actually happened." said Rick.

"Well, she did get shot, and she is in hospital. It's all over Facebook." repeated Jake.

"Oh right, well if it's on Facebook it must be true." said Rick sarcastically.

They got home and went into the kitchen. Laura was sitting at the kitchen table, waiting for Rick.

"Mum, have you heard about Mrs Cole? She was shot in the head." said Jake while getting a bottle of juice from the fridge.

"Yes, Jake I have. How was tennis? "replied Laura.

"It was ok, what's for lunch?" said Jake.

"It's not lunchtime yet Jake, get a bag of crisps and go into the other room. I want to speak to dad alone." said Laura. Jake took his drink and a bag of crisps with him into the living room.

"So, I've heard through the Javea grapevine that Marie was supposed to be staying in our apartment last night, with Mollie and Penny, is this true?" asked Laura.

"Yes. They asked me at the last minute if the apartment was free. Sorry darling, I forgot to tell you." replied Rick. He had his back to Laura washing his hands at the kitchen sink.

"Do you think you could at least look at me Rick when you're lying to me." said Laura. Rick turned round and looked at Laura.

"Honestly Laura, I just forgot. I went there this morning. But they weren't there, their overnight bags are in the apartment, but they didn't stay there." said Rick.

"So, Mollie and Penny are missing then. I saw that someone had put that rumour on Facebook." replied Laura, feeling even more angry with Rick than she already was.

"Yes. It looks that way. I'm sorry Laura." said Rick.

"Why are you sorry? have you got anything to do with their disappearance?" asked Laura.

"What? No of course I haven't. I'm sorry we're involved in it all, that's all." Replied Rick.

"No. I'm not involved Rick, you are. What the fuck do you think you're doing anyway, giving them the keys to the apartment without asking me?" shouted Laura.

"Sorry Laura. What should I do with their bags? They are still in the apartment," said Rick.

"I take it you've tried to ring Mollie. To find out where they are?" asked Laura.

"Yes, she's not answering her phone or reading her messages. I went to see her aunt and uncle at the English Bakers. Did you know they own it?" replied Rick.

"You have been busy, yes I know who they are." said Laura.

"They haven't heard from Mollie either. Mollies aunt has reported both Mollie and Penny missing to the police, do you think they will want to see the apartment?" asked a worried Rick.

"They won't do anything for 24 hours. They are both grown adults. They're probably sleeping in someone else's apartment, and yes, the police will probably want to see the apartment. You can deal with it, it's your problem" replied Laura. Rick decided to wash the car. He left his wife sitting at the table scrolling on her phone, reading the latest Facebook gossip about last night's goings on.

CHAPTER 8

Auntie Brenda and Sandy walked in to Javea police station.

"Hola." said Sandy to the officer behind the desk.

"Hola." replied the officer.

"We want to report 2 missing girls. They were with the woman that got

shot last night in Javea." said Sandy.

"Ok, wait here." said the officer. He went into the office behind him it has

glass windows, Brenda and Sandy could see him talking to two other

police officers, they both came out with him.

"Hola, I'm Officer Garcia, can I help you?" said Officer Garcia.

"I hope so." replied Brenda.

"My niece and her friend have gone missing. They were out last night

with Marie Cole, the lady that was shot. They didn't sleep in the

apartment that they were staying in, and no one has heard from them.

We are very worried." Said Brenda. Officer Garcia spoke good English and

understood everything Brenda was saying.

"Ok, I understand what you are saying. I need you to give me some more

information. I need the women's names, their addresses, and the address of the apartment you say they were staying in last night please." Said Officer Garcia, he got a pad of paper and a pen ready.

"The girls names are Mollie Lane and Penny Smith. They are both 24 years old and are teachers at the Elizabeth School. They were supposed to be staying the night in an apartment at The Golden Beach Apartments. The apartment is owned by the headmaster of The Elizabeth School, Mr Rick Wozniak. He came into my Bakery about 30 minutes ago, to tell me the girls hadn't stayed at the apartment." replied Brenda.

"I need the address of the apartment, and do you have Mr Wozniak phone number?" asked Officer Garcia.

"Shall I write the phone number down for you? I can tell you Mollies address she lives in my under build but I don't know Penny's address. I know she lives in the old town I think Mr Wozniak will have it somewhere at school. And you'll have to ask him the number of his apartment." replied Brenda. she wrote down her address and looked for Ricks phone number in her bag.

"Thank you. Can you write your name and phone number down as well? We are the officers dealing with the shooting last night. We will speak to Mr Wozniak and make further enquiries." said Officer Garcia.

"You will keep me updated, won't you?" asked Brenda "I own the English

Bakers I'm going back there now."

"Yes. we will keep you informed. Thank you for coming in." replied Officer

Garcia. Brenda and Sandy left the station.

"Thank you for coming with me." said Brenda to Sandy as they walked

back to Sandys

car.

"No problem. You're welcome. I'll drop you back at your shop." replied

Sandy.

 Rick washed his car quickly. He decided to go back to the apartment and

pick the girls overnight bags up and take them to the school. He thought

they would be better left in the staff room or in his office. He drove back

to the apartment and had lined the bags up by the front door. He was just

leaving again when his phone rang.

"Hello." said Rick.

"Hello, can I speak to Rick Wozniak?" asked Officer Garcia.

"This is Rick Wozniak. how can I help you?" replied Rick.

"I'm Officer Garcia. I'm looking into the possible disappearance of Mollie

Lane and Penny Smith. They are teachers at your school, yes?" asked

Officer Garcia.

"Yes. They are." replied Rick. Really wishing he wasn't involved in all this.

"I need the address of Penny, have you got that? Also, the address of your apartment." said Officer Garcia.

"Ok. I will have to go to the school to get Penny's address. Why do you need the address of my apartment? They didn't stay here last night." replied Rick.

"We would like the address of your apartment anyway. Don't touch anything in it. We would like to come and see it when you can be there?" asked Officer Garcia. Rick closed his eyes Laura is going to be pissed off about this.

"I'm here now." replied Rick.

"Ok what number is it? We will come now." said Officer Garcia.

"Number 4, block D." replied Rick.

"Thank you. We will be with you in 10 minutes." said Officer Garcia. Rick put the girl's bags back into the bedrooms where he had taken them from and waited for the police to arrive. He thought about phoning Laura to let her know what was going on. But decided against it. She might not need to know he thought.

 Back at the English Bakers. Brenda was telling Ant about the visit to the police station.

"I need to phone Sue and Bill. I think they need to know Mollies missing." said Brenda. Sue and Bill are Mollies Parents.

"Yes. I think you should do it before they see something on bloody Facebook." said Ant. Brenda phoned her sister and explained the situation. She tried her best not to worry Mollies parents after all, Mollie might walk through the door any minute. But they knew this wasn't like Mollie, something was wrong. Brenda finished the call. She had made the call from the kitchen out of the customers earshot.

"Well. They are coming over on the next available flight. I tried to tell them not to worry, but they knew something wasn't right when Mollie didn't message Sue back this morning." said Brenda to Ant.

"Let's hope the girls just met up with some other friends last night. And stayed over somewhere else." said Ant hopeful.

"I don't think that's what's happened Ant. I'm worried. Do you think Penny's Parents know what's going on? "asked a tearful and worried Brenda.

"Wont the police tell them?" replied Ant.

"I'll phone Mr Wozniak when we get home. The police will have to get Penny's parents details from him." said Brenda.

The police arrived at Ricks apartment in less than 10 minutes. Rick was looking out for them. He opened the door.

 "Hi. I'm Rick Wozniak. Come in" he said.

"Hello. I'm Officer Garcia this is Officer Gomez." replied Officer Garcia. The officers walked into the apartment.

"Their bags are in the bedrooms." said Rick. He showed the officers the bags in the bedrooms.

"There's nothing else here to show you. They must have dropped the bags off and walked to the Arenal. But obviously they didn't come back here last night." said Rick. The 2 officers walked around the apartment. When they were satisfied the missing girls weren't there, they opened the front door.

"Ok. Can you go to the school and send us the contact details of Penny's parents? We need to contact them. And we need Penny's address." said Officer Garcia.

"Yes. I will go there now." replied Rick. He looked at his watch, he knew he had to be quick Laura would expect him home soon to go to the supermarket with her. They always went supermarket shopping on a Saturday. Rick said goodbye to the officers and locked up the apartment. He drove as quickly as he could to the school then he ran to the school office to find Penny's details. He had to use Laura's computer. He was careful not to move anything out of place. Laura didn't like anyone touching her workspace. While he was waiting for the computer to boot up, he opened Laura's desk drawers, he didn't need anything from them, he was just being nosey. They were incredibly tidy, just like Laura. There were elastic bands in little bags, paperclips in a small box, multi coloured high lighter pens lined up neatly, and a little brown envelope with his name on it. He picked it up and looked inside, there was 1 large gold hoop earring. He knew who's earring it was. It was Mollies. But why did Laura have it in her drawer? The computer was ready to use, so he put the earring back in the envelope and hoped he put it back in the exact same spot in the drawer. He printed off Penny's details, then emailed them on to Officer Garcia. He locked the school back up and ran to his car. He knew Laura would be waiting for him.

Artiom woke up and looked at his phone, it was 11.30am. He sat up in bed, normally he has a wakeup call from Mollie at 10am. He had no missed calls but a few messages, not from Mollie but from his gym buddies that he was out with last night. He read the messages. He couldn't believe what he was reading. Marie has been shot in the head and she's in hospital. No one has heard from Mollie or Penny. What the fuck has happened? Thought Artiom. He rang Mollies mobile, but it went straight to voicemail. He quickly got dressed and brushed his teeth then drove to Mollies apartment. He knocked at her door, there wasn't any answer, so he rang the bell on her aunt and Uncles front door still no answer. I'll drive to the bakery thought Artiom and see if Brenda knows what's going on. Artiom drove to the bakery. He still couldn't believe what he had read, Marie shot in the head? Why? Who would do that? And where was Mollie and Penny? By now him and Mollie would be at the Ondara shopping Centre. It was their Saturday thing, they would spend a couple of hours going from shop to shop with Mollie trying on different outfits and shoes, Mollie always asking Artiom what he thought. He thought she looked fab in everything she tried on, but then Artiom thought Mollie would look good in a potato sack. After the shopping they would have lunch in one of the restaurants there, a burger or tapas and a lunchtime beer. He parked his car and went into the bakery, Brenda was cleaning a table.

"Hi Brenda, what's going on? where's Mollie?" asked Artiom.

"Oh Artiom, I was just thinking about you. Mollie isn't answering her phone and her and Penny didn't stay at the apartment last night. No one has seen them." replied Brenda.

"I saw them last night, they were with Marie, it was about 11.30pm and they were just about to walk home. They were fine, a bit drunk but fine." said Artiom "When was Marie shot?"

"On the way to the apartment we think, but we don't know if the girls were with her." said Brenda.

"Mr Wozniak, the headmaster has been in here. He went to the apartment earlier and said the girl's bags are there, but they didn't stay there last night."

"Where are they then?" asked Artiom.

"We don't know. I've been to the police station, and I've reported the girls missing perhaps you should tell them you saw the girls heading home together last night?" said Brenda.

"Yes, I will go there now and see if they know anything yet" replied Artiom.

"Can you give me your number Artiom in case Mollie turns up." said Brenda still hoping Mollie was going to walk in the door, hungover and hungry. Artiom and Brenda swapped phone numbers and Artiom left the bakery. He walked back to his car, he thought about ringing one of his Spanish friends to see if they would come with him in case, he needed a translator. But he decided his Spanish was probably good enough and he didn't want to wait for anyone. He needed to find out where Mollie was, and he wanted answers now. Artiom parked near to the police station, and he went inside up to the help desk.

"Hola." he said to the officer behind the desk.

"Hola. How can I help You?" asked the officer.

"Do you speak English?" asked Artiom.

"Yes, I do, a little." replied the officer.

"Ok. My girlfriend and her friend have gone missing they was with the lady that got shot in Javea last night" said Artiom "I saw them all at just gone 11pm they were walking home together. They were fine, a bit drunk but they were together."

"Ok, hang on let me call the officers that are dealing with this. They are out." said the officer. He went into the office behind the desk and phoned officer Garcia and officer Gomez, he relayed to them what Artiom had said then came back out to Artiom.

"Ok. Leave me your name and contact details. The officers will be in touch with you." He gave Artiom a piece of paper and a pen Artiom wrote down his name and phone number.

"Do you have any more news?" asked Artiom.

"You would have to ask the officers that are dealing with this case." replied the officer behind the desk.

"Ok, thanks." replied Artiom and he left the police station. As he walked back to his car his phone rang, Artiom answered it,

"Hello."

"Hi, Artiom its Dan," Dan was one of Artioms gym buddies "I'm at the gym, and there's talk about last night's shooting. Rumour is a Russian gang is behind it." said Dan.

"Really, do you know who they are? Or where they are?" asked Artiom.

"No, sorry mate. But they go to a gym in Calpe. Hercules, I think." replied Dan.

"Ok, thanks Dan. I'll have a ride to Calpe and visit it, see if there's any talk." said Artiom.

"Ok mate, be careful. If I hear anything more, I'll let you know," said Dan.

"Thanks Dan, see you later." replied Artiom. He googled the Hercules Gym in Calpe on his phone. Ok let's go thought Artiom and drove to Calpe.

CHAPTER 9

There wasn't much traffic on the motorway. Gary took Sean home so he could pick up the spare keys for the car, and then drove Sean to the Golden Beach Apartments so Sean could pick up their car from where Marie had Left it. They saw the car straight away. Sean thanked Gary and got out of his car. He unlocked his car, got in and adjusted the seat and the mirror, then followed Gary back to his house where the girls were waiting for him. The girls both burst in to tears when they saw Sean

"Oh dad I hope mum will be ok." cried Grace. Sean put his arms around both girls and they hugged each other.

"Who would do this to mum?" said Hannah.

"I don't know, hopefully mum will be able to tell us what happened." said Sean.

"Can we go to the hospital now?" asked Grace.

"Yes, get your bags." replied Sean. The girls got their bags and hugged Katie and her parents goodbye. Sean thanked them for looking after the girls and Gary for picking him up from the airport. He promised to update them on Marie's condition. They left the house and got into the car. Denia Hospital was only a 10-minute journey away.

"Dad have you heard that mums 2 friends are missing?" said Grace.

"Yes, I know, it's all very confusing." replied Sean.

"Well. Miss Lane is having an affair with Mr Wozniak, that's why they were staying in his holiday apartment." said Grace.

"I can't believe anyone would have an affair with Mr Wozniak. That's so disgusting. Miss Lane is half his age. Why would she want to have an affair with him?" said Hannah pulling a face.

"And her boyfriend is well fit, I've seen his Facebook profile," said Grace.

"Do you think he will dump her now?" replied Hannah.

"Yes probably" replied Grace "That's if he finds her."

Sean was listening to the girls. What would they think about Tracey being with him? He was a lot older than Tracey. But the age difference didn't seem to be a problem between them, if anything he felt like he was a better dad to Ronnie. More patient he loved to just sit and talk to Ronnie. He can't remember doing that with the girls.

When they had parked the car in the hospital carpark, they made their way to the hospital entrance. There was a help desk just inside the door.

Sean asked directions to the intensive care ward, the kind volunteer gave Sean the directions in English.

"You will need to take the lift up to the 5th floor, you'll see the intensive care ward once the lift doors open, there will be a nurse at the desk outside the ward." Sean and the girls got into the lift and Grace pressed the button for the 5th floor.

"It's the top floor." she said.

"Mum doesn't like heights, don't tell her she's on the top floor." said Hannah. The lift door opened, and the intensive care ward was directly in front of them. They walked over to the desk outside the wards doors there was a nurse sitting there."

"Hello, my wife is on this ward, Marie Cole." said Sean.

"Hello, yes she is have you come to visit her?" replied the nurse.

"Yes, we have." replied Sean.

"Please, take a seat I will let Marie's doctor know you're here." said the nurse and she pointed to a row of plastic chairs. Sean and the girls sat down on them. The nurse made a phone call, a few minutes later a doctor came through the intensive care ward doors. He spoke to the nurse then went over to Sean and the girls,

"Hello, I'm Doctor Jamie Dura. You're Marie's husband?" he asked Sean.

"Yes, and these are our daughters." replied Sean.

"Ok. You know Marie was shot in the head? she has been very lucky, the bullet had lodged into her skull, if it had gone through her skull, she would most certainly be dead. She might not feel lucky being shot, but she has had a lucky escape from death. We've removed the bullet, and everything is good. She will have another brain scan tomorrow morning. But we see no damage. She is very sore she has bruising to her face and her body from falling to the pavement. But that will heal." said Doctor Dura.

"Thank you. Can we see her?" asked Sean.

"Yes, of course. Please remember Marie, will look sore and she will have a headache. So be quiet and gentle when you see her." replied Doctor Dura. He gestured to Sean and the girls to follow him into the intensive care ward. On the other side of the doors there was a hand sanitising unit, and they were told to sanitise their hands. Then they followed the doctor down the ward to Marie's room. They had to pass 6 other rooms, 3 on each side, each room was occupied with a patient. The rooms all had large glass windows with blinds on them, all the blinds were open, and all the doors were closed. Some of the patients had visitors. They reached Marie's room. From outside they could see Marie laying in the bed. She was asleep, she had a large bandage covering her head, and some stiches on her face, she looked battered sore and bruised. The doctor opened the door and Sean and the girls crept into Marie's room. The doctor followed them and quietly closed the door. Sean walked over to Marie's bed and bent down to kiss her, this woke Marie up.

"Sean," she whispered "hello."

"Hello Marie. How are you feeling?" asked Sean.

"Like I've been shot." whispered Marie, she tried to smile but it was too painful. She looked past Sean and saw the girls. She tried to wave at them but could only manage to wiggle her fingers. Seeing her girls standing there made her cry, the looks on their faces told Marie she must look shocking. Grace rushed to Marie and put her arms around her,

"It's ok Mum, you're going to ok. The doctor said you were really lucky, you could have died." she said.

"Where's Mollie and Penny?" asked Marie.

"They're missing. Was they with you?" asked Sean. Both him and Hannah had pulled chairs up to Marie's Bed. Grace was sitting in the chair that was already there.

"Yes, But the men put them in to the car" said Marie "I couldn't stop them, he shot me."

"Who shot you Mum?" asked Hannah holding on to her mum's hand.

"The man in the car. There was 3 men, all big men, Russian, I think. He got out of the car, and he shot me." whispered Marie. She was crying at the memory of what happened, and the realization that Mollie and Penny were missing.

Grace looked around Marie's room. There were so many machines next to marries bed, some were bleeping, others were beeping. there were machines with numbers flashing in red and a machine that looked like a tv screen with wiggly lines going across it. There was a large white board above the bed with Marie's name on it, her date of birth and instructions about her care, the doctor saw Grace looking.

"Don't worry about all the machines and equipment, they are here to make sure your mum gets the best care we can give her." said the doctor

"There's a lot of machines." said Hannah. There was a knock on Marie's hospital room door, Nurse April came in.

"The police are here Marie, they would like to talk to you. Are you happy to talk to them?" She asked Marie.

"Yes. I need to tell them about Mollie and Penny." whispered Marie and she nodded as best as she could.

"Ok, I'll go and get them." said Nurse April. She left the door open and a minute later returned with Officer Garcia and Officer Gomez.

"This is Marie Cole." she told the 2 officers. Nurse April and Doctor Dura left the room. The doctor closed the door behind him.

"Hello Marie. I'm Officer Garcia and this is my colleague Officer Gomez. What can you tell me about last night?" asked Officer Garcia. He got his little notebook and pencil out from his jacket pocket.

"We were walking back from the Arenal to the apartment, when a car stopped, a big man got out and pushed Mollie and Penny into the back seat, they were trying to get away, but he was really big, I could see them trying to open the doors, but they must have been locked, the man was sitting in between them. I couldn't get my phone out of my bag, I was so scared, I was shaking, I've never been so afraid, and I felt so helpless. I managed to find my phone but before I could call anyone another big man got out of the front seat and he shot me. He was looking straight at my face, he looked evil, he just looked at me, then shot me, I think he meant to kill me." whispered Marie, tears were silently falling down her bruised and swollen face.

Sean, Grace, Hannah and the police officers were all amazed at how Marie was able to recall what had happened last night.

"Can you remember what make or model the car was Marie?" asked Officer Garcia.

"Yes. It was a silver Mercedes a big saloon car, not brand new I don't think it was new. It was a nice car" replied Marie "There were 3 men, 1 in the back, 1 was driving and the bastard that shot me. You need to find them. You need to find the girls." whispered Marie. she wasn't crying now, she was feeling angry, angry that these men had taken Mollie and Penny and then shot her. Who was they? Where were the girls? What did they want with them? The thoughts Marie was thinking were too horrifying to share. Doctor Dura came back into Marie's room.

"Hi. I think maybe Marie should rest now." he said to the officers.

"Yes. Of course. You've really helped Marie. If you remember anything else, can you let us know. Here is my number, you can ring me or message me anytime." said Officer Garcia. Marie nodded at him.

"Please find them. Find Mollie and Penny before it's too late." said Marie.

"Thank you. If Marie remembers anything else, I'll let you know." said Sean. The officers said goodbye and left the room. Sean saw them pick something up in a plastic bag from Nurse April at the nurse's desk.

"What's the nurse giving them?" Sean asked Doctor Dura.

"It's the bullet from Marie's skull. Hopefully it will help with the investigation." replied Doctor Dura. He checked Marie's pulse.

"How's the pain Marie?" he asked.

"My head is pounding and my face hurts. My body hurts all down this side." replied Marie pointing to her left side.

"You must of fell to your left Marie, that's why you're so bruised and sore. I will ask nurse April to bring you some more painkillers." said Doctor Dura. He left the room and a minute later nurse April came in with Marie's painkillers.

"Here you go Marie, these will help with the pain." she gave Marie the tablets with a glass of water. "You've got 2 beautiful daughters." She said to Sean and Marie, Grace and Hannah both smiled at Nurse April.

"Yes, they're good girls." replied Marie. She took the tablets and gave the glass back to nurse April.

"Try to rest a bit now Marie." said Nurse April.

Marie closed her eyes and nodded off. Sean and the girls decided to go to the hospital café. They crept quietly out of Marie's room in search some lunch.

CHAPTER 10

Sergei and Vlad returned to the villa in Pedreguer at 7am on Saturday morning in a silver Mercedes van. The saloon car they were driving the night before was halfway to Russia by now. They drove to the back of the villa so they wouldn't be seen. Then they entered they villa and went down to the under build. Paval was waiting for them to knock at the steel door once they had unlocked it their side, Paval opened the door and let them in.

"All ok?" asked Sergei.

"Yes, no problems." replied Paval.

"Good. Let's move them now." said Sergei. Paval unlocked the door of the room Mollie and Penny were in. The girls were both awake they hadn't really slept, they had been waiting for the door to open again with fear. Penny gave a little cry.

"Get up. We're leaving here in 5 minutes. Use the toilet, we have a long journey ahead." said Paval.

"Where are we going?" asked Mollie.

"Russia." replied Paval and he closed the door. Mollie looked at Penny.

"Russia? why Russia?" asked Penny sobbing.

"I think we are the victims of people trafficking Penny. We are probably going to Russia to be used in a brothel or sex club" replied Mollie "Artiom told me once that St. Petersburg is full of sex clubs and brothels."

"Oh my god! please be wrong about that Mollie. I can't do that sort of thing." cried Penny.

"Look Penny, we need to stay alive so use the toilet and let's get to Russia alive. Once we're there we will get help from someone, ok?" said Mollie.

"Ok." replied Penny. She was in shock at what Mollie had just told her. But she knew Mollie was right about staying alive. Once they get to Russia, they would get help. She used the toilet while Mollie washed herself in the sink. Mollie felt dirty and grubby, she looked at her face, it was puffy and red, and it didn't help that she had the hangover from hell. Penny didn't look much better, but at least Penny was wearing more clothes than Mollie. Mollie was regretting wearing the mini dress now, she wished she had on her comfortable tracksuit or her unicorn onesie pyjamas that Artiom had bought her for Christmas. She had bought him a tiger onesie and they had spent all day in them, even eating Christmas dinner with the family. The girls finished in the bathroom and was

drinking some water when the door opened.

"Out." ordered Paval. Mollie and Penny walked out of the room. The two

other men were standing at the steel door.

 "We are going up the stairs and getting into a van. Don't try to escape,

you will be shot if you do." said Sergei. The girls followed the driver up the

stairs and out to the van. The sun was shining in the sky. Vlad opened the

back of the transit style van.

"Get in." he ordered. The girls climbed into the van. There weren't any

windows in the sides of the van or in the doors, there was a pile of old

grey blankets and a bucket with a lid on it in the corner. the girls sat on

the blankets.

"Oh my god, it's going to be really dark in here Mollie." said Penny.

"I think some light will come in from above the seats in the front." replied

Mollie. Penny looked at the row of seats there was a clear plastic screen

separating the seats from the back of the van.

"That's so they can see us without having to stop and open the van

doors." said Mollie. The vans back doors closed. It was dark in the back of

the van it took Mollie and Penny a few minutes for their eyes to adjust to

the darkness.

"Is the bucket in case we need the toilet?" said Penny.

"Yes, I think so." replied Mollie. The three men got into the van and Vlad started the engine. The girls could feel the van driving over the weeds and rubble outside the house and down the bumpy road, the van stopped. They could hear a few cars driving past then the van pulled out on to the road.

"What do you think is happening Mollie? do you think anyone knows we're missing yet?" asked Penny.

"Yes, loads of people knew we was out with Marie last night. They will all be looking for us Penny. We just need to hope that someone saw something. Someone saw Marie shot. I can't believe that animal shot her what a bastard, Marie wouldn't hurt anyone." said Mollie.

"I know poor Marie. I feel so sorry for her girls and Sean. I can't believe this is happening it's like a nightmare." said Penny. Mollie could hear talking from the front of the van,

"Shhhh" said Mollie, she put her ear to the plastic partition "Where's Perpignan? is that in France? They are saying its 7 hours to Perpignan."

"Yes, it's in France." replied Penny.

"Ok, that must be where we will stop, and they will need to stop for petrol." said Mollie. The girls got as comfortable as they could. They wrapped the rough dirty blankets around themselves and leaned against the side of the van. Penny dropped off to sleep and rested her head on Mollies shoulder. Mollie tried to sleep but all she could think about was what was going to happen to them. She knew it wasn't going to nice. But she knew if they were going to have any chance of getting out of this alive, they needed to get to Russia alive. She just hoped that someone saw them getting abducted and has reported it to the police. The police and their families will find them she had to believe that. Mollie put her hands together and prayed. She asked God to look after her and Penny. To give them the strength to get through this and she asked him to help their families and the police to find them. To help Marie's family with the loss of Marie. The last time Mollie had prayed was when she was 9 years old at Sunday School. She hoped God was listening to her now.

Chapter 11

On his way to Calpe Artiom decided to pop into the English Bakers and see if Mollies Aunt and Uncle had any more news.

"Hi Brenda. I've been to the police station I've told them that I saw Mollie, Penny and Marie last night just before their walk to the apartment. The 2 officers dealing with this weren't there, but they have my contact details now. Have you heard anything else from the police?" asked Artiom.

"No, nothing yet. I've phoned Mollies Parents, they are getting the next flight out." replied Brenda.

"What about Penny's parents? Will the police inform them about Penny being missing?" asked Artiom.

"I have thought about ringing Penny's parents myself. I will need their contact details. I thought I'd phone Mr Wozniak he will have them" said Brenda "Why don't you come to ours later Artiom? Mollies parents will be here. You don't want to be by yourself. You can stay in Mollies apartment."

"Thank you, Brenda. Yes, I will be round later. I've got a few things to do no. See you later." said Artiom and he left the bakery. He didn't want to tell Mollies Aunt the rumour about the Russian involvement until he knew more. He got into his car and carried on to Calpe. Brenda and Ant finished tidying up the bakery then went home.

Rick was shopping in the supermarket with Laura when his phone starting ringing, he answered it,

"Hello."

"Hello, Mr Wozniak?" asked Brenda.

"Hi, yes, it is." replied Rick.

"It's Brenda. Mollies Auntie from the English Bakers. Do you know if the police are letting Penny's parents know about Penny?" asked Brenda.

"Yes, they asked me for their contact details, I had to go to the school to get them," said Rick. Laura gave Rick a dirty look and tapped her watch "Is there anything else Brenda? I'm in the supermarket." said Rick.

"Can you send me Penny's parents phone number. I'd like to speak to them." replied Brenda.

"Yes, ok I'll send you it Bye." said Rick and he hung up "Sorry Laura, that was Mollies Aunt she wants Penny's parents phone number. I'll just send it to her."

"You didn't tell me you went to the school. Did you use my computer?" asked Laura.

"Yes sorry, I didn't think it was a big deal. The police had a quick look around the apartment, then asked me to get Penny's personal details from the school computer." said Rick. Trying to act as though this was an everyday occurrence.

"Did you touch anything on my desk?" asked Laura. Feeling pissed off that the police had been in their apartment "So they didn't find Mollie and Penny dead rolled up in bin bags in the cupboard in the apartment then? They will be searching our house next." she said angrily.

"No. I didn't touch anything on your desk. And I don't think we will hear from the police again." replied Rick. Not telling Laura that he had seen Mollies earring in her drawer. Laura walked off with the trolley wondering if Rick had found the envelope in her drawer. She would get rid of it on Monday.

Artiom parked his car outside Hercules Gym in Calpe. It wasn't a place he'd been to before. He didn't really visit Calpe very often. He walked into the gym, straight away he could hear conversations in Russian. He went to the desk.

"Hi, can I buy a day pass." he asked the pretty receptionist.

"Yes, 6 euros please. Can you fill in this form." she gave Artiom a form and a pen Artiom gave her the 6 euros and began filling in the form. Once he'd finished, he gave it back to her and she buzzed him through the turnstile. Artiom went over the weights, he put his gym bag down and started to get himself ready for a weightlifting session. There was already 2 men using the weights, they were talking in Russian. Artiom listened in, they were discussing the shooting last night, calling the gang stupid and mad, they didn't need to shoot the woman, the car would have been on its way to Russia within an hour of the abductions. The 2 men stopped talking when they saw 3 big men walk into the gym, in fact, Artiom noticed the whole gym fell silent. The 3 men said hello to the receptionist in Russian, she spoke Russian back to them and buzzed them into the gym. They came over to the weights, the 2 men that were already using the weights had tided up and moved somewhere else. Artiom stayed where he was, the conversations in the gym started again but it was a lot quieter than before. Artiom carried on with his weight training, the 3 men didn't speak to Artiom, or anyone else in the gym. They started to get themselves ready for the weights, they were talking quietly about last night's events. Artiom listened without looking at them, they were mentioning names, Sergei, Vlad and Paval. Were these the men that abducted Mollie and Penny and shot Marie. They spoke about a derelict safe house a hiding place in Pedreguer, and St. Petersburg was mentioned more than once.

He decided he was going to ask the men what they knew about last night.

First, he packed up his gym bag, then he spoke to the 3 men.

"Hi. My girlfriend and her friend went missing last night. They were with the woman that got shot. Can you tell me anything about where they might be? Or who the gang are?" asked Artiom in Russian, the gym fell silent.

"No." replied one of the 3 men and they turned their backs to Artiom. Artiom took this as a sign to leave. He had three names now though. That's a start he thought. As he was passing the reception the pretty receptionist asked him for his pass back, Artiom gave her the plastic disc and she pressed a small, folded piece of paper into his palm, he nodded to her and left the gym. He opened the piece of paper once he was in his car and driving away. It had written on it the same 3 names as he had heard in the gym and their surnames, with the mention of St. Petersburg he was sure that Mollie and Penny had been abducted for sex trafficking to Russia. He knew all about the Soho of St. Petersburg. It had grown massively in the last 5 years even though prostitution is illegal in Russia there are thousands of prostitutes working in St. Petersburg. Many of them are foreign woman abducted from the streets and made to work in brothels, strip clubs and sex clubs. They are kept against their will, too afraid to escape they've seen what happens to woman that ask for help.

He had been to St. Petersburg on a friend's stag party a few years ago, it

was outrageous. They all visited the strip clubs and bars but a few of the

stags went on to the sex clubs. Artiom and the rest of the stags including

the groom to be didn't go. The other stags were full of it over lunch the

following day. Artiom and the stags that didn't go to the sex clubs were

secretly pleased they didn't go and advised the stags that did go to book

in for STD tests when they got back.

Artiom drove straight to the police station. It was the same officer behind

the desk at the police station.

"Hi, I came in earlier. My girlfriend and her friend are missing. I spoke to

you this morning." said Artiom.

"Yes. Hang on. The officers that are dealing with it are here." the officer

went into the office behind the desk, he spoke to Officer Garcia and

Officer Gomez. They came out to the desk.

"Hi. I'm Mollies boyfriend. She went missing last night" said Artiom "She

was with her 2 friends, Penny is missing, and Marie was shot in the head. I

think I know who did this. Who shot Marie and I think they abducted

Mollie and Penny." said Artiom.

"Ok. You need to come through to a room. I'll open the door." said Officer Gomez and he opened the door to let Artiom through to the other side of the desk. They walked up a short corridor and went into a small room, there was a table and 4 chairs. Artiom and the 2 officers sat down.

"Tell us what you think you know." said Officer Garcia to Artiom.

"Ok. First, I saw Mollie, Penny and Marie last night just before they walked back to the apartment together. They were happy, a little drunk but happy together. Today I heard a rumour that a Russian gang are involved and that they use The Hercules Gym in Calpe. So, I went to Calpe, and I went into the Hercules Gym. I was listening to the conversations in there, they were all talking about last night and 3 names came up. I asked the men talking if they could tell me anything about the men that shot Marie and I think took Mollie and Penny, but they wouldn't. Then as I was leaving, the receptionist gave me this, Artiom put the piece of paper on the table.

"These are the names of the 3 men that were in the car last night." The 2 officers looked at the names.

"Yes. These men are known to us. We will print off a E fit photo of each of them and take them to Marie. Hopefully she will be able to confirm that these are the men involved." said Officer Garcia.

"We need to act quickly, the girls are probably already halfway to Russia by now." said Artiom.

"Yes. We will do it now." replied Officer Garcia. The officers got up Artiom read this as his time to leave the station. He walked to his car and decided to go and visit Marie in hospital himself to see if she could tell him anything about what happened last night.

Brenda phoned Penny's parents Steve and Karen, they didn't answer, but Brenda was able to leave a message.

"Hi, this is Brenda. I'm Mollies Auntie. Mollie lives with me in Javea. Can you call me back? Thanks Bye." Brenda didn't really know what else to say, she presumed the police had contacted them and told them about Penny being missing with Mollie, and Marie being shot. She thought they would probably be at the airport. Or even on a plane. They will ring her back, she was sure.

Artiom reached the hospital, he parked his car and found the Intensive Care ward. He stopped at the nurse's desk.

"Hi, Can I see Marie Cole please?" he asked the nurse behind the desk.

"Are you a relative?" she asked.

"No. But can you ask her if she will see me, it's important. Tell her its Artiom." replied Artiom.

"Ok, wait here." said the nurse. She went through the door on to the ward. Artiom waited outside. The nurse came back and held the doors open.

"Marie is in room 7. Please be quiet." said the nurse. She let Artiom on to the ward. Artiom walked along the corridor until he found room 7. He could see Marie lying in bed she looked terrible. With her bandaged head and bruised face. He opened the door slowly, Sean stood up,

"Hi Artiom come in. Marie wants to see you." said Sean. Artiom walked into the room as quietly as he could. He smiled at Grace and Hannah they both gave him a little wave.

"Here sit down Artiom." said Sean. He pointed to the chair he had been sitting in. Artiom sat down next to Marie.

"Hi Marie, how are you feeling?" asked Artiom.

"Hi Artiom, I feel battered and bruised but I'll be ok. You need to find the girls." whispered Marie.

"Do you remember what happened last night?" asked Artiom.

"Yes" whispered Marie "We were walking back to the apartment, just after we saw you, then a car stopped. There were 3 men in it. They were Russian. 1 man got out of the back of the car, he was really big he pulled Mollie and Penny into the back of the car and shut the door. I couldn't do anything to help them, they were trying to escape but they couldn't."

Marie started to cry.

"Marie, it's not your fault. You couldn't have stopped it. What happened next?" asked Artiom.

"I was trying to phone someone for help. I had my phone out then the man got out of the passenger door and shot me in the head. The last thing I remember is seeing a gun pointing at me" sobbed Marie, "I don't remember anything else. I must have passed out when I hit the pavement."

"I think I've found out the names of the 3 men. I've been to the police station they know these men, they are going to show you some photos of them. If they are the same men, can you message me. If they are, Then I think Mollie and Penny have been taken to Russia." said Artiom.

"Russia? Why Russia?" whispered Marie.

"To work in the sex trade. I think this gang that took Mollie and Penny are sex traffickers. And if this is what's happened, I'm going to drive to Russia and look for Mollie and penny." said Artiom.

"Oh, my God. The poor girls, you've got to find them Artiom. Where in Russia will they be?" asked Marie.

"St. Petersburg. I've been there before on a stag party. I'm going to find them Marie don't worry." said Artiom.

"When are you going?" whispered Marie.

"In the morning. I just need to make sure the men I think took the girls are the right men. So, once you've seen the photos let me know." Said Artiom.

"Yes. I will get Sean to message you. Give Sean your number." said Marie.

Artiom gave Sean his number then said goodbye and left the hospital. He passed Officer Garcia and Officer Gomez as he drove out of the carpark. By the time he reached Javea Sean had messaged him with a thumbs up. They were the men that shot Marie and took the girls. Artiom was angry now, he was going to find Mollie and Penny.

Brenda's phone was ringing she looked at the phone number, she didn't recognize it.

"Hello." she said.

"Hello, is that Brenda? It's Steve, Penny's Dad. You left a message to call you back." said Steve.

"Hi Steve, Yes I'm Mollies Auntie, have the police phoned you?" asked Brenda.

"Yes, we are at the airport, lining up to board a plane now." replied Steve.

"Ok. When you get here do you want to come to my house for an update? Mollies parents will be here and Mollies boyfriend." said Brenda.

"Yes ok. Can you message your address to my phone?" replied Steve.

"I will do it now. Hope you have a safe flight. See you later. Bye." said Brenda.

"Thanks. Bye." replied Steve. Brenda messaged him her address and put her phone down.

"Who was that?" asked Ant. They were clearing up the bakery ready to close for the day.

"That was Steve. Penny's dad. They are just boarding the plane, I've messaged him our address, they are coming round later. Right let's get cleaned up and get home. I need to make the bed up for Sue and Bill." said Brenda.

"Yes, let's get on with it." replied Ant. They carried on clearing up the bakery, Brenda locked the door and turned the open sign to closed. They were closing shop earlier than normal this meant there was more cakes, pies and sausage rolls left over than usual. Brenda bagged them up along with some filled rolls and sandwiches. She was taking them home to feed everyone later. They wouldn't be wasted, she was sure.

CHAPTER 12

Penny woke up with a jolt.

"What was that?" she said. She had fallen asleep and forgotten where she was, she soon remembered when she opened her eyes.

"We've stopped. I think we're in a petrol station." said Mollie, she was trying to listen to the noises outside.

"Shall we call out for help?" asked Penny.

"I don't think we should. We will probably get shot like Marie. We need to get to wherever we're going and then we will get some help. Everyone will be looking for us now Penny. Someone would have seen something last night I'm sure of it." Said Mollie.

"I hope so. I need a wee, do you think they will let me go to the toilet," said Penny.

"No. That's what the bucket is for Penny. Go now if you need to go, before the van starts moving again." said Mollie. Penny got up slowly and got the bucket, she managed to sit above it and emptied her bladder.

"This is so wrong. I'm sorry Mollie but I was bursting." said Penny.

"It's ok Penny, just make sure the lid is on it properly. We don't want wee everywhere." said Mollie. Penny made sure the lid was back on the bucket securely. She sat back down next to Mollie, the van doors slammed, and the engine started they were on the move again. Penny fell back to sleep quickly, Mollie closed her eyes and prayed again.

"Dear God, please save us. Please help us to get through this. Please look after my family and Artiom. Please. Thank you." Mollie hoped God was listening.

Tiredness and exhaustion finally won, and Mollie fell asleep. She woke up when the van stopped again.

"Wake up Penny, we've stopped again." said Mollie. Penny was laying on the floor she sat up. "Where are we?" she said trying to adjust her eyes to the darkness.

"Shhh, I can hear talking." whispered Mollie. Vlad had got out of the van. He was standing at the back doors of the van and was talking to another man in Russian.

"Hi Dimitri. Do you have the packages?" asked Vlad.

"Yes" replied Dimitri "Let's see the cargo." Vlad opened the van doors. The brightness made the girls cover their eyes.

"Move your hands." ordered Dimitri. The girls moved their hands but were still squinting, they could see Vlad standing next to the other man, Dimitri. He was like Vlad a big Russian man, younger than Vlad. He looked only in his twenties. He looked at Mollie and Penny.

"Ok good. Get out." he said to Mollie and Penny. The girls slowly climbed out of the van, their legs were almost numb from being in the van sitting on the hard uncomfortable floor for so long.

"Hurry up." ordered Dimitri. Mollie looked about they was parked in a closed down service station. There was no one else about apart from a van like the they had just been in. It was parked next to them. Mollie realized what was happening they were being traded. For what? she wondered. Dimitri pushed the girls over to the back of the other van. Mollie could see he had a gun tucked in his trouser waistband. He opened the van doors.

"Get in." he ordered them. A rancid smell of sweat and fear came from the van. The girls looked in, there was 6 other women huddled in the van all shielding their faces from the daylight.

"Move." shouted Dimitri at Mollie and Penny. They climbed into the van and sat down. Dimitri slammed the doors closed and locked them. The 2 men walked to the front of the van. There was another man sitting in the passenger seat. Alex, another big Russian man. He too was in his 20s, Vlad

spoke to him.

"Hi Alex, all good?"

"Hi. Yes, all good for me. These are yours." said Alex and he handed 2

house brick size packages to Vlad. Vlad took them and said goodbye. He

got into his van and drove out of the petrol station. Dimitri got into his

van and drove away too.

Mollie and Penny looked at the other 6 women already in the van. There

was 1 woman who looked their age. The others were younger 3 were very

young.

"Hi" said Mollie.

"I'm Mollie this is Penny. How long have you all been in here?" she asked

them. The woman that looked nearer their age spoke.

"I've been in here since early this morning, the others have been collected

throughout the day, like you two." she said.

"What's your name?" asked Mollie.

"Michelle. I was kidnapped in Barcelona I was kept in a house overnight

then they put me in here this morning. Where are you from?" said

Michelle.

"We are from Javea we were taken last night. We were walking home with our friend Marie. They shot her in the head." said Mollie, the other women all gasped.

"Why did they shoot your friend?" asked one of the younger women.

"I think they could only fit us 2 in the car, she was a witness." said Mollie.

"That's awful. I'm Chloe, I was taken in Barcelona last night too." said Chloe.

"You look young Chloe, how old are you?" asked Penny.

"I'm 16"replied Chloe.

 "I'm 16 too" said Kara "I was taken from Madrid. On my way home from college yesterday afternoon."

"I'm 19, I was taken from Paris on Thursday night. I was walking home from work I feel like I've been travelling around for days. this is the third van I've been in." said Charlotte.

"Really that's terrible. I wonder where we're going?" said Penny.

"Russia" said Michelle "We're being trafficked to work in the sex clubs. I'm not sure but I think we're in France now."

"I heard the men that took us talking about Perpignan, that's in France." said Mollie.

The other 2 girls introduced themselves to Mollie and Penny. Ava is 17 and from Madrid. And Kelly is 21 also from Madrid. They swapped their stories of where they were when they were taken and where they've been kept before being put into this van. The more that's said the more Mollie and Penny realize that they are part of a sex trafficking crime. They were only in the van for an hour when it slowed down, turned a few corners then stopped. They could hear what sounded like gates opening then a garage door opening. The van moved slowly down a ramp then stopped on flat ground the front doors opened then closed, then the vans back doors opened. The women once again all put their hands over their eyes. The lights outside were bright.

"Come on out." ordered Dimitri. The women all climbed out of the van. Mollie looked around it looked like they were in a garage of a house, it was a big double sized garage. There was a laundry area in one corner and a set of stairs in the other. Alex pointed to the stairs.

"Up the stairs please." he said. It was the first time any of the men had said please. The women all went up the stairs. They arrived in a large living area of a house it was open plan and very modern. There was a large lounge area with 2 big black leather sofas, glass coffee tables and a huge tv on the wall. A long dining table was set with plates dishes and glasses. And in the modern top of the range kitchen area an old woman was stirring something in a large pot on the stove it smelt like a stew. Alex and Dimitri went to the old woman, she kissed them both on the cheeks then spoke quietly to them Dimitri turned to the group of tired and hungry women.

"Ok. Dinner will be ready in 10 minutes go and use the bathrooms in the bedrooms on this floor. Don't go upstairs. We are staying here tonight. Tomorrow we are going to Russia. Use the bathrooms then come back for dinner." Mollie turned and looked down the hallway there was 4 rooms all with open doors, the women walked down the hall. Mollie and Penny went in the first room, there was a double bed, bedside cabinets and nice bedding and towels on the bed. The windows were locked, and Mollie could see there was shutters down on the outside of the window. Penny went into the en suite.

"There's toilet roll and soap, and shower gel in the shower. I think I'm going to have a shower later." said Penny.

"It's actually a really nice house. Let's use the loo and wash our hands before dinner it smells like a Russian stew. Who do you think the old woman is?" said Mollie.

"Maybe she is the nan of one of them, do you think she knows what's going on?" replied Penny.

 "Definitely this isn't the first time she's done this." said Mollie. They used the toilet and washed their hands and faces before going back to the lounge. The other women were already sitting up the table there were 2 chairs left empty for Mollie and Penny. They sat down. The old woman called Dimitri in to the kitchen area, he picked up the large stew pot and carried it over to the table. The old woman followed with plates of bread. Dimitri put the pot down on the table, the old woman put the bread down then started to dish out the stew to the women. She didn't look at any of them but when she had served them all she said,

"Enjoy your meal." in Russian.

"Thank you, it looks delicious." replied Mollie in Russian. The old woman looked at Mollie she looked like she wanted to say something more to Mollie, but she stopped herself and returned to the kitchen area.

The women ate the stew in silence. It was good and they were hungry, they used the bread to clean their plates. Once they had finished the old woman came over to the table and cleared away the plates. Dimitri and Alex were eating their dinner in the lounge area, they were sitting on the sofas with the TV on. Mollie could smell the coffee, she was hoping it was for them she needed a coffee. The old woman came back with coffee

cups, a jug of cream and sugar in a bowl, then came plates of biscuits and

fresh coffee. The old woman looked at Mollie and said,

"Please serve yourselves."

 "Thankyou." replied Mollie. She started pouring the coffee in to her cup

then passed the coffee pot around. Once the coffee and biscuits had gone

Dimitri came over to the table.

"Tomorrow we will go to Russia." he said to the women. The women left

the table and returned to the bedrooms to shower and try to get some

sleep. They all knew tomorrow would be another long journey.

CHAPTER 13

Sean, Grace and Hannah left the hospital at 6pm. They were getting hungry again and Marie had been sleeping for the last hour. They all kissed Marie goodbye. Marie opened her eyes.

"Sorry, have I been asleep?" she asked.

"Yes, but that's ok, you need to rest as much as you can Marie. We will be back in the morning. The Nurse said you're going for another scan in the morning, so we might be here when you get back. Is there anything you want from home?" asked Sean.

"My face cream. Some clean underwear and clean nighties please." replied Marie.

"Ok, have you got that girls? In case I forget anything." said Sean. Grace and Hannah nodded. They said goodbye to Marie again and left the hospital. Once they were in the car Sean asked the girls what they wanted for dinner.

"Mc Donald's." said Hannah.

"Yes, a Mackie's Dad." agreed Grace.

"Ok, Macie's it is then." replied Sean. The nearest McDonalds restaurant was only a 5-minute drive away.

"Do you think Mum will be ok?" asked Grace.

"Yes, I do" replied Sean "Your Mum is stronger than we think. She is going to be ok. She was very lucky if that bullet hadn't got stuck well, it could have been a different outcome."

"I can't believe Mollie is cheating on Artiom with Mr Wozniak." said Grace making a face.

"I know he is well fit, do you think he will dump her when he finds out?" replied Hannah.

"He might not find out. Unless someone tells him, or Mollie tells him. If she ever comes back." said Grace.

"Cheats always get found out, don't they Dad?" said Hannah. Sean looked at Hannah, he didn't know what to say to that.

"I think people should be honest with each other. But sometimes it can be difficult, you don't want to hurt the people you love. It's not always easy." replied Sean feeling guilty. What will the girls think when they find out about Tracey and Ronnie, will they understand? He knew he needed to tell Marie and the girls soon. They pulled into McDonalds and went inside. Once they'd ordered their meals they sat at a table.

"Do you think Mum had to have her hair shaved off?" asked Grace.

"Yes, I think they must have shaved some off to remove the bullet." replied Sean.

"She's going to go ape shit if they've shaved it all off. She's only just had the colour done on it, she was moaning because it cost her 50 euros. She said next time she's going to buy a box of dye for 7 euros and do it herself." replied Grace.

 A McDonalds staff member brought their meals over on a tray. Sean had ordered a Big Mac meal, Grace had a Chicken Wrap meal and Hannah ordered a nugget meal. There was silence as they started eating. Once they'd finished and put their rubbish in to the bin, they got back into the car.

"Ok, do either of you know if there's any milk, bread etc at home?" asked Sean.

"Nope." Replied Grace.

"I think the cupboards are pretty bare actually" said Hannah, being more helpful, "Mum does the shopping on a Saturday."

"Ok, we will pop to the supermarket now. Buy the basics, then we can always go again." said Sean. They drove in to Javea and pulled in to the Mercadona supermarket. Sean got a trolley, and they went inside.

"Right Girls, we need the essentials." said Sean.

"Crisps, chocolate, coke and peanut butter." said Grace.

"I was thinking milk, bread, bacon, eggs that sort of thing," replied Sean smiling "I'll get the basics you two can get the crisps and stuff." Sean went off to get his list of food. The girls found him a few minutes later with their arms loaded up with bottles of coke, crisps, chocolate peanut butter and toiletries, they put it all into the trolley. Sean looked at the toiletries.

"Does Mum buy all that normally?" he asked he counted the bottles in his head six in total and a red nail polish.

"Yeah, every week" lied Grace "You can check with her tomorrow." Grace knew her Dad wouldn't remember to check it with Marie.

"Ok, I believe you. I think that's it. Come on let's get home." said Sean. They headed towards the checkouts.

"Sean!" shouted a middle-aged woman with bleach blonde hair and a yearlong suntan from a bottle. "How's Marie? Is it true what everyone is saying? Is she in hospital?" Sean and the girls stopped, Sean didn't recognize the woman who was now blocking their way with her trolley.

"Sorry do I know you? Sorry, bad memory." said Sean.

The blonde woman looked surprised.

"I live 3 doors up from you Sean" she replied looking a bit shocked," You came to our house last New Year."

"Oh, yes sorry, I'm shattered. I only had 1 hours sleep last night and yes, we've been at the hospital all day. Yes, Marie is in hospital. She is ok, she will be ok. She was shot in the head last night." said Sean.

"OH MY GOD!" shouted the woman, "Who would want to shoot Marie?"

"Well, we don't really know." said Sean.

"The Russians." said Grace. Sean looked at Grace and raised his eyebrows.

"We don't know for certain. So, let's just wait and see what the police find out. But Marie is doing well. Thanks for asking about her. Sorry can we get passed?" said Sean. The woman moved her trolley.

"Tell Marie, I send my love and if you need any help, you know where I live." said the woman.

Sean and the girls hurried to the checkouts before they saw anyone else. Sean paid for the shopping. "I didn't recognize the woman from up the road, did you two?" asked Sean back in the car and driving home.

"Yes, I did. Mum doesn't like her she says she's a right old gossip. Mum calls her the Javea Gazette." said Grace.

"Oh, right. Perhaps I shouldn't have told her Mum was shot then." said Sean.

"Well, everyone knows about Dad, it's all over Facebook. So, I don't think you've given away a secret." said Hannah.

"Well, if it's all over Facebook then obviously it's not a secret." said Sean.

They arrived home and Sean parked the car. After putting the shopping away Sean looked in on the girls, they were both laying on the sofa watching TV, Hannah was munching the crisps and Grace was eating the peanut butter from the jar with a spoon.

"Shouldn't you eat that on bread?" Sean said to Grace.

"I've eaten too many carbs today already." replied Grace. Hannah rolled her eyes at Sean.

"I'm going up to have a shower." said Sean the girls both said OK without taking the eyes off the TV. Once upstairs Sean closed the bedroom door and went into the en suite, he closed the door and switched the shower on, then he phoned Tracey.

"Hi Tracey, it's me." said Sean.

"Hi Sean, How's Marie?" asked Tracey.

"Marie is ok. She is bruised and sore, but she's ok." replied Sean.

"What happened? Was she actually shot?" asked Tracey.

"Yes. She was shot in the head, but the bullet got lodged in her skull. If it hadn't, she would be dead." replied Sean.

"Oh my God! Who did it? do the police know?" asked Tracey.

"Well, it seems like it was a Russian trafficking gang. They took the 2 friends Marie was with. The police think they've taken them to Russia." said Sean.

"Russia? Why?" asked Tracey.

"To St Petersburg, to work in the sex clubs I think." said Sean.

"Really? that's terrible." said Tracey.

"Artiom is one of the women's boyfriends. He wants to go and look for them in St. Petersburg, he is Russian." said Sean.

"God. I hope he finds them, how terrible. What a nightmare, are you ok? and the girls?" asked Tracey.

"We're ok. We've spent all day with Marie. We left at 6 O'clock and went for a McDonalds. Then we popped to the supermarket to pick up some things, home now. We're going back to the hospital in the morning. How's everything there? How's Ronnie?" asked Sean.

"We're fine. Don't worry about us Ronnie is in bed already. He had enough excitement last night." said Tracey.

"I'm shattered myself, early night I think." replied Sean.

"Yes, me too. I miss you already." said Tracey.

"I miss you too and Ronnie. I'd better go, the shower is running. I'll message you tomorrow." said Sean.

"Ok. I love you. Good night." said Tracey.

"Love you too. Give Ronnie a kiss from me, night Tracey." replied Sean and he hung up. He sat there on the side of the bath thinking about his life, he needed to tell Marie about Tracey and Ronnie, he needed to tell the girls they had a baby brother. He knew he was living a lie out here in Spain, he would tell Marie about Tracey and Ronnie once she was out of hospital. He needed to come clean. He quickly jumped in the shower before the hot water run out.

CHAPTER 14

Artiom popped to his apartment before going to Mollies Aunt and Uncles.

He packed a small bag with enough underwear, socks and a few t shirts to

last him a week. He decided if he run out of clothes while he was looking

for Mollie, he would just buy some cheap stuff. He had a quick shower

and made a coffee, while he was drinking his coffee, he looked at his

appointments for next week, he was good at his job as a Personal Trainer

and he had a steady list of clients, he messaged the ones booked in for

sessions next week and explained he would have to cancel all lessons next

week for personal reasons. He got a reply from all his clients, they all

knew what had happened to Marie and that the girls were missing, they

all replied with no problem and hoped he was ok. Artiom finished his

coffee and put his passport in his bag, he wanted to pop to the service

station to check his tires and fill up with petrol, then he would go to

Brenda's. He needed to fill Mollies family in on what he'd found out. And

to see if anyone wanted to travel to St Petersburg with him. He parked his car on Mollies drive, he noticed there wasn't a car outside Brenda's house. He rang the doorbell and Brenda answered.

"Hello Artiom. Come in, Ant has gone to the airport to collect Mollies mum and dad and Penny's parents are coming here as well. Come into the kitchen I'm just putting the kettle on, would you like tea or coffee?" asked Brenda, Artiom sat down at the table.

"Tea please." replied Artiom. Brenda opened the fridge and took a large plate of cakes out, she put them in front of Artiom.

"Have a cake." she said. Artiom looked at the cakes they all looked delicious, he chose a custard tart.

"They're Mollies favourite." said Brenda. She put the rest of the cakes back in the fridge.

"Yes, I know. I hadn't ever had one until I met Mollie." replied Artiom. Brenda made the tea and sat at the table.

"Have you anymore information?" asked Brenda.

"Yes. I have been to see Marie at the hospital, and she remembers everything that happened up when she was shot." said Artiom.

"How is Marie? What does she remember?" asked Brenda.

"She is going to be ok. She said they were walking home, and a car stopped and there were 3 big Russian men in it. Then a man in the back of

the car opened the door and managed to pull Mollie and Penny inside.
The man in the passenger seat got out and shot Marie in the head. Marie
was ringing Sean her husband at the time, and he heard the gunshot."
said Artiom. Brenda sat there in shock.

"But why would they take Mollie and Penny off the street like that?"
asked Brenda.

"I have found out who the 3 men are. They are part of a Russian gang.
They traffic women to Russia to work in the sex clubs. It's not great news I
know, but at least we know they are alive and where they are going." said
Artiom. Brenda put her hand up to her mouth.

"Oh my God. Artiom, are you sure?" said Brenda.

"I was told the names of the three men earlier and I went to the police
station and told them, they took E fit photos of the men to Marie, and
she's identified them." said Artiom.

"Oh my god, what are the police doing?" asked Brenda "They need to get
to Russia and find the girls."

"I'm sure they will have the Russian police looking for the girls and the
gang. But I'm driving to St. Petersburg tomorrow. I'm going to look for
them myself. I've been there before. I can't just wait for the police to find
them." said Artiom. Brenda was still digesting what Artiom had told her.

"We will come with you. Me and Ant, and I know Mollies mum and dad will want to come as well. Penny's parents will probably want to too will that be, ok?" asked Brenda.

"Yes. The more of us looking for them the better." said Artiom.

"How long does it take to drive to St. Petersburg?" asked Brenda.

"Last time I went it took me 17 hours. I stopped in France overnight. I have the directions saved in my sat nav, I stayed in Narbonne in an Ibis hotel it was about 50 euros for the night. The hotels in St. Petersburg are roughly the same price, we might be able to find a cheaper one." said Artiom.

"I think 50 euros a night is fair. It's not a holiday, so we don't need anything posh" said Brenda "I'll have a google and see what I can find while we're waiting for the others to get here."

Ant was waiting in his car outside the arrivals at Alicante airport for Bill and Sue. The airport was busy. But not as busy as it in the summer holidays. He wasn't waiting for very long before Bill and Sue came rushing out of the airport doors. Ant saw them and got out of the car, he opened the boot so they could put the small bags in it then hugged Sue.

"Hello Sue, are you ok?" he asked.

"Hello Ant. No not really, I feel so helpless and worried." she replied. Ant could see she had been crying, her face was normally calm, today it was red and puffy. Ant hugged her tighter.

"Come on let's get you home. Artiom is coming round he has been out all day trying to find the girls." said Ant.

He shook hands with Bill and opened the back door for Sue, then got in the car and began the journey home. There wasn't much conversation in the car, Ant could see Sue crying quietly in his rear-view mirror. There wasn't much traffic, and they were in Javea in 45 minutes. Ant parked the car but before they had opened the car doors Brenda was outside. She hugged Sue as soon as Sue got out of the car. The two sisters hung on to each other sobbing. Brenda had been dreading seeing her sister, she knew she would cry.

"Come on Sue, let's go in and have a cup of tea, Artiom is here he has some news." said Brenda. Bill and Ant got the bags from the boot of the car. Brenda hugged Bill then they went into the house.

"We're in the kitchen." said Brenda. They went into the kitchen, Artiom got up and greeted Sue with a big hug.

"Hello Artiom, we've heard so much about you." said Sue. Artiom shook Bills hand.

"Hello Artiom, so what news have you got?" asked Bill.

"Sit down. I'll put the kettle on." said Brenda. Ant, Sue and Bill sat down at the table with Artiom.

"Ok, well there's good news, I think Mollie and Penny are still alive and I think I know where they are heading." said Artiom.

"Where are they heading?" asked Sue.

"To Russia. St. Petersburg." replied Artiom.

"Russia? why?" asked Bill.

"Ok. This is the bad news, earlier today I went and visited Marie in hospital, she remembers what happened last night, up to being shot," said Artiom. Sue, Ant and Bill sat holding their breaths waiting for Artiom to carry on. "They were walking back to the apartment they were staying in for the night when a car stopped. in the car was 3 men all Russian, they are part of a sex trafficking gang." said Artiom. Sue gasped and put her had up to her mouth.

"Oh, my god" she whispered. Artiom carried on.

"They managed to get Mollie and Penny into the car, then as Marie was phoning her husband for help one of the men shot Marie in the head. It's a miracle she is alive, the bullet got stuck in her skull." Sue, Bill and Ant sat letting it all sink in. Artiom carried on "I was told the names of the 3 men earlier. I went to the police station and told the 2 officers in charge of the case, they knew the names and printed out E fits of these men. They took them to Marie, and she identified them as the men from last night. I was also informed that they are taking the girls to St. Petersburg. I'm going to travel there. I'm leaving in the morning." said Artiom. Sue, Bill and Ant were still digesting what Artiom had just told them. Brenda put the teapot and cups and saucers on the table, then sat down herself.

"I think we should all go with Artiom. The more people looking for the girls the better don't you think so Sue?" said Brenda.

"Yes. I want to come with you Artiom. We have got to find Mollie and Penny. Have the police said anything else? are they going there to look for them?" asked Sue.

"We've not heard anything else from the police." replied Brenda.

"I expect they've informed the Russian police to look out for the gang and the girls." said Ant.

"We need to come with you Artiom. Do you think Penny's parents will want to come as well?" said Bill, "What time are they arriving? Do you know Brenda?"

"They were boarding the plane around the same time as you, I think. Or just after, so they should be arriving soon I think" replied Brenda, "I've sent them our address."

"Do you know how long it is to drive to St. Petersburg Artiom?" asked Bill.

"Its 17 hours, I've done it before. We will have an overnight stop in a hotel in Narbonne in France, that's about half of the way. I was telling Brenda that I booked into an Ibis hotel it's about 50 euros a night. There's lots of hotels in St. Petersburg prices star from about 40 euros. We only need a cheap one as close to the red-light area as we can get." replied Artiom.

"I've already looked at the Ibis hotel in France, they have rooms available at 50 euros, and I've found a few in St. Petersburg that are 40 to 50 euros a night. How many nights do we think we will need?" asked Brenda. They all looked at Artiom, he shrugged his shoulders.

"I hope not many. It will take us 2 or 3 days to cover all the clubs and bars. But if we all go and split up then hopefully, we will find the girls quicker." said Artiom. They all felt more positive than they did before listening to Artiom. They felt like they were in with a good chance of finding the girls.

Brenda decided it was time to eat. Sue helped her clear away the tea things and make some sandwiches to go with the sausage rolls and cakes.

The men were discussing tomorrow's journey. Ant and Bill were pleased to hear Artiom still had the directions saved in his sat nav. Artiom said he would send them to Bill later. Sue and Brenda put the food on the table and Brenda sent Ant to the garage to fetch some wine. He was just pouring the wine when there was a knock at the front door.

"This could be Penny's parents." said Brenda. She got up and answered the door. Brenda knew it was Penny's parents straight away. Penny's mum was a little woman with blonde hair, just like Penny. Brenda could see she had been crying by her red eyes and puffy face. Penny's dad was good looking too. He looked sporty and fit, he too had red eyes.

"Hello, you must be Penny's parents?" said Brenda.

"Yes. Hello, we're Steve and Karen are you Brenda?" replied Steve.

"Yes. I'm Mollies aunt, come into the kitchen we are just about to eat, there's enough for you too." said Brenda.

"Oh no, we don't want to disturb your dinner." said Karen. They walked into the kitchen and saw the others sitting at the table. They all got up to say hello.

"Please sit down, it's not dinner it's just sandwiches. You must be hungry. Ant get 2 more glasses please." said Brenda. Ant got the glasses from the cupboard and poured Karen and Steve some wine.

"Here you go, you look like you need this." said Ant.

"Thankyou. Have you heard anything more?" asked Steve.

"What do you know? What have the police told you?" asked Artiom.

"Only that Penny was missing, she went out last night with Mollie and Marie and that Marie is in hospital and Penny and Mollie are missing, that's all we know for definite. Karen has seen some things on Facebook about a Russian gang shooting Marie." replied Steve.

"Yes, that's true. It is a Russian gang that's involved," replied Artiom "I was told the names of the 3 men from last night. They are Russian criminals known to the police. They took Mollie and Penny and shot Marie." Karen and Steve had the same reaction as the others did when they heard what had happened last night.

"Are you sure Artiom?" asked Steve.

"Yes, and Marie remembers it all up until she got shot." said Artiom.

"But where have they taken them?" asked Karen "We need to rescue them."

"They will be trafficking them to Russia. To St. Petersburg," replied Artiom "To work against their will in the sex clubs." Karen put her hands over her face and shook her head.

"No, we need to find them we can't let this happen." she said crying into a tissue.

"We are going to start driving to Russia tomorrow, we will stop in France overnight and then reach St. Petersburg on Monday, will you be coming with us?" asked Artiom. Steve and Karen looked at each other.

"Yes of course we will." replied Steve.

"Good, the more of us looking the better. You can travel with me in my car if you want, I've driven there before." said Artiom.

"Yes, that would be best. We've got a hire car and Penny's car is getting on a bit." said Steve. Brenda started handing out the sandwiches.

"Come on let's eat these before they curl up." she said.

They all started eating the food. None of them really tasting it. On a different day under different circumstances the food would have tasted delicious. Once the cakes had also been eaten, Brenda booked the hotels and Artiom shared the sat nav directions with Bill.

"What time shall we leave in the morning?" asked Steve.

"I think we need to leave here at 8am." replied Artiom.

"Ok, we will be back at 7.45 in the morning. Thank you for all for the food and the hospitality. We will go now and try to get some sleep." said Karen.

"Where are you staying?" asked Sue.

"We are going to stay at Penny's house." replied Karen.

"Have you got keys?" asked Brenda "Mollies car is still at the Arenal. Her keys are in her bag at the apartment, and she doesn't have a spare car key. I've phoned Mr Wozniak, the headmaster. It's his apartment, he is going to meet us when we are back from Russia, so we can pick Mollies bag up and bring her car back."

"Oh. Yes of course, Penny's car will be at the Arenal too. We don't need her car. It will be ok there until we get back. Penny normally leaves a spare house key in the key box next to her front door. We're hoping it's still there." said Steve.

"If you have any problems, come back here. I'm sure we will fit you in." said Brenda. They all hugged Steve and Karen goodbye and Brenda saw them out to the front door.

"What a lovely couple." said Brenda coming back into the kitchen

"Yes, they are very nice, Penny's a lovely girl too." said Ant.

Artiom got up from the table and looked at his watch,

"Thank you for the food Brenda, I'm going to go to bed. Early start tomorrow." He said.

Brenda looked the time,

"Oh, my goodness its 11 pm. I didn't realise it was that late, Night Artiom.

Come in here for breakfast. We will be having breakfast at 7." said

Brenda. She got up and hugged Artiom.

"Thank you Artiom, for everything you've done today." she said. Sue

hugged Artiom as well, the men waved him goodnight. Artiom left the

house, got his bag from his car and let himself in to Mollies apartment. It

felt strange being there without Mollie. He brushed his teeth and climbed

into Mollies bed, he could smell Mollies perfume on the pillow. He was so

worried about Mollie, he knew she sounded tough, but she wasn't really.

He knew had to find her and Penny, he had to save them. He closed his

eyes and prayed. He wasn't religious and he had never prayed before in

his life, he didn't even know if he believed in God. But tonight, he asked

him to look after the girls and to keep them safe and to help them find

them.

Steve parked the hire car near to Penny's little town house. it was in Javea

old town. The town is made up of narrow roads all entwinning with each

other. Some of the roads aren't wide enough for a car Penny's house is in

one of those roads. It is only metres away from the church and Penny can

hear the church bells ringing in every room of her little house. There's lots

of little Tapa's bars and crafty type shops around her, and on a Thursday it's a 5-minute walk to the local market. Penny loves her little house. She was lucky enough to buy it outright from money left to her from her Nan. She'd had a choice of a little terrace town house here or a modern new apartment near the beach. She chose this house and has never regretted it. Steve and Karen stood outside Penny's front door, it was very late but there were still people walking about. It felt strange knowing Penny wasn't in the house to greet them. Steve opened the key box, he knew the code, it was Penny's year of birth. He opened the front door, and they went inside. It was dark so Karen switched on a light. Penny kept a tidy little home. She had painted the walls white in every room. There were only 4 rooms, 2 downstairs and 2 upstairs and the bathroom was a little extension added on to the back of the house behind the kitchen. The floor tiles and the wall tiles in the kitchen were the original 1940s tiles Penny loved them. The floor tiles were a different colour in each room. All of them patterned in bright colours orange, blue and green. The kitchen tiles were bright blue with white flowers, Penny had painted the brown wooden kitchen cupboards white and added blue ceramic knob handles. The rest of the house was furnished with a mix of modern and old furniture that Penny had bought cheap or found at the side of bins, she loved painting old furniture giving it a new lease of life. On the walls hung lots of photos all in unmatching frames. Photos of all the places she had travelled to as a child with her parents and her brother. Precious memories.

Steve and Karen used the little bathroom then went up to bed. They had decided to sleep in the spare room, there was clean sheets on the bed and clean folded towels on the sideboard. It was as if Penny knew her parents were coming. Steve set an early alarm on his phone, and they got into bed.

"Good night Karen. Love you." said Steve.

"Love you too. Good night. We need to get up early to go and find our daughter." said Karen tearfully.

"We will find her." said Steve. They both laid in Penny's lovely spare room lost in their own thoughts. Too scared to share them.

CHAPTER 15

Sean woke up at 9 am. He got up and dressed and went down to the kitchen to put the kettle on. He opened the cupboard and got out his Emma Bridgwater mug it was decorated with a robin, Marie had bought it for him 3 Christmas's ago and every year they would see a little Robin in the garden. They always say it's sent to visit them from loved ones in heaven. Sean called the girls, was they coming to visit their mum? If they were, they needed to get up. He got a muffled reply from one of them, he didn't know if it was a yes or no. He decided to make himself some toast to go with his coffee, he opened the back door and was sitting in the morning sun when Hannah appeared. "Morning Hannah is Grace up?" asked Sean. Hannah was yawning,

"Yes, she's in the bathroom. She'd better not be long I need the loo." yawned Hannah.

"Use our toilet if you're bursting." said Sean.

"Ok I will, she could be asleep on the toilet for all I know." said Hannah. She went upstairs to use the en suite in her parent's bedroom. While she was on the toilet she heard Sean's phone ringing, he must have left it upstairs, thought Hannah. She finished in the en suite and picked Sean's phone up off the bedside cabinet, there was 1 missed call. I'd better take dad his phone to him she thought, then as she was leaving the bedroom a message came through it read,

"Morning Sean, hope you got some sleep. I've just rung you, nothing important. just wanted to tell you I love you. Ronnie sends his love to

Daddy. Speak later Tracey xxxxxxxx." Hannah read the message twice, she

didn't know what to do. She wished she hadn't seen the message. Oh my

god she thought, my dad is having an affair with someone called Tracey,

and who is Ronnie? is it a child? maybe it's a dog? dad always wanted a

dog. He wanted a brown Labrador he was going to call it Roxy though not

Ronnie. Hannah put her dads phone back on the bedside cabinet and

went downstairs. Grace was in the kitchen eating the peanut butter from

the jar with her finger.

"For god's sake Grace, at least use a spoon. You wouldn't be doing that if

Mum was here." said Hannah angrily.

"Ok, keep your hair on. What happened to you? Get out of the wrong side

of the bed." replied Grace.

"Oh, fuck off Grace." said Hannah. She was looking in the cupboard for

cereal.

"Ooooo you wouldn't say that if Mum was here." replied Grace. Hannah

slammed the cupboard door shut. There wasn't any cereal they had forgot

to buy any last night. Hannah went back upstairs and slammed her

bedroom door. Sean came into the kitchen,

"What was all that shouting?" He asked Grace, who was still sitting on the

kitchen side eating the peanut butter with her fingers.

"It was Hannah swearing, she told me to Fuck off." replied Grace. Sean looked at Grace,

"That doesn't sound like Hannah, she was ok 10 minutes ago." replied Sean.

"Well, a lot can happen in 10 minutes. She's probably found a split end or broken a nail." said Grace.

"If you two are coming to the hospital with me, you need to get ready. I'm leaving at 10 can you tell Hannah?" asked Sean. Grace looked at him and raised her eyebrows,

"No way, you can tell her, I'm not talking to her until she apologies to me." said Grace. She jumped down from the side, put the jar of peanut butter back in the fridge and took out the carton of orange juice, she was just about to drink it from the carton,

"I don't think so, do you?" said Sean "Get a glass Grace." Grace tutted and got a glass out of the cupboard,

"Mum lets me drink from the carton." she said.

"Well, I'm not mum, and I don't think she does Grace, now start getting ready please." said Sean.

He went upstairs, Hannah's bedroom door was shut, he knocked on the door,

"Hannah, if you want to come to the hospital you need to get ready, and please don't swear at your sister." he said through the door. Hannah didn't answer, she was sitting on her bed messaging her best friend Katie, telling her about the message she saw on her dad's phone.

Sean went into the bedroom and picked up his phone, he could see he'd missed a call from Tracey and read her message, he replied telling her he'd slept well, and that he loved her and Ronnie too.

Sean and the girls finally left the house at 10.30 am. Hannah was still in a mood,

"What's up Hannah?" asked Sean.

"Nothing." replied Hannah. Sean decided to leave it. Hannah was 15, she wasn't a little girl she was a teenager. Normally it was 13-year-old Grace that had the strops, Stroppy Lil, they called her behind her back. They drove to the hospital in silence, both girls had their earphones plugged in and Sean turned the radio off, it was tuned in to Bay Radio, he hated that radio station, they only have 6 songs that they're played repeatedly. He liked to listen to Radio 5 in his cab, and Tracey had the radio tuned in to Capital in the kitchen, he didn't mind that.

Sean parked the car, and they went up to the intensive care ward. Marie was in bed asleep. They said hello to the nurses at the desk, Nurse April was there,

"Hi, Marie has been for her head scan, Doctor Jamie Dura will be in to see Marie today with the results, but he said he was happy, so I wouldn't worry too much." she said.

"That's good, thank you." replied Sean. They crept into Marie's room and sat down in the chairs next to her bed, Marie opened her eyes,

"Hi," she said, she wasn't whispering today "Did you remember my things?" she asked Sean, Sean picked up a bag and put in on the end of Marie's bed.

"Yes, underwear, nighties and your face cream," replied Sean "I couldn't find your toiletry bag?"

"It's at the apartment, in my overnight bag. You'll have to go and get it." said Marie.

"Oh of course it is. I'll get in touch with the headmaster later and pick it up for you." said Sean.

"Thanks, all ok girls?" asked Marie looking at Grace and Hannah, they were both on their phones,

"Yes, all good, apart from Hannah swore at me this morning." said Grace.

Hannah looked at her sister,

"Yes, I did. Because you're annoying. She was eating peanut butter out of the jar with her fingers." said Hannah. Marie looked at Sean for help.

"Come on girls, give it a rest, Mum doesn't want to know all this." said Sean.

"Sorry." said Grace giving Hannah a dirty look Hannah returned the look to Grace

"Sorry Mum." said Hannah.

"The nurse just said the results of the scan this morning is ok. Well, she said Doctor Dura will be round later to see you about the scan, but that he was happy with the results." said Sean.

"That's Good, I feel a lot better today my headache isn't as bad." said Marie. Sean's phone pinged with a message, he took it out and read it, he smiled.

"Who was that?" asked Marie. Sean put his phone back in his pocket, "Just work." replied Sean. Hannah looked at her dad's face, was he lying? She was still upset about the message she had read earlier on her dad's phone. She had told her best friend Katie about it. Katie thought that Ronnie was probably a little dog or a kitten. But it did sound like her dad was having an affair with Tracey, whoever she was. Hannah didn't know

what to do, should she ask her dad who Tracey is? She knew her Mum

would be devastated if she found out. Maybe if she asks her dad about it,

he will finish it with Tracey and her mum will never know. Yes, decided

Hannah she will ask her dad who Tracey is, later when they get home.

CHAPTER 16

Mollie woke up. She opened her eyes it was dark in the bedroom, the

shutters were down, and the light was off, for a few seconds she forgot

where she was. She could hear plates and cutlery being moved about.

Breakfast, she remembered Dimitri telling them they would have

breakfast before they leave the house. She switched on the light it was

bright, Penny moved,

"Wake up Penny," said Mollie gently shaking Penny, she opened her eyes

and immediately put the sheet over her head.

"Turn the light off." she groaned. Mollie climbed out of the bed and went

in to the en suite,

 "Come on Penny get up. I don't know what the time is, but I heard plates

being moved about. We can have breakfast before we go." said Mollie.

"I'm not hungry." replied Penny. She got out of bed and went in to the en suite. Mollie was sitting on the toilet. They weren't worried about privacy between the two of them anymore.

"Well, I think you should have something to eat Penny, it could be a long drive. Listen Penny, once we get to Russia St. Petersburg or wherever we are going, we will be able to get a message to Artiom or our parents. They will all be looking for us now. We just need to get there alive, ok?" said Mollie. She finished on the toilet and began washing her hands Penny took her turn on the toilet,

"I hope you're right Mollie. I hope they are looking for us. You hear about people going missing and they're never found." said Penny. Mollie had washed her hands and was now washing her face.

"That's because those people are probably dead buried in a hole in the middle of nowhere or under a bloody motorway. We're not dead Penny. We were taken but we will be found. Now come on hurry up and get washed. I could murder a coffee." said Mollie. Sounding more confident than she felt. Penny got washed and both girls got dressed back into their dirty clothes.

"I hope there's a way we can get some clean clothes soon." said Mollie.

The girls opened the bedroom door, the smell of toast and coffee wafted in.

"Breakfast." said Mollie. They walked along to the dining table. The other girls were already there, they were sitting in the same seats as last night.

"Oops, last 2 again." said Mollie. They sat down, the same old woman was in the kitchen area, she carried over 2 large plates of toast, then returned with pots of coffee and tea, there was already butters and jams on the table.

"Serve yourselves." she said to Mollie. Mollie smiled at her the woman looked away quickly.

"Thankyou." said Mollie and poured herself a coffee. The other women helped themselves to the breakfast. Once they'd all finished Dimitri came over to the table, he had been eating toast sitting on the leather sofas with Alex, the TV was on.

"Use the toilets. We are leaving in 15 minutes." he said. And moved his hand in a gesture to say come on, get up. The women all got up and returned to the bedrooms where they used the toilets again. All hoping they wouldn't need to use the bucket in the back of the van today. 15 minutes later

Alex walked along the hallway and opened all the bedroom doors.

"Ok, we're going. Come on." he said. The women were all sitting on the beds in the rooms waiting for the call. They went out into the hall.

"Ok, back downstairs." Ordered Alex. The women all followed Alex down the stairs, to their surprise the van had been replaced with a minibus, "Upgrade," said Dimitri he already had the side door open "Get In and put the seatbelts on. You're travelling in comfort today." The women climbed in the minibus, the windows were all blacked out, they could see out, but no one could see in. They all put their seat belts on. Mollie and Penny were sitting at the back of the minibus.

"Well at least we have seats to sit on." said Mollie.

"Thank god. I'm not sure I could have lasted another day in the back of that van." replied Penny. Alex and Dimitri got into the minibus, Dimitri started the engine and put the air con on. He opened the garage doors and the women all looked out of the windows. Dimitri pulled out of the garage and then the gates opened. Mollie looked back at the house they had been in. It was a nice, detached house. There were houses on both sides to it and houses opposite. They pulled out on to the road the house was situated in the middle of a residential street, there was people jogging along on the path, and a woman walking her dog. How can these people not know what's going on in that house thought Mollie? How can people be living next door and opposite it and not see the vans and minibuses go in and out. She knew they weren't the first van full of women to stay in the house and probably not the last. Soon they were travelling on the motorway, as they overtook other vehicles the women would all look out of the tinted windows pleading with their eyes "please help us." But the people just looked at the minibus they couldn't see the women's desperate faces.

Most of them nodded off. Penny was asleep within 20 minutes of them driving on the motorway. Mollie just sat looking out of the window, she was thinking about what might happen to them once they arrived at their destination. She knew that there was lots of sex clubs in St. Petersburg and strip clubs and brothels. She tried to work out what the difference was between the clubs, she decided the strip clubs were where women danced naked, the sex clubs were where the woman probably danced naked and had to have sex with men and the brothels were where men went for sex, no dancing involved. Oh god, she thought to herself what we are going to end up in. She started to talk to God again.

"Please God, don't let them put me or Penny in a brothel or a sex club, we can handle a strip club, but please, don't let us go anywhere where we have to have sex, please, please, please." She was talking to God in her head, she put her hands together and closed her eyes, "Please help

Artiom and our families find us, I know they will be looking for us. Please

help us get through this, please God, Amen." She opened her eyes again,

she knew she had to believe they would be rescued. It was the only way

she could get through it.

CHAPTER 17

Artiom knocked at Brenda's front door. He had showered and put his bag back in his car boot. Brenda opened the door.

"Morning Artiom, come in I've made some bacon rolls, sit down and help yourself." said Brenda. Artiom sat at the table. Brenda had made 2 plates of bacon rolls, the others were already sitting around the table drinking tea and coffee. Brenda got Artiom a mug.

"Here you are Artiom, help yourself to tea and coffee. And eat a bacon roll or 2, Come on everyone eat the rolls while they're still hot." said Brenda. She sat herself down and took a roll, she thought maybe if she started eating the others would too, it worked soon the plates were empty of bacon rolls, and the tea and coffee drunk.

"Right then, are we ready to rock and roll.?" asked Ant. Brenda started to clear the table.

"Let me stick all this in the dishwasher, and then we can go." said Brenda. Sue and Karen helped Brenda tidy up.

"I'm just going to use the loo before we go." said Sue. The others all decided visiting the toilet quick would be a good idea. Soon they were all outside putting their bags in to the car's boots.

"Ok Brenda, you have got my phone number. If you need us to stop or anyone wants the toilet message or phone me, ok?" said Artiom.

"Yes, I will message you. Drive safely, not too fast, Ant doesn't like driving too fast." replied Brenda. They got in to the two cars. Artiom started up the engine of his BMW, he loved his car. Normally he would drive fast on the motorway, but he would take it steady on this trip. The sat nav started to tell him the directions and soon they were travelling on the motorway towards France.

Marie woke up from a short nap. Sean and the girls were still there, all looking at their phones.

"Hi Marie, you dozed off do you want anything? a drink?" asked Sean. Putting his phone away.

"I would love a cup of tea, Hannah do you think you and Grace could go and buy me a cup of tea from the canteen?" said Marie. Hannah looked up from her phone.

"Yeah ok. Do you want it in a takeaway cup? I'm not sure I can carry a cup and saucer all the way back here." replied Hannah.

"A takeaway cup is fine. Make sure you put milk in it, do you want one Sean?" asked Marie.

"Yes please, I'll have a cup of tea, here is some money." said Sean. He gave Hannah a handful of change, Hannah looked at it and tutted.

"can't I take a note instead of all this change?" she said.

"It might be a vending machine you will need change if it is." replied Sean.

"Oh, ok." said Hannah.

"Are you going Grace?" said Marie. Grace looked up from her phone and looked at Hannah.

"You don't have to. But I can only carry 2 cups." said Hannah. Grace stood up.

"I'll come, is there enough money for some crisps or chocolate. I'm starving." said Grace. Sean opened his wallet and gave Grace a 10 euro note.

"Buy a few bags of crisps and some chocolate. For us all to share." he said to Grace.

 Grace rolled the note up and looked through it like it was a telescope.

"Ok, see you soon." she said. Marie and Sean watched the girls leave the room and walk pass the nurse's station.

"Hannah was in a right mood this morning." Sean told Marie.

"Was she? Normally it's Grace that gets the hump. It's probably nothing, I wouldn't worry too much, it's her age and her hormones." replied Marie.

Sean thought Marie was probably right it was her age. Doctor Jamie Dura came into Marie's room.

"Hello Marie, how are you feeling today?" he asked.

"I'm feeling better than yesterday, but I'm so sore I feel bruised and battered." said Marie.

"You will very sore for a while. I've looked at your scan from this morning. I'm happy to say its fine there's nothing apparent to worry me. Your brain looks normal, and your skull looks like it will heal ok. So good news." said the doctor.

"I'm just pleased you could find my brain." laughed Marie. She felt relieved the scan showed everything was ok.

"How long will I have to keep this bandage on for?" asked Marie.

"Probably a few more days, is it uncomfortable?" asked the doctor.

"It is a bit uncomfortable, but I wondered how much of my hair has been shaved off?" replied Marie.

"Not that much. Don't worry about your hair it will grow back in no time." said the doctor. He smiled and nodded at Sean then left the room. Marie looked at Sean.

"I hope I'm not bald under this." she said pointing to the bandage.

"I'm sure they only shaved off what they needed to." said Sean. Hannah and Grace came back with the cups of tea for Marie and Sean, a hot chocolate for Grace and a can of coke for Hannah. Grace tipped a plastic bag out on Marie's bed it contained 2 bags of cheese and onion crisps, 2 mars bars and a Reese's peanut butter chocolate bar.

"That's all I could get with 10 euros." said Grace picking up the Reese's chocolate bar. Hannah picked up a Mars bar.

"Didn't they have any plain crisps?" asked Marie "Cheese and Onion will stink the room out."

"Erm, I didn't look, I just saw cheese and onion." said Grace. Hannah looked at her sister.

"There was every flavour. I told her to buy the plain ones, but she said she likes cheese and onion." said Hannah. Grace poked her tongue out at Hannah, it was covered in chocolate.

"You're a disgusting pig Grace. I don't know how we are related you must have been adopted."

said Hannah. She turned her back to her sister and opened her coke. Sean picked up the other mars bar and gave it to Marie.

"You have it Marie I'm ok, I'll go and get a sandwich or something in a minute." said Sean.

"Let's have half each, I'll eat the first half." replied Marie. She opened the Mars bar and started eating it. Sean took his phone out of his pocket.

"I'm just popping to the toilet, I won't be long." he said and left the room. Once he was outside of the intensive care ward, he looked at his phone at the earlier message from Tracey.

"Hi Sean, just checking everything is ok? All ok here xxxxx" Sean messaged back, saying everything was ok and he would ring her later. He put his phone back in his pocket and walked back to Marie's room. Marie was talking to Hannah and Grace.

"Behave you two, you are not little girls anymore dad said you got into a strop this morning Hannah, is everything ok? It's not like you to get stroppy. I know you do Grace." said Marie. Grace gave her Mum a surprised look.

"Mum, you should have heard her she was really swearing." said Grace.

"No, I wasn't really swearing, I swore that's all. Everything is fine mum don't worry." said Hannah "I just had the hump, I'm ok now."

"Good. Your Dad doesn't need to play referee, it's bad enough I'm stuck in here." said Marie.

Sean walked back into the room.

"That was a quick wee." said Marie "I wonder if they sell magazines in the hospital shop?"

"Do you want us to go and have a look?" said Hannah.

"Yes please, thank you. You know what I like, gossipy rubbish and real-life stories." said Marie. Sean got his wallet out again and gave Hannah a 20 euro note.

"Do you want anything else? biscuits? asked Hannah.

"Yes, if they sell biscuits buy a packet of biscuits, you know what I like, nothing too chocolatey and not too crunchie." said Marie. The girls went off to the shop.

"Got over your strops yet?" Grace asked Hannah.

"Yes. I didn't have the strops, I saw something that upset me." said Hannah.

"What? you haven't been watching those videos about the chickens bred for KFC without legs or wings again have you? "asked Grace.

"No, nothing like that. I can't tell you, you will tell mum. And I don't want mum to know." said Hannah. Grace looked hurt that Hannah didn't trust her.

"Hannah, I wouldn't tell mum something if you told me not too. You can trust me. I promise I won't say anything." said Grace linking her arm through Hannah's arm.

"Ok, but don't say anything to mum ok. I saw a message on dads phone this morning, it was from someone called Tracey, it said her, and Ronnie missed dad and had love and loads of kisses in it." said Hannah. wishing already she hadn't told Grace. Grace stopped and looked at Hannah.

"Really. What like Tracey is a girlfriend or something? And who's Ronnie?" said Grace.

"I wish I knew. Maybe he is a dog? or a cat? I'm going to ask dad later who Tracey and Ronnie are." said Hannah.

"Let me be there. Maybe Ronnie is Tracey's child?" said Grace "I wonder how old he is?"

"He might be a dog or a cat. I'm going to tell dad he has got to finish it with Tracey, or I'm telling mum." said Hannah. They arrived at the shop, it wasn't much of a shop. It did have the trashy magazines Marie liked to read and some plain biscuits, not too crunchy. Grace bought herself another Reece's chocolate bar. There wasn't enough money for anything else so Grace said she would give Hannah a bit of the Reece's bar. They walked back to Marie's room.

"Don't say anything to dad about Tracey" said Hannah "I want to talk to him later when we get home."

"Ok, keep your hair on I will try not to ok." replied Grace. Hannah really regretted telling Grace.

"Here you are, I was going to send dad to look for you both." said Marie to the girls. Hannah gave Marie the magazines and biscuits, "Thanks love, I haven't read these ones either. Well done, and I love these biscuits, and they have my name on them MARIE." laughed Marie.

"That's why I picked them." Lied Hannah she hadn't even noticed her mums name on the biscuits.

Sean and the girls stayed until 4 o'clock, then Marie sent them home. She was feeling more like herself, still sore, but she decided she would sooner read her magazines in peace. And dinner tonight was salmon with vegetables, she was looking forward to that. The canteen was crap according to Sean, so she thought it was better all-round if they went home for dinner. Sean and the girls kissed Marie goodbye, they would be back tomorrow. Hannah had charged up one of her old mobile phones for Marie so she could phone them if she wanted anything brought in.

Once they were home Sean looked in the freezer, there were pizzas or fishfingers, he decided on pizzas. He got them out and switched the oven on. Hannah and Grace were both in the kitchen.

"Alright girls? what's up? pizza, ok?" asked Sean. The girls both nodded. Grace looked at Hannah and lifted her eyebrows, Hannah took a deep breath.

"Dad can I ask you something?" said Hannah.

"Yes, what it is?" replied Sean. He was unwrapping the pizzas.

"Who are Tracey and Ronnie?" asked Hannah. She breathed out. Sean froze for a second, then carried on putting the pizzas on to baking trays.

"What do you know about Tracey and Ronnie?" asked Sean quietly.

"Nothing, I saw the message on your phone this morning when I was in your bedroom." replied Hannah. Sean put the pizzas in to the oven, should he tell the girls now? before he told Marie? He didn't want Marie to find out from Hannah or Grace.

"Ok. Sit down." He said to the girls. They both sat at the table. Sean sat down and took his phone out of his pocket. "Mum doesn't know about what I'm going to tell you two. I was going to tell her on this trip back, but now she is in hospital. I don't want either of you telling her." Said Sean. Both Hannah and Grace were holding their breath, they both nodded at Sean. "I live with someone called Tracey in the UK, and we have a little baby named Ronnie." Said Sean. He showed the girls a photo of Baby Ronnie with Tracey on his phone. Hannah and Grace looked at the photo.

"How old is Ronnie?" asked Hannah.

"12 weeks old, he is really cute, you will both love him." Replied Sean.

"Is he our brother?" asked Grace.

"He is our half-brother." Said Hannah.

"Yes, your half-brother." Said Sean.

"Where did you meet this Tracey, and how long have you been living with her" asked Hannah.

"I met her 18 months ago. She was a fare in my taxi. She used to live in Javea." replied Sean.

"Oh my god, does Mum know her?" asked Hannah.

"No, no they don't know each other." replied Sean.

"Does she know about us, about Mum?" asked Hannah.

"Yes, she knows all about you two. You would like her she's really nice." replied Sean. He could tell that Grace was ok with it all but Hannah, he wasn't sure what she thought.

"So, what's going to happen now dad? are you leaving mum and us? to live full time with your new family?" asked Hannah tearfully, Grace looked worried now too.

"I will never leave you two. You're everything to me. But I think once Mum knows about Tracey, she won't want me coming back to Spain anymore so you two will have to come and stay with us in the UK, you will meet your little brother. Tracey wants to meet you both too." replied Sean. Both girls were crying now, "Come on girls, I'm really sorry this has happened. I love you both so much, you're going to love Ronnie." Hannah looked at her dad.

"But mum is going to be so upset dad, you've cheated on her with another woman, and you've had a baby with her." cried Hannah "When are you going to tell mum?"

"I will tell her when she comes home from hospital. Please don't tell her while she's in the hospital," said Sean.

"But she will think we've kept it secret from her." said Hannah.

"No, I will tell her I asked you not to say anything, she will understand." replied Sean.

"I don't think she will." replied Hannah. Grace picked up Sean's phone again and looked at the photo.

"Do you have any more photos of Ronnie? not her just of Ronnie?" asked Grace. Sean took the phone from Grace and found photos of Ronnie when he was first born, he gave the phone back to Grace.

"Start here Grace, that's when he was first born you can flick through all the photos. Tracey is in a lot of them." said Sean. Hannah moved closer to Grace and looked the photos with her.

Sean watched his girls looking through his photos. He was relieved that they knew about Tracey and Ronnie. He just had to hope they wouldn't tell Marie before he did. There was a lot of photos to look at. Lots of the photos were of Sean, Tracey and Baby Ronnie together, a little family. It was difficult for Hannah and Grace to look at Tracey without disliking her. But they had both fallen in love with Ronnie. He looked like their dad.

"When can we meet him dad?" asked Grace. She had stopped crying and was now feeling desperate to meet her baby brother.

"Soon Grace, soon." replied Sean. He checked the pizzas in the oven "Pizzas are ready, set the table please." he said. Hannah and Grace put Sean's phone down and set the table between them. Grace was feeling excited about having a little baby brother, but Hannah was feeling sad. Sad that her mum didn't know what they knew. Sad that her mum was going to be heartbroken when she finds out about dads secret family.

CHAPTER 18

The journey in the minibus was long. But it was much more comfortable than sitting in the dark on the floor of a van, with a bucket of urine threatening to spill over. Dimitri had obviously done this journey before, he knew where to stop one time on the motorway. It was in a small carpark where there was a single shed with a toilet in it. There wasn't anyone else about and the toilet was disgusting. There was a dirty toilet without a seat on it, no paper, no sink or soap, it didn't look like it had been cleaned for a very long time. The floor was flooded with dirty water and who knows what else. There were cobwebs hanging from the ceiling so thick they looked like curtains. Dimitri stopped the minibus and said if anyone needed to use the toilet they could do now. All the women needed to use the toilet. Alex escorted each one to the shed and he waited at the door, the door was stuck half open. Alex stood on the outside of the door. Dimitri stayed at the minibus at the open door, he had his gun tucked into his waistband, so no one was going to try to run away. Once the women had all used the toilet Dimitri and Alex took turns in going to the toilet themselves, they didn't go in to the shed they

relieved themselves around the side of the shed.

Four hours later the minibus pulled off the motorway. Mollie could see a

road sign for St. Petersburg, the roads they joined were all busy, there

was lots of traffic lights and queues of traffic, once again the women all

looked out of the windows desperately willing someone to read their

minds.

"SAVE US!" they were all shouting silently.

They stopped at the gates of a large apartment block, it wasn't in the red-

light district of St. Petersburg, it looked more of a residential area. There

were children riding bikes in a park opposite. The gates opened and

Dimitri drove into an underground carpark, he drove to the back of the

carpark next to a lift and parked. Alex got out and called the lift, once it

had arrived Dimitri opened the minibus door.

"Out you get, go straight to the lift and get in." he ordered. The lift was 4

steps away from the minibus, all the women got into the lift and Alex and

Dimitri squeezed in with them. Alex had a key card that he tapped on the

button that said PENTHOUSE, the doors closed, and the lift travelled up to

the top floor. Already the women could tell it was a posh apartment

block, the lift was huge, it was mirrored on the walls, the floor and the ceiling, and was pristine clean. All the women tried to avoid looking at themselves in the mirrors, they knew they all looked a mess. But it wasn't easy when everywhere you looked you could see your reflection. The lift came to a stop and the doors opened on to a hallway. The women all stepped out into the hallway there was only one large door there, Dimitri opened it using the same key card. The women could hear other women talking inside the apartment. Dimitri held the door open until they were all inside a large lounge area. He called out.

"Hello."

The talking stopped and two young women appeared in the lounge area. "Hello Dimitri, hello Alex," they both said to the men "Hello." they said to the women standing looking around. They all thought the house they were in yesterday was nice, but this penthouse apartment topped it. There was so much glass and mirrors and a glitterball hanging over a big dining room table. The furniture was all white leather, shiny chrome and black gloss.

The two young women in the apartment were slim and attractive, they were wearing pink tight fitting jogging suits, and had pink fluffy sliders on their feet, their blonde hair was tied up in ponytails. Their faces showed only a hint of makeup, and their finger and toenails were immaculate painted in glossy neon pink varnish. Dimitri spoke to them both.

"Take the women to the bedrooms, give them clean clothes, and shoes, bin what their wearing." The two young women nodded at Dimitri. Alex and Dimitri walked into the kitchen area.

One of the two young women spoke.

"Hi, I'm kitty this is Lola. We have got to give you new clothes, come this way." Kitty and Lola turned and walked in the direction they had appeared from they stopped at a door.

"Ok, four of you go with Lola, the other Four come in here with me." said Kitty. Mollie, Penny, Michelle and Kara all went in to the first room with Kitty, the others followed Lola into a room next door. The rooms were big, they had king sized beds, fluffy cushions, and large en suites. Kitty opened a floor to ceiling wardrobe that covered the whole wall, the doors were mirrors. Hanging inside the wardrobe were lots of pink jogging suits, the same as what Kitty was wearing, and on the shelves were t shirts and underwear down on the floor of the wardrobe were pink fluffy sliders. All the clothing and sliders were brand new.

"Ok, tell me your dress sizes and your shoe sizes. You go first what's your name?" asked Kitty pointing to Mollie.

"I'm Mollie, I'm a size 12, and shoe size 5." said Mollie, happy that she was going to get clean clothes, but thinking this was surreal. Who were these young women and who owned this apartment? Kitty picked a size 12 jogging suit, t shirt and knickers, no bra, thought Mollie, she looked at Kitty's chest, was she wearing a bra? she couldn't really tell. Kitty picked up a pair of size 5 sliders and passed it all to Mollie.

Ok", you need to get changed into these clothes, you all showered last night, yes?" asked Kitty.

"Yes, I did. I think we all probably did." replied Mollie.

"Good, get changed then." said Kitty. Mollie looked around her where was she meant to go?

"Get changed in here Mollie. Just so you know, there are cameras in every room even the bathrooms, there's no privacy." said Kitty. The women looked around the room, the cameras weren't visible.

"Who's watching us?" asked Mollie. She started to take her dress off.

"They are watching. The people that now own you. Put your dirty clothes in a pile on the floor." smiled Kitty. She asked Penny for her name and sizes, then Michelle and Kara. Soon all four women were wearing the matching pink tight fitting jogging suits and fluffy sliders.

"I feel like we're at a Barbie sleep over." said Mollie to Penny. They were all looking at themselves in the giant mirrors.

"What is this all about?" said Michelle to the others.

"God knows, it must be the uniform or something, at least we're in clean clothes. I'm glad I'm more covered up, apart from the lack of a bra, why?" replied Mollie. Kitty picked up the pile of dirty clothes and shoes and put them in to bin bag, she tied up the top.

"Ok, two of you will sleep here tonight, there's another three bedrooms, two to a room." said Kitty.

"Do you and Lola live here?" asked Kara.

"No, we live somewhere else. We're just here to kit you out with clothes, and we're going to cook your dinner tonight." replied Kitty.

"You can use the bathrooms in the rooms if you need to, then come down to the lounge area."

Kitty walked out of the room with the bin bag of dirty clothes and shoes.

"Me and Penny will sleep in here, if that's Ok?" said Mollie to Michelle and Kara. They both nodded and went to look for another bedroom.

Mollie closed the bedroom door, she looked above their heads.

 "The cameras must be in the light, do you think they can hear us as well?" asked Mollie.

"Yes, probably. This is so weird, it's like our identity has just been taken away. Do you think that's their real names? Kitty and Lola?" replied Penny. Both girls were looking at the enormous chandelier above the bed, it was huge there could easily be cameras and bugs in it, watching and listening to everything they did and spoke. Mollie went into the bathroom, it was the nicest bathroom she had ever been in, there was an open shower big enough for a football team, a free-standing roll top bath with gold taps, a double sink, and two toilets.

"I've never ever seen two toilets in one bathroom, that's Just weird." said Mollie. The two women looked for the cameras, the lights in the ceiling were all spotlights.

"Well at least we don't have to wait for the loo, we can have a shit together." said Mollie. Penny had a little smile at this remark.

"I don't know why I'm laughing Mollie this is so strange. What the fuck is all this about?" she pointed to their jogging suits.

"I have no idea, but I'm sure we will find out soon." said Mollie. She hugged Penny tight and whispered in her ear.

"Stay strong Penny, don't forget we are being spied on." Mollie let Penny go and penny nodded at her.

"Right, come on then let's have a wee together and then go down to the lounge." said Mollie.

Mollie and Penny went to the lounge area, the other women were already there, they were sitting on the white leather sofas.

"Where did Alex and Dimitri go?" Mollie asked Michelle.

"They've just left, they said they will be back in the morning." replied Michelle.

"Was you told about the cameras?" asked Mollie.

"Yes, weird, eh?" replied Michelle. They all looked up at the three large chandeliers hanging from the ceiling.

"Whoever owns this apartment loves a statement chandelier." said Mollie. Kitty and Lola appeared from the kitchen area.

"Ok ladies, we have prepared a lasagne for you with a salad, hope you all eat meat, if not it's a nice salad." smiled Kitty.

"You can sit up at the table, there's water and juice, help yourselves." The women all sat up at the long black glass dining table. The big glitterball above the table was slowly turning, making it feel as though they were in a disco, Mollie suspected whoever was watching them was doing it now. Kitty and Lola started to bring in plates and cutlery. Mollie and the others had helped themselves to water and juice, obviously alcohol is off the drinks list, thought Mollie. She could murder for a glass of wine right now.

Once Kitty and Lola had brought in the lasagne, salad and bread they too sat down to eat. Lola plated up the lasagne and Kitty passed the salad and the bread round.

"Hope none of you are professional chefs, Lola made this lasagne." laughed Kitty.

"Ha very funny, at least I can actually cook." replied Lola. The women all began eating, the food was all very good.

"It's all lovely, thank you." said Mollie.

"Do you know what's going to happen to us next?" she asked Kitty. Kitty looked at Lola, and Lola shrugged her shoulders.

"Can they, whoever they are, hear us?" asked Mollie.

"Yes" replied Kitty "We don't know where you will end up tomorrow, I think I can say, there are many clubs and brothels that you could end up in. You will need to wait until tomorrow to find out where you go. We both work in the same club, it's a strip club." The women all stopped eating while listening to what Kitty was saying.

"So, what do you do in the strip club? Sorry I've never been in one" asked Mollie.

"Well, we dance and then we take our clothes off, Lola is an expert in pole dancing." said Kitty.

"I wouldn't say I'm an expert. I don't think you can be an expert at pole dancing, I just like dancing around a pole." laughed Lola. Mollie and the other women didn't know what to think. Kitty and Lola didn't seem to mind that they are working as strippers in a sex club, was it their choice? "Were you taken, like we all were, against your will?" asked Michelle. Kitty looked at Michelle and nodded.

"Yes. You do have a choice you know, the girl I arrived with decided she wasn't going to cooperate, she disappeared fairly quickly." said Kitty.

"I don't see that as a fair choice, work in the sex industry or die? is basically what you are saying. Our friend we were with on the night we were taken was killed. She was shot in the head. She didn't have a choice." replied Mollie. Kitty looked at Mollie with a forced smile.

"It is what it is." she said. But her eyes showed sadness. The women finished the dinner, it was followed by fruit and ice cream, and then coffee. By now they were all feeling very full and well fed. "Thank you." said Michelle to Lola and Kitty.

"You are welcome. Hopefully we might see one or two of you again sometime." said Lola. The women helped to tidy up the table and the kitchen that was out of this world, all white marble and glitter, even the floor, it was like something a famous film star would show off in OK magazine. Once it was all tidy Kitty said they all needed to use the showers or baths and go to bed they were to be up for breakfast at 8 am. The women all said goodnight to each other and went into their bedrooms once they were inside Kitty and Lola locked the doors from the outside.

"Have we just been locked in?" asked Penny. Mollie tried the handle,

"Yes. Bastards locking us in the rooms, we really are like prisoners now." said Mollie.

"I'm going to run a bath."

"Don't forget they are watching us." said Penny pointing to the lights in the bathroom.

"Well let's give them something to watch." replied Mollie. She started to run a bath, the bubble bath smelt like vanilla, she poured some in the bath and swirled it around.

"Right" she said "I'm stripping off, let them have a good look I'm sure they are going to see it all soon anyway, but this is my choice to strip off tonight. I'm doing it because I want to." she took all her clothes off and used the toilet, then once the bath was ready, she climbed in it and laid back in the bubbles. She decided that even though these people had taken her from the street and were going to make her work against her will, she wasn't going to lose herself, she wasn't going to change, they won't break her, she will survive this.

CHAPTER 19

Artiom pulled into the carpark of the IBIS hotel in Narbonne France. Ant

pulled up next to him, they all got out of the cars and stretched their arms

and legs.

"Well, that's the first leg of the journey done." said Brenda. They got their

bags from the cars and walked into the hotel reception. Once they had

booked in and got their room keys they had a quick look in the restaurant,

it was basic but looked ok and there was a menu of the day on the door. A

three-course meal for 19,95 euros.

"That's not bad for France," said Steve, "it always costs more to eat out

here than Spain and the UK" "Let's see if we can book a table." said

Brenda, "what's the time now?"

"It's 10 to 8 Brenda," said Sue "Book it for 8.30, give us all time to freshen

up." The restaurant manager came over and Brenda booked the table.

"Ok all booked for 8.30. Let's check our rooms are ok." said Brenda. They

all went and found their hotel rooms. They were basic but fine with clean

beds and fluffy towels, that's all they needed. Artiom was first back down

to the restaurant, he could see no one else was there yet so he went to the bar and ordered a coke, he sat up the bar and checked his phone. He was hoping there might be something from Mollie. He had messages from some of his clients, asking how he was, and from his gym buddies, wishing him luck in finding Mollie. He had a quick look on Facebook, the events of Friday night had been replaced with other gossip, nothing as Shocking as a shooting and abduction. Artiom put his phone away. Steve and Karen were next to arrive, two minutes later the others were there too. They all went through to the restaurant and the waiter showed them to their table. The menus were on the table ready for them to look at. The waiter took the drink orders, 2 bottles of the house white wine and 2 bottles of water. Artiom still had his coke, he wasn't going to have any wine. Ant said he would just have the one glass. The menu looked good, on it was vegetable soup or prawn cocktail for starters, fish of the day or chicken casserole for mains and apple pie or fruit salad for dessert then coffee. The waiter brought the wine and water back and they ordered their food. They chatted about today's journey, how the French drive too fast, especially the lorries. Soon the food arrived, they all enjoyed their meal choices. It was a strange situation to be in, they had been thrown together quickly. All desperate to get to St. Petersburg and all determined to find the girls. Artiom was the first one to leave the table.

"See you all at breakfast, 7.30." he said.

"Goodnight Artiom love, see you in the morning." said Brenda. The others all waved him goodnight. Once he had gone Brenda told the others she thought Artiom was a lovely young man, they all agreed with her, and they meant it. Once the last of the wine was finished, they all went to bed, hoping sleep would come quickly so they could get on the road and reach St. Petersburg as quickly as possible.

The following morning Steve and Karen were the first down to breakfast. The table they were sitting at last night was set up for them, the waiter came and showed them the buffet breakfast then left them to it, they helped themselves to coffee then decided to wait for the others before getting any food. They didn't have to wait long the others all arrived within a minute or two, it wasn't 7.30 yet, they all wanted to get today over with. The breakfast was good, they all had a hot breakfast of bacon, eggs, sausages, tomatoes and mushrooms plus toast and Brenda took a few pieces of fruit and some pastries for the journey.

Once they had checked out of their hotel rooms, they put their bags back in to the cars."

"Ok, same plan as yesterday, if you need to stop let me know ok Brenda?" said Artiom.

"Yes, we will Artiom, drive carefully won't you." replied Brenda. They got into the cars and started the journey to St. Petersburg. It was an easy drive until they hit the city then it got very busy, Ant lost Artiom at a set of traffic lights, but the sat nav got him to the hotel. Artiom, Steve and Karen were there already.

"Hi, we got stuck at the lights." said Ant.

"The traffic is mad, isn't it, we forget what traffic jams are living in Javea." said Artiom.

"Until the summer, when all the holiday makers arrive." replied Ant.

"Yes, that's true. Shall we book in?" Asked Artiom.

They all nodded and walked into the hotel reception. Artiom took over and booked everyone in. Once they had their room keys, they looked for the hotel restaurant. Once again there was a meal of the day menu, it was in Russian so Artiom translated it. Again, it was a good selection the starters were blinis, basically pancakes that you fill with different savoury fillings or pampushki, a dumpling made from potato and stuffed with cheese. For the main course there was plov which Artiom explained is chicken and rice in a pot, or pelmeni Artiom described as meat filled dumplings, and there was beef stroganoff, everyone knew what that was.

The desserts were Russian biscuits and coffee. Artiom booked a table for them for 15 minutes time, it was already 8 pm.

They went off to their rooms to freshen up, Artiom was first back to the restaurant, and he sat at the table and checked his phone, no messages from Mollie. He was still hoping to see something from her, he had messages from friends and from Mollies friends asking where she was. There was a message from Officer Garcia, he said they had located a house in Pedreguer that they believe the girls were kept, he called it a safe house, the girl's bags were found there, and that he would keep Artiom informed of any more developments. The others arrived in the restaurant.

"Artiom, have you had a message from the police?" asked Brenda, she was waving her phone around.

"Yes, about the safe house in Pedreguer?" replied Artiom.

"Yes, what's that supposed to mean? safe house? and found the girls bags in there." said Brenda.

"We said that Brenda, safe house? didn't keep them safe, did it?" said Sue.

The waiter came and took their drinks order, two bottles of wine and some water again, then they gave him their food orders. While they were waiting for their food, they started planning the search for Mollie and Penny, Artiom said he was going to start tonight after dinner. He said he was going for a walk about, that the first bars and clubs were about a 15-minute walk away, the others all said they wanted to come with him, so they ate their meals skipping dessert and changed into comfortable shoes, they all left the hotel at 10pm. Artiom said the clubs and bars would be getting busy now and so would the streets so watch your pockets and bags, the pick pockets will be working.

They walked towards the first street full of bars and strip clubs, it was an eye opener for all of them apart from Artiom who had been there before. Brenda wasn't sure she wanted to actually go into any strip clubs, Sue and Karen agreed with her. Bill, Ant and Steve said they didn't mind going in, just to look for Mollie and Penny of course, they weren't going to stay in there for any longer than they had to. Artiom decided it would be best if they all split up and went into as many clubs and bars as they could. Brenda had printed off some flyers with photos of the girls on them, she gave everyone a hand full each, the women decided to stay together and visit the bars. Artiom and Steve teamed up together and Ant and Bill made the other team. Artiom and Steve crossed the road they decided to go into all the strip clubs on the opposite side of the road to Ant and Bill, the women were covering the bars on both sides. They agreed to meet up back outside the first bar in an hour they all had their phones on them in case they spotted the girls or needed help. Bill and Ant went in the first strip club. The Flamingo Club. It was an eye opener, they were let in the entrance door by the tough looking door men, then they had to pay 400 Rubel, about 5 euros each to a scantily clad young woman, luckily Artiom had given them some Russian currency at dinner. They went through some double doors and into the strip club, the music was loud, and the lights were flashing, they stood on the spot for a few minutes taking it all in trying to adjust their eyes and ears, a young topless woman walked over to them.

"Hello" she shouted above the music, "Can I get you handsome guys a drink?"

Artiom had already warned them not to order a drink or buy a drink in the strip clubs, that's where they make money, that and paying for lap dances etc. Artiom had said just pay to get in, then walk around the club to look for Mollie and Penny then leave, if you see Mollie or Penny, don't make a scene, just let the others know and Artiom will phone the Russian police. These people are not going to just let the girls walk out of a club. Ant shook his head at the hostess.

"No thank you." he replied to the topless woman, and quickly walked away from her.

"Well, this is busy." said Ant to Bill, they were standing still again, taking it all in. There were 4 different platforms they all had shiny silver poles reaching up to the ceiling, each pole had a pole dancer sliding naked up and down it. Then there were 6 large metal cages hanging down from the ceilings each with naked dancers in them, and a large jacuzzi on a platform had naked women in it washing each other with sponges and bubbles. There were lots of topless women walking around with silver trays, ready to take the customers drinks order. It was super busy, there was leather sofas and booths around the edge of the club, they were all occupied. There were single men sitting talking to the hostesses drinking champagne and then there was groups of men sitting in booths watching a hostess give a striptease or private dance. It was what you would expect to see in a strip club. Ant and Bill got their bearings and started to walk around the club, they stopped every now and then and did a full 360 degree turn, the club was big and there was a lot of women working in there, they didn't want to miss spotting Mollie or Penny, they concentrated on just looking at the women's faces, but it was difficult.

Once they had covered the whole club they headed to the exit, once outside both men took a deep breath in.

"Well, that was an eye opener" said Ant" I don't really know what I was expecting, there were a lot of men in there wasn't there?"

"Yes, and a lot of girls, some of them looked so young" replied Bill "I'm not sure Sue or Brenda should go into a strip club. I think they'd be shocked."

"I was shocked to be honest, I just thought there would be a stage with a stripper, do you think they will all be like that?" asked Ant, still trying to get over what he had just seen.

"Yes, I expect they will all be similar do you want to go in to the next one?" asked Bill.

"I'm not sure I want to, but I will. Come on, nothing will shock us now." said Ant.

They went in to 2 more strip clubs, they were all very similar to each other, within a minute or two of walking in a topless hostess would ask to take their drink order, they would decline, and then start the slow walk around the club, searching for Mollie and Penny. The second club had a dancer performing on a stage with a huge snake and the third had naked women painting each other with large paintbrushes on a stage, it looked a messy said Bill. They left the third strip club and decided they'd better start walking back to meet up with the others. The streets were busy, lots of stag parties rushing about. There were women standing about, dressed in high heels, short skirts with stockings and suspenders on show and very low tops, when you looked at their faces you could see these were women in their forties and fifties, too old to work in the strip clubs, they would quietly offer their sexual services to the men as they walked past them, there was lots of busy dark alleys next to the bars and clubs. Brenda Sue and Karen were waiting for the men to come back. They had been into lots of the bars, they all thought the bars were sleazy. They showed the people working in the bars the photos of the girls, no one had seen them. There were shops in between the clubs and bars but they had closed earlier so they decided to come back in the morning and show the flyer to the shop staff when they opened again. Ant and Bill and Artiom and Steve arrived back to the meeting place at the same time.

"How did it go?" asked Artiom "How many clubs did you go in?"

"We went in to three. It was an eye opener for us I can tell you, I don't think you should go in any Brenda," said Ant "We didn't realize they would be so busy. We didn't see the girls."

"Well, to be honest the bars are sleazy enough, I wouldn't want to go into a strip club, but I will if it means finding the girls" said Brenda "How did you two get on Artiom?"

"We went in three clubs too, they were all busy, we didn't see Mollie or Penny either, but that's only six clubs there's so many more, we will come back tomorrow, the strip clubs open at 6pm, but the bars open at lunchtime, so we can ask around in them first." replied Artiom.

"What time do the clubs close?" asked Steve.

"They won't close until 4am," replied Artiom.

"4am! bloody hell, they can't be busy until 4am?" said Sue.

"There are some people won't get here until 2 or 3am." said Artiom.

"Jesus, that's mad" said Ant "We could stay out tonight, and cover a few more clubs? You can go back to the hotel." he said the women, they all looked at each other.

"Well, I don't mind carrying on" said Artiom, "But I think maybe you three should go back to the hotel, it's really busy now. It's probably not the safest place for you to be without us men." Artiom said to Brenda, Sue and Karen.

"Ok, we will go back to the hotel, do you think we will be safe walking back there?" asked Brenda.

"Yes, I think if you walk back the way we came you will be fine." replied

Artiom, the women said goodbye and started walking back to their hotel

once they arrived there, they all agreed they needed to get a drink in the

bar. They found a little table in the corner of the bar and ordered large gin

and tonics each.

The men walked back to the last strip clubs they had been in, they had all

spent about 1200 roubles each so far, they had enough rubbles each for 3

more clubs, then they would need to get some more Euros and Sterling

changed up into Russian roubles. The men split up again, with Artiom and

Steve crossing the road and Ant and Bill going into the next strip club

along their side of the street, they had arranged to message each other

when they had run out of money. Ant and Steve messaged Artiom at 1am

to say they'd been in 3 more clubs, but no sign of the girls, so they were

heading back to the hotel, Artiom messaged back saying they was just

leaving the 3rd club and they would see them at the hotel. Brenda, Sue

and Karen were still in the hotel bar when Ant and Bill got back there. The

men spotted the women in the bar.

"Hello Brenda, why didn't you go to bed?" asked Ant.

"I wouldn't have been able to sleep, not until you all got back, no joy?"

she replied.

"No, but there's plenty more clubs to look in, is the bar still open?" asked Ant, looking at the empty gin glasses on the table, there was also empty pots of tea and coffee.

"Sorry it's just closed" said Brenda "I can make you a cup of tea up in the room."

"I'm parched, I would have liked a beer, but a cup of tea sounds good." replied Ant. Artiom and Steve arrived back.

"Hi Artiom, no luck?" asked Sue, Artiom shook his head.

"No, but there's a lot more clubs to search in." he said.

"That's what Ant just said" said Sue "Right then, let's go to bed, it's another day tomorrow." The women all stood up, they all wished each other good night and arranged to meet for breakfast at 9am. The shops didn't open until 10am. They went to bed disappointed that they hadn't found the girls yet.

CHAPTER 20

After her bubble bath Mollie dried herself with a giant fluffy towel, put on her knickers and t shirt and climbed into the king size bed. Penny was already in it she had had a quick shower, trying to keep the front of her body facing the wall the whole time away from any cameras. Once Mollie was under the quilt, she took her t shirt off.

"Why don't you take yours off Penny? then they will be clean when we get dressed in the morning." said Mollie. Penny decided if she stayed in the bed and under the quilt all night it was a good idea, she took her t shirt off and dropped it on the floor her side of the bed.

"What do you think they are going to make us do?" she asked Mollie, whispering under the duvet.

"Do you want me to be honest with you Penny?" whispered Mollie.

"Yes." said Penny. She wasn't stupid she knew what was going to happen, she just needed to hear it.

"I think, some of us are going to be working in a strip club where we will have to basically strip and dance in front of men, some will be put in a sex club, basically it's a night club but you can have sex there either in rooms or in certain areas in the club, and men will pay to either have sex or watch other people having sex, the last option will be a brothel, you know what a brothel is, it's a house or an apartment, where men go and pay to have sex with women in private rooms, this apartment is probably used as a brothel it would a high end brothel. To be honest Penny, I'm hoping for the strip club, I can get used to stripping I think." whispered Mollie.

"I hope we stay together Mollie, I don't think I'll cope on my own." whispered Penny. She started crying quietly, Mollie put her arm around her.

"Don't cry Penny, we don't know what's going to happen tomorrow, I know we will be rescued I just know we will, we've got to keep it together. I think the younger girls are going to be put in the sex clubs and the brothels, I feel really bad saying that, but I think that's what is going to happen." whispered Mollie. Penny stopped crying.

"I think that as well. I hope so, and that makes me such a bad person." whispered Penny.

"No, it's called survival Penny. And we have got to look after us. Let's try to get some sleep, once we're out of here we will look for ways of getting a message to Artiom." whispered Mollie. Penny fell to sleep soon after, but Mollie couldn't sleep, she was worried about what was going to happen tomorrow. She was praying again, that her and Penny would be put into a strip club and wouldn't have to have sex with strangers. She felt guilty, hoping it would be the younger girls put chosen to put be put into the sex clubs and brothels and forced to have sex. She decided that if she managed to get help to be rescued then she would come back and save these girls. She asked God to save them all before anything bad happens to them. She asked God to give them all the strength to carry on and she asked God to help Artiom and her family to find them.

She must of fell asleep eventually because a loud bang woke her up, she didn't move, she had heard that noise before, it was a gun shot, she looked at Penny, she was still asleep, it was dark, and her eyes were trying to adjust to the darkness. She could hear talking, it was men talking in Russian, she didn't know if the cameras would be watching them sleeping so she decided to stay in the bed. The voices got louder, until they were in the hall outside their bedroom door. Mollie froze, Penny opened her eyes.

"Shhhh" whispered Mollie "something is happening, I heard a gunshot." Mollie and Penny both lay dead still, listening to the commotion in the hallway.

"Get her out of here" said a man's voice in Russian "we need to clean this mess up." Mollie told Penny what she heard, she thought it could have been Dimitry, but she wasn't sure, they listened to what they must thought was a body being moved, then a tap being run and a scrubbing noise, they didn't go back to sleep. It didn't seem much later when their door was unlocked from outside.

"Morning, up you get, breakfast is ready." said Kitty popping her head in the room. Mollie climbed out of bed and pulled her t shirt on, she switched on the light, Penny put her head under the quilt and groaned. Mollie walked to the door and opened it a crack to look out, there wasn't anything to see at first, the marble floor looked as glossy and clean as it was before, then Mollie spotted something, it was a bright red smear about the size of a small fingerprint on the wall, she looked closer, she knew the cameras would be watching her, it was blood she was sure of it. She went back into Penny and climbed back in bed and put her head under the quilt.

"Penny, there's a fingerprint in blood outside on the wall its about 4 inches up from the floor opposite our door." whispered Mollie.

"Oh, my god, what happened?" Penny whispered back.

"Let's get up and see if we can find out. Breakfast is ready." said Mollie. Both girls got up and dressed, they used the bathroom and even brushed their teeth, using the new toothbrushes they found in the bathroom. They left the bedroom, Penny saw the blood on the wall and nodded at Mollie.

They walked down the hall to the living space, they weren't the last ones to arrive today, Michelle wasn't there, they sat down, and Lola and Kitty came out from the kitchen area with bowls of fruit, plates of toast and pots of tea and coffee. Mollie looked at Michelle's empty seat, she looked at Kara,

"Where's Michelle?" asked Mollie. Kara and Michelle were sharing a bedroom, Kara looked at Mollie, she had been crying, her face was red and blotchy, tears started to fall down her face, she wiped them away with a tissue

"I don't know, I woke up in the night and she was gone." she said. All the women were looking at Kara.

"Where has she gone." asked Mollie. Kara shrugged her shoulders and started buttering a piece of toast. Kitty and Lola sat down at the table, Mollie looked at them.

"Where has Michelle gone?" she asked them.

"She was needed last night for a job." said Lola, helping herself to coffee.

"What sort of job?" asked Mollie, the other women were all silent, listening to what Lola would say next.

"Listen, we don't ask questions ok, and you shouldn't either, sometimes girls get picked for jobs, sometimes they come back, sometimes they don't, we can't tell you anything else because we don't know anything else, do you understand this, Mollie?" replied Lola. Mollie looked at Kitty and Lola, she knew, they knew exactly what had happened to Michelle, it was probably them that had to clean up last night.

"Ok." said Mollie. She knew when it was best to shut up. The women finished the breakfast in silent, all thinking about Michelle, and what could have happened to her? Kitty stood up.

"Ok, you all need to get yourselves ready, you're getting picked up in 20 minutes." She said. They all left the table, Mollie looked at Kitty and moved her head slightly towards the hallway.

"Do you think I could have a clean t shirt, I've got jam on this one?" asked Mollie. Kitty looked at Mollie she could tell Mollie wanted to show her something.

"Yes, I'll come and get you one." she replied. They walked to the hallway and just before they opened the bedroom door Mollie kicked a slider towards the blood on the wall, Kitty looked and saw the blood.

"Ooops." said Mollie. She put her foot back in the slider. Kitty opened the bedroom door and got a new t shirt out for Mollie when she gave it to Mollie their hands touched, and Kitty squeezed Mollies hand. She didn't say anything but the look in her eyes told Mollie that she was saying thank you. Kitty left the room, Mollie and Penny used the bathroom again and then went down to the lounge area, they both saw that the blood on the wall had disappeared. Dimitry and Alex were waiting in the lounge area drinking coffee, they didn't look tired or worried, they were laughing about something on Alex's phone. Soon the remaining seven women were all in the lounge, standing there in their matching pink jogging suits and fluffy pink sliders.

"Ok let's go." said Dimitry. He called out goodbye to Kitty and Lola, they came out from the kitchen area and took the coffee cups from the men. "Bye, girls, good luck, hopefully we will see some of you again." said Kitty, she was looking at Mollie, "Bye, take care." said Mollie. Lola and the other women all said goodbye to each other. The women followed Dimitry and Alex out of the penthouse apartment to the lift, it was open ready for them, they all got in, Mollie looked at their reflections in the walls and ceiling, there was too much pink going on. The doors of the lift opened and the minibus from yesterday was parked up, Dimitry opened the minibus door and the women all climbed in soon they were outside on the road, they drove for 10 minutes then stopped, they waited while a large metal gate opened then drove in, they stopped on the driveway of a large house. Dimitri waited until 2 men came out of the front door, they came to the minibus and opened the side door, Mollie and the other women all held their breaths, the 2 men looked in and pointed to Ava, Kara and Chloe, the 3 youngest women.

"Out." ordered one of the men, the 3 girls got out, they all looked terrified, Mollie called out to them.

"Girls, stay strong." she called. They didn't reply, Mollie and Penny looked at each other, they were both thinking the same thing. This is a brothel. Dimitry turned the minibus around and drove out of the large gates, another 10 minutes later and they were driving through the red-light district of St. Petersburg. It was busy with people walking about, the clubs and bars were closed but there were coffee shops and shops open.

Dimitry drove down a backstreet and pulled up behind a club, the women couldn't tell what sort of club it was, he parked the minibus and both men got out, the minibus door was opened, and the 4 remaining women were ordered to get out. Then the back door of the club opened and a blonde woman in her 50s came out, she was slim and attractive. She was wearing a black trouser suit and her hair was on top of her hair in a neat bun, she had a friendly smile on her face.

"Hello Dimitry, hello Alex," she said and kissed the two men, they said hello back. "Come in girls." she said to Mollie, Penny, Charlotte and Kelly.

"I'm Margot, welcome to the Pink Kitten Club." She went back through the door Mollie and the others followed her in, the door was closed and locked behind them from the outside then they heard the minibus drive away. They were in a long corridor with doors on either side of it, all the doors were closed, and they had numbers on them. Margot walked past them all until she reached the end of the hallway, there was 12 doors in total 6 either side.

"Ok, as you can see there are 12 rooms off this corridor, each room is a dressing room with toilets. You will be given your own space in one of the rooms. That's your space, keep it tidy, and don't touch anything on any other of the spaces, ok?" she said. Mollie and the others all nodded, Margot opened door number 1. "You will all be in this room. Go in." She waited for them to walk into the dressing room, it was huge, there was 8 dressing tables around 2 walls of the room, in the centre was two pink sofas back-to-back. The dressing tables all had mirrors on them and there were full sized mirrors along another wall. Margot opened one of the mirrored wardrobes behind it was full of sparkly and sequined dresses all pink and black, and so many pairs of shoes, all stiletto shoes, all shiny. There was a single door leading into a large bathroom with 4 showers and toilet cubicle.

"So, you can see there are lots of dresses and shoes in here." said Margot pointing in the cupboard, "You can choose 1 dress and 1 pair of shoes each. Hang them on the hooks next to your dressing table." They looked and saw that the four empty dressing tables had hooks on the wall, the other 4 dressing tables had lots of makeup and hairbrushes on them and on the hooks next to them there was dresses hanging and shoes below on the floor.

"Can you see what I mean about you all having your own personal table and space? Don't take anyone else's things, I've seen hair pulled out by the hand full, just because one girl has taken a lipstick without asking first," said Margot, they all nodded. "Ok, you can come back in here after I've given you a tour of the club. And you will be given some training." Margot opened the door and held it open and waited for them to leave the room. Then Margot opened the door that was at the end of the corridor, it opened into the club, the women walked in, it was huge it had mirrored walls and giant glitterballs were hanging from the ceiling. There were 6 stages positioned around the club, all with poles on them running from the floor of the stage up to the ceiling. There was a bar that run along one wall it was in a black glittery glossy marble, there was black leather and chrome stools in a line in front of the bar. All around the club there was black leather sofas and low black and chrome coffee tables. In the areas at the front of the stages there were rows of black chairs, for a good view I suppose thought Mollie.

"Ok, so as you can see this is the club. Obviously when its open it will look different, the lights will be on, and the disco balls will be spinning. And of course, it will be full of men, wanting to have a good time, and you girls are going to give them what they want." said Margo. She wasn't speaking aggressively or even forcefully, but she wasn't asking them she was telling them, they didn't have any choices, this is what they were going to do.

"In about 10 minutes, some of the other girls are coming in to practice their dance routines. Work starts at 5pm. You will be escorted here with the girls from your house, they are the ones coming into practice. Once they have finished practising you will go back to the house with them, that will be where you will be living. Then you'll be back here later, ok? Got all that?" They all nodded at Margo, what would happen if they hadn't got it all? it's not like they could just say. "Well actually, I don't fancy this job, see you later."

"You can go and choose your dresses and shoes now, there's a box of makeup and hairbrushes etc next to the shoes help yourselves to what you want, no fighting." said Margo. Then she turned and headed towards the bar area. The girls could see that 2 men were standing behind the bar restocking the bottles.

"Ok, let's go and have a look." said Mollie. They walked over to the door that led them to the corridor, Mollie opened it and they all walked through it, she could see the back entrance door at the end of the corridor was closed. If only that was open, they could have escaped she thought. Mollie opened the door they were in earlier, no one was in there, they all went in and started to look through the dresses. They were all in 2 parts, a bra type top and a skirt bottom part, they were made from stretchy Lyra fabric with lots of sequins and sparkly gems and crystals sewn on. They were all one size.

"One size fit all." said Charlotte. The others laughed at this, rarely does one size fit all. There wasn't much fabric in any of the outfits, Mollie picked up a black sparkly outfit, a bra top with a mini skirt that had a daring split up to the waist.

"Wow, now I like to wear daring outfits but even this is a bit much for me." she said. She looked through the other outfits, but they were all similar, there wasn't anything that covered anymore flesh up, a few showed off a bit more flesh. She stuck with the black one and picked up some shoes. Penny chose a black too. Charlotte chose a pink outfit and

Kelly went for a black 2-part sparkly dress. They all hung the outfits on an empty hook and stood the shoes on the floor under it. Kelly went and got the box of makeup. There were 2 big boxes of make-up and a box of hairbrushes and hair accessories, they opened them all up and started to look through, all the make-up was new and unused. They all chose what they would normally use at home there was nail polish as well, so they all chose a couple of them too, they put their chosen make up on their dressing tables

"This is so weird." said Mollie.

"I know. It's like we're in a dream or something, it's not real life anymore." Said Charlotte.

"More like a nightmare." said Penny. They started to look through the box of brushes when the door opened and 4 young women wearing the uniform of pink tracksuits and fluffy sliders walked in.

"Hi, you must be the new recruits" said one of the women "Welcome to the family." She walked over to her dressing table and sat on the chair.

"Well, tell us your names then?" she said while looking at herself in her mirror.

"I'm Mollie, this is Penny, that's Charlotte and Kelly." said Mollie.

"I'm Shelly." said a small blonde-haired woman.

"Hello, I'm Zoe." said a tall slim red headed woman.

"Hi, my names Ana." said a small dark-skinned woman.

"And I am Cherry." called out the last woman from the bathroom. She came back in wearing just her knickers, she was a slim blonde-haired woman, they were all in their early 20s. Cherry walked over to her dressing table and put the bottom half of her outfit on, it wasn't a skirt it was a pair of skimpy hotpants, she didn't put the top on but put some stiletto heels on. The other women got changed too, also just into the bottom half of the outfits.

"You will get used to it, don't worry" Said Zoe "It is what it is, the sooner you just get over the fact that you're going to be walking around half naked the better. Believe me, you could be working somewhere much worse."

"Is this club a strip club? you don't have to do anything else?" asked Charlotte.

"Yes, it is a strip club, so you don't have sex with any of the men, they are not allowed to touch us. If they want that, they have to go to one of the sex clubs, or to a brothel." replied Zoe "Now we've been told you have got to come and watch us. our routines, if I were you, I'd put the outfit on now, and the shoes, you'll be wearing it later."

The other women were getting changed, Mollie decided she would just do it, and started to get herself changed. Charlotte and Kelly followed her lead, but Penny didn't move.

"Come on Penny, let's just get on with it." said Mollie.

"I really don't think I can walk about without a top on, I'm just not comfortable with it." replied Penny.

"Look, I'm not comfortable either. I don't suppose Kelly or Charlotte want to do this anymore than you do but come on Penny this is going to be the only way we are going to get through this. We have got to do what we're told." said Mollie. Charlotte and Kelly were changed into the bottom parts of the outfits, Mollie looked at Zoe.

"Zoe are there cameras in here watching us?" she asked.

"Oh yes, there's cameras watching us everywhere, here and at the house, they listen sometimes too" replied Zoe "and they don't like troublemakers or whingers, so if I was you Penny, I'd get over your embarrassment now, and toughen up." Zoe walked to the door, the other women were already there. "Come on, let's go. The other thing they don't like is lateness." said Zoe. Penny stood up and quickly got changed, she put the bra like top on as well as the mini skirt, she knew it might cause her trouble, but at that moment in time she just couldn't be topless.

They all went into the club, Margo walked over to them.

"Hi girls" she said to Zoe and co. "You've met your new housemates then? All, ok?" she asked.

"Hi Margot, yes everything is fine. Penny is a little bit shy, but she will be ok, won't you Penny?" said Zoe. Margot looked at Penny, she had noticed she was wearing a top, she was pleased the other 3 wasn't.

"Listen Penny, if you're going to stay here, you will have to work topless, the tops are worn sometimes to start a routine, but they always come off. So do the skirts or hotpants if you are pole dancing naked. Tonight, we want you to serve the customers. You will be topless, the men don't come here to look at girls with tops on" said Margot "If you prefer, I can you transferred to one of the sex clubs or a brothel?" It was a loaded question, Penny didn't answer Margot, she undid the hook at the back of the top and took it off, she knew she was stuck between a rock and a hard place. Zoe and the other girls had gone over to a stage and had started to slide up and down the poles, they were expertly swinging themselves around the poles and hanging upside down. Margot told Mollie and the others to go and watch.

"You will all have to learn to do that. I'm going to bring you all a tray so you can practice walking around holding a tray." she said. She walked to the bar to get 4 silver trays. The trays were round and heavier than they looked. Margot showed them how to walk with the tray up high in the air, wiggling their bottoms and a hand on their hip, she was good at it. Mollie wondered if maybe she was once standing where they were now. Margot told each girl to practice walking around the club, Mollie didn't find the task too hard, she was used to wearing high heels, Charlotte and Kelly had both done a bit of waitressing, so they were getting the hang of it. But Penny was having a nightmare, she couldn't walk in the shoes, and found the tray heavy to hold up in air.

"You'll be alright Penny, you just have to practice walking in the shoes. See if you can take them with you and practice in the house." said Mollie. Penny nodded, she didn't want to be here, and she was terrified about coming back later. Margot called out to Zoe.

"Zoe, do you want to see if the new girls are any good on the poles?" Zoe stopped dancing around the pole.

"Who wants a go?" she called out. Charlotte walked up to the stage.

"Ok Charlotte, you need to jump a bit off the ground, wrap you knees around the pole, then grab the pole up high with your hands, then cross your ankles over each other, all at the same time! It sounds hard but believe me it isn't really, it just takes a bit of practise, go on have a go."

Said Zoe. Charlotte jumped up grabbed hold of the pole and wrapped her legs around it, she didn't know what to do next, so she just hung on to the pole. Zoe laughed.

"Well, you know how to get on to the pole well done, now you've got to learn how to swing yourself around it, but I think you will be good at it, a lot of girls can't even hang on a pole straight away." Charlotte carried on practising, she was enjoying it, but that was because there weren't any customers in the club, she didn't know how she would feel being watched swinging around a pole naked. Penny was trying her best at walking in the high stiletto shoes, she didn't think she would ever be able to walk in them properly, she had tripped up so many times. How was she going to walk in these stupid shoes and carry a heavy tray full of drinks? She wasn't feeling positive that it would happen. Margot was watching Penny.

"Well done Penny, and yes take the heels back to the house and practice wearing them. It's time for you to go girls, I'll see you all later." said Margot. The girls all went back to their dressing room and changed into their matching jogging suits. They hung their costumes on the hooks for later. Penny kept hold of her shoes.

"Ok, the minibus will be here soon." said Ana.

"So does the minibus pick you all up and take you back to where you live?" asked Charlotte.

"Yes, we can only travel to here and the house, and only by the minibus." replied Ana.

"So basically, you're kept like prisoners?" asked Charlotte.

"Yes, we are. You'll get used to it." replied Ana. There was a knock on the door, Ana opened it.

"Hi. Yes, we're ready." She said to a large Russian man standing at the door. They all followed Ana out of the room and down the corridor, one of the other doors opened and Mollie could see the girls inside getting dressed and chatting. The big man unlocked the back door to the club, outside was a minibus just like the one they were dropped off in. They must have a fleet of them, thought Mollie. Another big man was standing at the open minibus door, Ana and the others got in first Mollie, Penny, Charlotte and Kelly climbed in after them. The two men got into the front of the minibus. The driver started the engine.

"All ok girls?" he said, looking at the girls in his rear mirror.

"Yes, all ok. These are our new house mates." said Zoe. The man in the passenger seat put his hand up and waved.

"Hello." he said. The driver did the same, Mollie and the others all waved back and said hello. It was a short journey no more than 10 minutes. They stopped outside some tall gates, the gates opened, and the minibus drove in, it stopped on the drive outside a nice-looking house, there was a house either side and a high fence all the way around it. The man in the passenger seat got out of the minibus and opened the front door of the house. The girls all got out of the minibus and went into the house, Mollie and the others 3 followed them.

"See you at 10 to 5." said the man shut the front door, Mollie heard him lock it three times.

 The house was modern and clean, the floors were all tiled and had rugs on them. They walked through the hall into a lounge, there was a couple of sofas and armchairs all black leather, with fluffy pink throws on them and furry pink cushions, Mollie noticed there wasn't a TV.

"Are you not allowed to watch TV?" she asked Zoe.

"No, it's one of the things we all missed to start with, but you get used to it. We are allowed books, we read a lot of books." replied Zoe. This pleased Penny, she could live without TV, but she couldn't live without books.

"We are both teachers" said Penny "So I'm glad we are allowed to read."

Zoe looked impressed.

"You're both teachers? what do you teach?" she asked.

"We are primary school teachers, so we teach everything. We work in the same school." replied Penny.

"Oh, ok so you're used to dealing with children all day?" replied Zoe.

"Yes, we are." said Penny.

"Well just imagine that the men are just little boys in the classroom, don't let them intimidate you, be in charge of them." said Zoe "Come and see the kitchen, and your bedrooms." They followed Zoe into the kitchen, it was big. It had a long wooden table in the middle and worktops along two walls. There was a dishwasher, a fridge freezer and a large oven and stove.

"It's a nice kitchen isn't it?" said Zoe. Mollie and the other 3 girls all nodded, it was a nice kitchen. Then Zoe showed them 2 bedrooms. Both had a double bed, bedside cabinets and wardrobes.

"We're lucky here, each bedroom has an en suite, unfortunately we have to share a bed, but at least it's not with a man." said Zoe.

"What do we do about more clothes?" asked Mollie.

"We are allowed to ask for more clothes. Our wardrobe consists of jogging suits and t shirts, it's like a uniform, but to be honest when you've been dancing about either naked or in a tight outfit and high heels, it feels like heaven wearing a comfy jogging suit and fluffy sliders. We have a laundry area downstairs, we wash our clothes, do our cooking and clean the house. We all muck in, everyone has to do their fair share." replied Zoe. Mollie and the other girls all nodded.

"What about the food shopping? Who does that?" asked Penny.

"We give a shopping list to Margot on Monday and the shopping is delivered on Tuesdays.

We can ask for chocolate and crisps, just no alcohol, all our shampoo and shower gel go on the list as well" replied Zoe "Now it's time to start on what we call linner, its lunch and dinner combined. Come on, back to the kitchen I think the others will have started making it already." said Zoe. She left the bedroom and went back to the kitchen. Ana, Shelly and Cherry were cooking.

"Hi, sit down we've made pizzas with nachos and dips." said Ana. They all sat down at the table. There were already bottles of water and cola on the table. Penny was still carrying her high heeled shoes.

"You should put them on." said Mollie.

"I will after we've eaten." replied Penny. Ana brought over the nachos and dips.

"The dips are homemade, they are the best" said Ana "I made them." she laughed and sat down at the table. Cherry and Shelly put 4 large pizzas down on the table.

"Bon appetite" Said Cherry "Tuck in girls before it goes cold." The girls all started eating the pizzas and nachos, the food was good. They started talking about themselves, nothing too personal just things like their favourite foods and favourite animals, for a minute Mollie forgot they were all the victims of sex trafficking and that they were being held prisoners against their will. She remembered that she couldn't just get up and walk out of the front door. This is how they cope, thought Mollie, they have got to make the best out of a bad situation, she looked at Zoe, Cherry, Shelly and Ana, even though they seemed ok, she could see they all had one thing in common they all had a sad look in their eyes, like they were waiting for someone to arrive, to find them. To save them.

CHAPTER 21

Marie was awake early, physically she was feeling sore still, but mentally she was back to her normal self. She wanted to go home, she was bored stuck in hospital. She wasn't hooked up to any hospital equipment now, so she had been moved out of the intensive care ward and was on a general ward. She was still in a room on her own, but at least there was more happening on the ward. Marie had got out of bed and was sitting in a chair by the door, just being nosey really, watching the doctors and nurses doing their jobs. She had phoned Sean and told him what ward she had been moved to, she was waiting for him and the girls to arrive.

Sean was up early, he phoned Tracey, he had spoken to her last night and talked about Hannah reading the message she had sent him. Tracey said she was sorry, it was all her fault, she shouldn't have messaged him, but Sean told her it wasn't her fault, it was his mistake leaving the phone upstairs. But what was done was done. The girls know about Tracey and Ronnie now, he said Grace was quite excited by it all, but Hannah was more concerned about how Marie will take it. After his phone call to

Tracey, Sean called the girls up, they both came downstairs in their school uniforms.

"We have decided to go to school. There's no point in falling behind in our studies, Mum will want us to go to school." said Hannah.

"Oh right, Ok. Does mum know you're going to school today?" asked Sean.

"No, you can tell her. She will be pleased. She's always telling us we shouldn't miss school." replied Hannah. The girls made their breakfasts and sat down to eat it.

"We will need some lunch money. Mun normally makes us a packed lunch." said Grace. Sean opened his wallet and gave both girls 10euros.

"I'll pop to the supermarket later and buy some packed lunch stuff. What do you want?" he asked.

"Ham, cheese, white rolls, crisps, penguins, and kit Kats. You will have to go to the Iceland's Supermarket for it all." said Grace.

"I always take an apple and a banana as well. But don't buy them there, get them from Mercadona." said Hannah. Sean got the note pad Marie keeps on the kitchen side and started to write a shopping list, he read it back to the girls.

"Anything else?" he asked them, they both shook their heads.

"When are you going to tell Mum?" asked Hannah.

"I want to wait until Mum is back home" replied Sean. Hannah didn't reply. "It isn't fair on Mum to drop this on her at the moment, let's wait until she is back here, ok?" said Sean.

"Ok." replied Hannah. Grace nodded. They both finished eating their breakfasts. They picked up their school bags.

"Do you want a lift to the bus stop?" asked Sean. The bus stop was only a 5-minute walk.

"No. We will walk. see you later say hello to Mum from me." said Hannah.

"Bye dad, say hello to Mum from me too." said Grace. The girls left the house to walk to the bus stop. Sean tided up the breakfast dishes and glasses the girls had left on the table then made his way to the hospital. Marie was surprised to see only Sean walking down the corridor.

"Where are the girls?" she asked Sean as he approached her room, she was sitting in the doorway still being nosey.

"They decided to go to school." replied Sean. Marie looked at him in surprise.

"Really? Normally they can't wait to have a day off. Well, that's good I suppose." said Marie, she was a bit disappointed, she was looking forward to seeing the girls. She really missed not being at home with them.

"I hope they are behaving themselves, I know Grace can be a little madam sometimes." she laughed.

"They are being as good as gold, well as good as any good teenage girls can be." smiled Sean "I gave them lunch money today, but I'm going to pop to Iceland supermarket and buy the stuff for their packed lunches on my way home." said Sean.

"Yes, it's better to get what they like, otherwise it just stays in their lunchboxes for weeks." said Marie "Have you heard anything from Artiom?"

"No, I haven't, why don't you message him?" said Sean.

"I was thinking of it, do you think he will mind?" replied Marie.

"No, I don't think he will mind." said Sean "Marie, there's something I need to tell you, I was going to wait until you were out of hospital, but I can't keep it from you any longer. It's not right, I need to tell you now." said Sean nervously. Marie looked at him, what could he possibly need to tell me,

"What is it Sean, are you ill?" asked Marie, feeling really worried about what it was Sean had to tell her, Sean shook his head. He wished he hadn't started this conversation now.

"No, I'm fine, it's nothing like that. The thing is, I've met someone else." Sean blurted it out. The look on Marie's face will stay with him forever, pure devastation.

"You what?" said Marie. She had heard him, but she needed him to say it again, to make sure she heard him correctly.

"I'm so sorry Marie. I wasn't looking for someone else, I was happy with you, with us, it just happened, I'm so sorry." replied Sean.

"When did this happen? Who is she?" asked Marie crying. She felt gutted, heartbroken. She had only ever loved Sean. He was her first true love. She didn't want to stop loving him, she wasn't ready to stop loving him.

"18 months ago, she was just a fare in my cab." replied Sean. He felt terrible, he felt like this was the worst thing he could ever do to Marie. He could tell she was shocked and heartbroken. He had doubts suddenly, what am I doing? he asked himself, but then he thought of Tracey and Ronnie waiting for him in the UK, he knew this was the right thing to do.

"A fare in your cab? what's her name?" asked Marie.

"Her name is Tracey." said Sean. Marie could see his eyes lit up when he said her name, her heart sunk, she knew he didn't love her anymore. He loved Tracey.

"How old is she?" asked Marie.

"She is 30. We have a baby boy." replied Sean. He thought he might as well tell Marie about Ronnie. Marie's chin dropped.

"What?" she had stopped crying. She was feeling a bit angry now.

"He is 3 months old. His name is Ronnie." Said Sean.

"Ronnie, you named him after your dad. You always wanted a son. Where do you live? in our little flat?" asked Marie.

"No. When I picked Tracey up from Gatwick airport, she was flying in from Spain, to see her Mum. She was in hospital she had had a stroke. Unfortunately, her Mum died, and Tracey inherited her Mums house, we live there." explained Sean.

"What about our flat then? is it just sitting there empty?" asked Marie.

"No, I've rented it out to a student, he pays the rent on time." said Sean.

"Was she on holiday in Spain?" asked Marie. She wanted to know more.

"No, she lived here, in Javea. But we didn't know her." replied Sean.

"What? She lived in Javea? What on her own?" said Marie.

"Yes, she moved to Javea with a boyfriend, but the split up. He went back to the UK, and she stayed here. She worked in an estate agent in Javea." explained Sean. He wanted to show Marie a photo of Ronnie. "Do you want to see a photo of Ronnie? you don't have to." Marie nodded.

"Yes." she replied. Sean found a photo of him holding Ronnie, it was one of his favourite photos, he showed it to Marie. She looked at the photo, her Sean, the one man she loved more than anyone in the world, apart from the girls, had another baby, a little baby boy, a beautiful baby boy. Sean looked so happy in the photo, so proud, she needed to see a photo of Tracey, she swiped the phone, a picture of Sean with a young woman and Ronnie was next, this must be Tracey thought Marie, she zoomed in, she's not ugly but she's not all that, average looking really, Marie showed Sean the photo she was looking at.

"Is this Tracey?" she asked Sean.

"Yes, that's Tracey, you would like her Marie." replied Sean.

"I always thought that if you ever left me, it would be for a little blonde bimbo" said Marie "So what are you going to do now? You've been living a double life for 18 months, does she know your married with 2 girls? asked Marie.

"Yes, I told her on the first day I met her. We started out, just me picking her up each day and taking her to the hospital, so she knew all about you and the girls, but then things just happened." said Sean. Marie was trying to get her head around it all.

"So, she knew you were married with kids? didn't that put her off? what sort of woman sleeps with a married man, knowingly?" asked Marie, she wanted to make Tracey the bad person "Or did you say you were unhappy, your wife doesn't understand you, you're trapped in an unhappy marriage?" asked Marie. She was angry again.

"No, it wasn't like that, Tracey feels terrible. She has always felt bad about the situation." said Sean.

"Obviously not that bad Sean, you're living together, and you've got a baby together!" Marie was getting pissed off now "And what about the girls? our girls? what are you going to say to them?" asked Marie. Her voice was getting louder.

"They already know." replied Sean.

"What? How do they know? did you tell them before you told me?" asked Marie. She felt like punching Sean in the face, he had cheated on her for 18 months. All those lies he must have been telling her, and that bitch Tracey was in on it. They must have laughed at Marie behind her back. How did she not know Sean was cheating on her? Ok, so they don't have much of a sex life, but they've been married for 27 years, surely that's normal when you've been married for that long. Marie noticed that Tracey was slim, she was nice and slim, like Marie used to be when she was 30. she hoped Tracey got fat, really, really fucking fat. And the girls already know?

"What do the girls know?" asked Marie. Fighting the urge to punch Sean.

"Hannah, saw a message on my phone from Tracey, I couldn't lie to her." explained Sean.

"Oh, but you're ok lying to me for 18 months? are the girls, ok? is that why they've gone into school? because they didn't want to see me, knowing what they know?" asked Marie.

"Yes, I think so. Grace is really excited about having a baby brother, and Hannah, well she was more worried about what you will think than anything else." said Sean.

"Half-brother, he is their half-brother." said Marie "You didn't answer my question, what are you going to do now?"

"I think it will be best if I go and live with Tracey and Ronnie, don't you?" replied Sean.

"Don't make this my decision Sean. If you want to leave us, then do it." said Marie. She had found an inner strength. She wasn't going to let this destroy her. She was going survive without Sean in her life.

"I'm not leaving the girls Marie, I'm leaving us. The girls will always be number 1." said Sean. He felt sad, he didn't think he would feel so sad, this is what he has wanted for 18 months, to be honest with Marie and to be able to live with Tracey out in the open, to be able to leave his phone on the table without worrying that a message or call from Tracey will catch him out. He didn't think he would feel so sad.

"When are you going to see the girls then?" asked Marie.

"They can come and stay with us, there's enough room." replied Sean.

"What in the school holidays?" said Marie.

"Yes, in the school holidays." agreed Sean.

"Well, you've got it all worked out, haven't you?" said Marie "I'm not staying in here, go and find the doctor, I'm going home today, and you can fuck off back to that slag." shouted Marie.

"Don't start shouting, you can't go home today." said Sean.

"Don't fucking tell me what I can or can't fucking do, I'll go and find the fucking doctor myself." shouted Marie. She got up slower than she wanted to, Sean tried to get her to sit back down.

"Take your fucking hands off me, don't ever touch me again. Now move out of my fucking way, you bastard." she was talking through gritted teeth.

"I'll go and find the doctor, sit back down." said Sean. He rushed out of Marie's room, he looked for the doctor, but he wasn't about, so he found a nurse and explained that Marie wants to go home today. The nurse came back with him to see Marie.

"Hi Marie, your husband tells me you want to go home today? I'm not sure that Doctor Dura will agree with that, you're still fragile." said the nurse kindly, she could see that Marie was upset "Has something happened at home?" she asked.

"Yes, I need to go home and look after my daughter. My husband has got to go back to the UK." said Marie. The nurse looked at Sean.

"Oh, that's a shame, you can't stay a few more days?"

"No, he can't he has to go today, so I need to go home. I don't care what the doctor thinks, I'm going to discharge myself, is there a form I have to sign? or can I just walk out?" asked Marie.

"You can discharge yourself Marie, but we urge you not to, you've had a head injury, it's still early days, you would be better staying here, at least for a few more days." replied the nurse.

"No, I'm going home now. So, if there's a form, get it please." replied Marie. She got up slowly from the chair and began packing her things in to her bag, the nurse said she would go and call Doctor Dura.

Marie didn't care, she'd made her mind up. She was going home. Sean tried again to reason with Marie, but she told him to fuck off. She was slowly walking down the hospital corridor when Doctor Jamie Dura showed up.

"Marie, where are you going?" he asked Marie. Marie didn't stop, she was limping slowly leaning against the wall.

"Marie, you can't leave like this, stay a few more days."

"No, sorry doctor, but I'm going home, now I said to the nurse if you want me to sign something, I will." said Marie. She had made her mind up.

"Ok, if you're determined to go against my advice and leave the hospital, then you will have to discharge yourself. There is a form you need to sign, can you get one, please nurse." said the doctor, he was shaking his head, he looked at Sean. "I really think Marie is making the wrong decision."

"So do I." said Sean. Marie looked at him, was he having a fucking laugh, what did he think she was going to do? Just smile nicely, and say, "That's ok Sean, you can have 2 families" Prick. Thought Marie. The nurse came back with the form, Marie scribbled her signature on it, she was too angry to even write properly. The doctor told Marie if she felt unwell, she must come back to hospital. Marie wasn't listening, she just wanted to go home. She knew he looked a sight, limping along in her pyjamas and slippers with a bandage on her head, the doctor was still talking to Sean, he was telling Sean that Marie would need to either come back to the outpatients or to her doctor to have the stitches removed. Sean said he would look after Marie. Then caught Marie up.

"Let me help you Marie, hold on to me." said Sean.

"I would sooner have help from Bin fucking Laden, fuck off, you can drive me home. Then you can fuck off back to the UK." growled Marie. she was in pain now, but she wasn't going to let Sean help her. Not now. Not ever. They got to the car eventually, Sean opened the door for Marie.

"I can open the fucking door myself." she said as she fell into seat. She was really in pain now, but she didn't care, she would take some painkillers when she got home. She hoped she had some. Sean got in the car, he knew better than to try and talk to Marie. She didn't lose her temper that often but when she did it was best to leave her to calm down. The drive home was uncomfortable for Marie, she was in pain. Sean stayed silent. Marie wanted to cry, she felt so angry with Sean, but she still loved him, it wasn't fair. He'd had 18 months to decide their marriage was over. She would forgive him. She knew she would. But he didn't want her, he wanted Tracey, skinny fucking Tracey. The mother of his baby. When they got home, Sean jumped out and opened Marie's door, she wouldn't look at him, she got out of the car slowly, Sean could tell she was in pain, he closed the car door and opened the front door. Marie hobbled

into the lounge and collapsed on to the sofa.

"Do you want a cup of tea?" asked Sean. Trying to build a bridge between

them.

"No. I want you to pack your things and fuck off. I don't want you here

anymore." growled Marie, through gritted teeth. Really, she wanted a cup

of tea and some pain killers, and she wanted Sean to tell her he wanted

her, he would choose her. Sean went up to the bedroom he packed a bag

and then went back the lounge, Marie was still on the sofa.

"I don't want to leave you like this, Marie." said Sean quietly.

"Just go Sean, you've been planning to leave me for 18 months, now's

your chance, just fuck off." said Marie, she was forcing back the tears.

"Phone me if you need me. I'm going to book into the Marriot Hotel for a

couple of days. I'm really sorry Marie, I didn't mean to hurt you." said

Sean. Marie couldn't look at him, she was on the edge of breaking down.

Sean left the house, as he closed the door, he heard a noise that sounded

like an animal, it was a howl. He realised it was Marie, he didn't know

whether he should go back in. He decided not to. He got into the car and

drove to the hotel, he felt as if someone had died, that he had lost

someone for forever, he should be happy. Now he can carry on with the rest of his life with Tracey and Ronnie and having the girls over in the holiday. But he didn't feel happy, or triumphant, he felt sad and lonely. Marie couldn't hold her grief in anymore, she heard the front door close, and the flood barriers opened, she heard a howl and realized it came from her. She sobbed and sobbed, she had never felt heartbroken before, this is what it must feel like when your heart breaks thought Marie. She actually felt a physical pain in her chest, it felt like a hand was squeezing her heart, it hurt. She stayed on the sofa crying until she couldn't breathe properly, she was in a mess, and still in pain, she climbed off the sofa and climbed up the stairs, she crawled into the bedroom. She knew she had some painkillers in her bedside cabinet, she climbed on to the bed. Sean had left a glass of water next to the bed, he always did that, always forgot to take his glass down to the kitchen in the mornings. She found the tablets, there was 40 paracetamol tablets. Marie took 2, she thought about Hannah and Grace, she loved them so much, she didn't think she could stand it if they went back to the UK and stayed with Sean. What would she do here on her own? She didn't want to live without Sean. She took some more tablets, she wasn't crying anymore, she wanted to die, she thought about Mollie and Penny, was they dead too? She wasn't religious, she didn't believe in heaven, once you're dead you're dead is what she always used to say. She took some more tablets, how many had she taken? she didn't know, she couldn't remember, she didn't care. She took some more tablets, she couldn't take anymore, she had drunk all the water. She closed her eyes and sobbed quietly.

CHAPTER 22

Karen and Steve were the first at the breakfast table, the others weren't far behind. They were all yawning, even after a little lay in.

"Ok, so let's get back out there." said Artiom "Let's split up again, so we can cover more pavement, it will be coffee shops and shops to start with, then the bars will start to open. Shall we meet back here at 2?" The others all nodded in agreement. "Shall we split into the same groups as before?" asked Artiom.

"Yes, that's a good idea, us women can stay together. How about we do the coffee shops, and you can do the shops?" said Brenda to the men.

"That sounds good Brenda, you can always stop for a coffee, if you need a break." said Artiom.

"Well, we can buy one to takeaway, I'm sure." said Sue. They finished breakfast and went to get on their walking shoes. Artiom had changed some euros into roubles at the reception, he handed the others their share of the money. They were all out of the hotel by 11am.

The weather was cloudy, but warm.

"I hope it doesn't start to rain." said Brenda. The women had started on the walk back towards the red-light district.

"Fingers crossed it won't." replied Sue. They came to a small coffee shop, all 3 women went inside. Karen showed the leaflet with the girl's photos on to the woman behind the counter.

"Have you seen these girls?" she asked. The assistant spoke a little English.

"No, sorry." she said shaking her head, "There are many girls here."

"These were taken against their will, they are stolen." replied Karen. The women seemed to understand what Karen was saying.

"Many girls are taken here, they are kept here." said the woman sadly. Brenda, Sue and Karen left the shop.

"Oh, my god, where can they be?" said Karen sadly. They all stood on the pavement looking around themselves, feeling hopeless.

"Come on." said Brenda. "Let's keep our hopes up, we will find them, I just know we will." The others nodded, and they carried on. They went into every open coffee shop they could find. They bought a takeaway coffee halfway through the search, soon it was ten to two.

"Let's walk back to the hotel." said Karen. Brenda and Sue agreed, the men were already at the hotel when they got back.

"Hi." said Artiom. "You all look tired out."

"We are, I can tell you." replied Brenda. "How'd you lot get on?"

"No luck yet, but there's still lots of places we haven't been to, let's have a sandwich and get back out there." said Steve. He sounded positive and determined, it rubbed off on the others.

"Yes, we will find them, we've just got to keep on looking." agreed Brenda.

Penny had practised walking in the stiletto shoes for an hour after linner. She wasn't getting any better.

"How do you wear these bloody shoes all the time Mollie?" she said. Taking the shoes off and looking at them as if she'd never seen stiletto heels before.

"Practice." said Mollie. "I've been wearing high heels since I was 13, not that high obviously, but high heels. You will get used to them." replied Mollie.

"I'm not sure I will. Oh God Mollie, I'm dreading it, I can't walk around topless." said Penny. She felt like crying, she was holding in the tears. She knew they were being watched, and probably listened to.

"Look Penny, it's mind over matter ok. Have you never been topless on the beach?" asked Mollie.

"That's different, I don't actually walk around topless on the beach." replied Penny.

"I do." said Mollie. "It won't just be us topless, it will be all the other girls as well, some of them will be naked. We've got to do it. We don't have a choice. Remember what we spoke about, we are survivors Penny. We will make it to the end." Penny nodded. She didn't know where she would be without Mollie. She knew she had no choice that she would have to take her clothes off to survive. She knew she had to be brave.

The driver knocked at the door, the girls were ready and waiting for their escort to the club, Zoe opened the door.

"Hi." said Sol. One of the men from earlier. Ready?"

"We are. Come on girls." replied Zoe. They all left the house and climbed into the minibus. They sat in the same seats as earlier. These must be our seats now, though Mollie. The driver smiled at the girls as they got in the minibus.

"Hello girls." he said.

"Hi Yanson." echoed the girls. Sol got in the minibus, and it drove out of the gates. They reached the club car park in the back entrance again. Sol unlocked and opened the back door of the club then opened the minibus door so the girls could all get out. They followed each other into the club, the door was shut and locked behind them and the minibus drove away. The girls walked up the corridor, some of the doors were wedged open by chairs, Zoe and the other girls waved to the girls in those rooms as they walked past. They opened their dressing room, room number one, and went in, everything was how they had left it earlier. Ana went to her dressing table and plugged a CD player in she put on a Beyonce CD. "Let's get into the mood girls." she said and started getting herself undressed. Ana, Sherry and Cherry were all doing the same, getting their "work" clothes on, Charlotte and Kelly followed their lead. Mollie looked at Penny.

"Come on Penny, let's get this done, we can get through this." she said. Penny wanted to cry, she wanted to run away from the situation. She knew she need to pull herself together, but this was the hardest thing she had ever had to do in her life. She watched Mollie stand up and take her clothes off, she looked around the room, all the others were topless. She made herself stand up and take her top off.

"Well done." said Mollie. She went over and gave Penny a hug. "When we get out of here, we're going to find those bastards that killed Marie, and make sure they go to prison for a long time, ok, we are doing this for Marie." she whispered in Penny's ear, Penny nodded.

"Yes, we will find them for Marie." she whispered back. Penny put the black sparkly mini skirt and killer heels, she looked at herself in the mirror. She wasn't looking at herself anymore, she was looking at someone else. A different Penny. This Penny had a sexy body, she hadn't thought of herself as sexy before. She sat down and applied her make up, she would never wear this much make up in her real life. She brushed her hair and styled differently to her normal natural look, then she added glittery combs and sprayed hairspray, something she never normally wore, her hair was stiff now, she looked at Mollie.

"What do you think?" she said. Mollie turned to look at Penny.

"Wow. Penny. You look so different." said Mollie, she had put her make up as she normally did when going on a night out and was just painting her nails. Penny looked at Mollies nails.

"I haven't done my nails!" said Penny.

"Do them now, it's a quick drying polish. Dries in 60 seconds apparently." said Mollie giving Penny the nail varnish.

"I can't remember the last time I painted my own nails." said Penny.

"I'll do them for you." said Mollie. She moved her chair over to Penny, and painted Penny's fingernails.

"There you go, you will have to take the varnish home and do your toenails to match." Said Mollie.

"Thank you, Mollie." replied Penny. All the girls were looking at themselves in front of the wall of mirrors. Penny looked at the other girls, they all looked good, even though they were wearing hardly any clothes. She looked at herself, she didn't see herself, she saw a young woman with a great body, for the first time ever she was happy with her small breasts. Mollie was much bigger in that department, and she looked good in a tight dress on a night out, but without a bra on they were wobbling about all over the place. The door opened and Margo came in.

"Hi girls ready for tonight's guests?" she asked. Looking around at the girls, she had a longer look at the new girls.

"You all look good. Now, there's no touching from any man in this club. The security men are everywhere, you might not even notice them. They are watching you, and the customers, they are there to protect you, if you feel threatened or a customer is getting out of order, you go to the bar and tell one of the men behind the bar. They will send someone to throw the customer out. Now I want the new girls to shadow you lot." she said to Zoe, Cherry, Sherry and Ana "Not on the poles, but the serving of

drinks, ok?" they all nodded. They had done this before, they themselves

had to shadow someone else to begin with.

"Right off you go." said Margo dismissing them all. Zoe opened the door

and walked into the club, it was early so there was only a few men in

there, she changed her walk into a swagger.

"Come with me Mollie." she said. Mollie looked at Penny.

"Good luck Penny. You can do this, see you in a little while." said Mollie.

They had been told they get a 15-minute toilet and drinks break every 3

hours, so Mollie and Penny arranged to meet up at 9pm in the dressing

room. Mollie followed Zoe. She swaggered her best swagger following Zoe

around the club, they did a whole lap, then swaggered to the bar and Zoe

gave Mollie a silver drinks tray.

"Now let's do a lap holding the tray." she said to Mollie. Zoe swaggered

off again holding the tray above her shoulder, Mollie copied her. What am

I doing? thought Mollie. She saw herself in one of the many mirrored

walls, she saw Zoe looking at her, Zoe smiled and put her thumb up,

Mollie returned the thumbs up, this is crazy, thought Mollie. She looked at

the front exit doors, what would happen if she just walked out of the door

right now? How would they stop her? Would they wrestle her to the floor? there were some customers in here, would they help her? She just didn't feel brave enough, so she carried on following Zoe around the club.

A few minutes later a party of young men entered the club, they were already half drunk, their eyes were popping out of their heads.

"Ok," said Zoe. "The children have arrived. It's probably a stag party, these are easy customers, they will just stand watching the pole dancers." said Zoe. She swaggered up to them, Mollie swaggered behind her.

"Hello boys. Can I get you a drink?" Zoe asked them, poking her tongue out and liking her lips as she spoke. The group of young men all stood there like naughty little boys. They were all grinning with their mouths wide open. Finally, one of them spoke, he looked a bit older, maybe the older brother, thought Zoe.

"8 beers please." He said. Trying to look at Zoe's face and not her breasts.

"Any particular beer?" asked Zoe licking her lips again.

"No." replied the man looking a bit hot and bothered.

"Where will you be?" asked Zoe. She knew the answer.

"Watching the pole dancing." he replied. Of course, you will be thought Zoe. She said they wouldn't be long and swaggered off to the bar, Mollie followed her.

"There you go." said Zoe to Mollie once they were up the bar "easy, now we have to order the beers, and take them back to them, then they have to pay, we have a card machine, or they can pay cash." The bar man came over.

"Hi Zoe, what can I get you?" asked a good-looking man, he was in his 30s with muscles and tattoos. He had long dark curly hair tied back into a ponytail.

"Hi Zac, 8 bottles of beer please. This is Mollie, it's her first night." replied Zoe.

"Hi Mollie, how's it going?" he asked.

"Ok, I think." she replied. Zac put 4 of the beers on Zoe's tray and 4 on Mollies tray, he gave Zoe the bill and the card machine.

"Thanks." said Zoe and she picked her tray up. Mollie picked her tray up too, Zoe made it look so easy, swinging her hips with a tray above her shoulder, Mollie did her best to copy, but she knew she didn't look as good. Zoe found the group of men easily, she put the tray down on a table, Mollie did the same, the men all picked up a beer each.

"Ok, that's 8,200 roubles please." she gave the man that ordered the beers the bill, they all stopped drinking the beers.

"That's 10 quid a beer." said one of the men.

"Yes, it is." said Zoe. "Cash or card?" the men all got their wallets out and paid in cash for their beer. "Thanks." said Zoe. She picked up her tray and walked back to the bar, Mollie followed Zoe back to the bar, Zoe put the cash machine back on the bar and the money for the beers. Zac came over and took the money, he smiled at Mollie. Zoe looked at Mollie. "See easy, they will drink their 1 bottle of beer, watch the girls on the poles then move on to the next club. If only all the customers were like that." said Zoe. Mollie wondered what she meant.

Penny didn't find the walking around in stilettoes as difficult as she thought it would be. She was shadowing Ana. Ana didn't swagger like Zoe she just walked, so it was easy for Penny to keep up with her but balancing the drinks on the tray, and then holding the tray up above her shoulder and walking all at the same time wasn't easy for Penny, she dropped a few glasses, luckily, they were empty champagne flutes. Ana had the bottle of champagne in an ice bucket on her tray, nobody seemed to think it was a big deal.

"Don't worry about it Penny, you're allowed to make a few mistakes on your first night, its ok." said Ana kindly. Zac came over and swept the glass up.

"Hi Zac, this is Penny, it's her first night." said Ana. Zac smiled at Penny.

He'd been watching all night, there was something about her that meant

she didn't fit in here. She had an innocent aura about her. Zac sees pretty

girls all the time in the club but there's a rule he must follow. No one

touches the girls, not even the bar staff. It's never bothered him before

now, but there was something about Penny.

"Hi penny, I can see you're having a smashing time." he smiled at Penny.

"Ha-ha very funny Zac. Penny why don't you follow Zac back to the bar

and get some more glasses, I'll wait here, this champagne bottle is bloody

heavy." said Ana. Penny followed Zac back to the bar, he put 6 more

glasses on her tray.

"Don't carry it so high, try to concentrate on balancing the glasses on the

tray. You'll soon get the hang of it." said Zac. Penny liked Zac. She just

wished she was wearing some more clothes. She carried the tray back

over to Ana and they took the champagne to a group of middle-aged men

sitting in a booth, all suited and booted, Penny could feel them looking at

her, it made her feel embarrassed. These men looked like normal men,

they are probably married, probably have children, grandchildren even,

why are they coming in to a place like this? What would they think if I was

their daughter? Being made to walk around topless. Having men staring at my breasts, saying lewd comments. These men are disgusting, thought Penny. They are the reason me and Mollie were taken, and the reason Marie was shot dead. It's because of men like this, if they didn't come to these clubs then we would still be free. I hate you all, thought Penny. She looked at them, sitting there with their champagne glasses, all red faced and sweaty. She felt sorry for the wives at home, do you know where your husbands have been tonight? Probably not, thought Penny. She hoped not, otherwise, the wives of these men would also be the reason her and Mollie were taken. She knows she could never knowingly allow a boyfriend or husband of hers visit a club like this. Ana finished pouring the champagne. One of the men gave her a credit card, she showed Penny how to put it through the card machine. Penny worked out that 1 bottle of champagne was 200 pounds. That was wrong as well thought Penny, the club and these men are exploiting us girls, and the club are exploiting these men.

"Company credit card." said Ana. reading Penny's mind "they will have 4 more bottles of champagne tonight." Ana gave the card back, and they went back to the bar. Penny looked at the time it was 9pm.

"Can I go for my break now?" she asked Ana.

"Yes, you don't have to ask me. If it's been 3 hours, which it has, you can have a break, I'll have mine when you come back." replied Ana. Penny put her tray on the bar and went out of the door that led to the dressing rooms, Mollie was already in there, she came over to Penny and hugged her.

"Are you ok?" she asked. Penny sat down and took her shoes off.

"I can't believe these places exist. The men are pathetic pigs, they must all have wives or girlfriends. Some are my dad's age, they must have daughters our age. Why are they here?" ranted Penny. Mollie had never seen Penny so irate about something.

"I totally agree with you Penny. They are just a load of sad bastards. You can see them getting a hard on from looking at our tits, honestly, we have the upper hand here, they can't touch us. I feel superior to the sad bastards, don't you?" said Mollie.

"I'll tell you what I feel Mollie. I feel disgusted that these men come to these immoral shit holes. It's their fault we were taken. It's their fault that Marie is dead. I'm going to get through this, and then I'm coming back to close these disgusting places down. If it's the last fucking thing I ever do in my life, I'm going to stop this happening to other girls like us." said Penny.

Mollie liked this new Penny, she had fight in her. She handed Penny a bottle of water.

"Here, I've got you a water." she said. Penny took the water and drank half of it straight down.

"Thanks, I forgot to get a drink." said Penny. "How's it been for you?" she asked Mollie. Mollie shrugged her shoulders.

"Well, it's been eye opening if nothing else. I've served a few stag parties, they were mainly little boys, just ordering 1 bottle of beer in each club they go in, pathetic little shits really." replied Mollie.

Soon their 15 minutes was up. Penny put her shoes back on. They used the toilet then went back into the club.

"Shall we team up together?" said Mollie. Penny looked at her.

"Do you think we will be allowed to?" replied Penny.

"Well, if we're not I'm sure someone will tell us. Come on grab a tray, let's serve these sad old bastards." laughed Mollie. Penny laughed and followed Mollie swaggering up to the bar to get their trays. They walked around together serving the sad old bastards. Mollie was playing the game, she was licking her lips and getting the men all hot under the collar. They took their break again at midnight, by 1 am the club was busy, and the sad old bastards had all had a lot of alcohol, Mollie and Penny witnessed a few of the customers getting escorted out of the club none too nicely by the security men, by 2am, it had started to quieten down again, the businessmen, all suited and booted started to leave. Need to get home to wifey, thought Penny. Sad bastards. There was a few more stag parties through the door, then it was 3am, and the club was empty. Margo had left at 2am, and by 3.30am most of the girls that are not on the stages swinging around poles were sitting around, tired out. At 4am the girls start to retire to their dressing rooms. Some take a shower, they all put the clothes they were wearing in a pile on the floor, they get cleaned after each wear. Then if they hadn't already done it earlier, they choose an outfit for tonight, by 4.30am they are ready and waiting for their chaperone minibus to arrive. Once home the girls make a cup of tea and go to bed. Mollie and Penny are completely wiped out. Penny can hardly walk, her feet are throbbing.

"Oh my god, my feet are killing me." said Penny. "I hate stilettos." Mollie climbed into their bed.

"Night penny, let's get some sleep." Penny climbed in next to Mollie.

"Night Mollie, love you." she said.

"Love you too." replied Mollie. The girls were both fast asleep within minutes.

CHAPTER 23

Sean arrived at the Marriott Hotel. He went into the reception area, there was a group of golfers booking in, so he sat down on a sofa and phoned Tracey.

"Hi Tracey." he said.

"Hi Sean, I was just thinking about you, how's things?" asked Tracey.

"Marie knows everything." replied Sean.

"What did she say?" asked Tracey.

"She is devastated, I feel so bad, she has discharged herself from the hospital. She is at home now." replied Sean.

"Oh, that's not good, where are you?" asked Tracey.

"I'm waiting to book in at the Marriot Hotel. Marie chucked me out, I can't blame her. She went mad. I've never seen her so angry." replied Sean.

"Will she be ok at home on her own? What about the girls?" asked Tracey.

"They are at school today, I'm going to message Hannah to let her know her Mum is at home, it's been a horrible day." said Sean sadly.

"I'm sorry I'm not there with you Sean, I love you so much." said Tracey.

The group of golfers had finished at the reception Sean stood up.

"I love you too, I'm at the reception now. I'll ring you back, bye." he hung up and walked to the reception desk. He booked a room for 4 days, he didn't know how long to book it for, the Marriott Hotel isn't the cheapest Hotel to stay in. But he thought 4 days would give him time to try to sort things out with Marie and find somewhere else to stay a bit cheaper. He went to his hotel room. it was a lovely hotel, he had stayed there a couple of times before with Marie, both times it was for the schools Christmas dinner and dance, the hotel offered the room and breakfast at a discounted rate. Sean sat on the bed. They were both good nights out. He sent Hannah a was sup message

"Hi Hannah. Mums at home. She knows about Tracey, she wasn't happy. I'm staying at the Marriott Hotel. Phone me when you can xxx" Sean looked at the time it was 2-30pm. Hannah will be in lessons, so she won't see the message until school finishes at 3.30pm. He decides to call Marie and phones the home phone, but there's no answer, he just wanted to check on Marie, he phones the mobile she is using, again she doesn't answer, maybe she's sleeping, thought Sean. He decided to ring her again later. Hopefully the girls will be home by then. He phones Tracey back.

"Hi, I'm in my room now, I've booked in for 4 nights. I've tried to call Marie but she's not answering." said Sean.

"She's probably sleeping. Have you told the girls, their Mum's home?" asked Tracey.

"I've left Hannah a message on her phone, they are on the bus together, so she will tell Grace." replied Sean. "I just feel so bad, I should have told her sooner. It's because it's been going on for so long behind her back that she's so upset."

"I don't think she would have been any less upset Sean, it was always going to end in tears. Stop beating yourself up about it, you've told her now. It's still what you want isn't it? To be with me and Ronnie, you haven't changed your mind, have you?" asked Tracey sounding worried.

No, it's what I want Tracey. I just feel bad about it all, at least the girls are happier about it than Marie." replied Sean.

"I wish I was there with you Sean, Marie will calm down, are you going to go and see her later?" asked Tracey.

"I will talk to her on the phone first. I wished she'd stayed in the hospital, she is in a lot of pain." said Sean.

"Now that she's home she will be ok. The girls will look after her, and hopefully she will forgive you enough to let you help her." said Tracey.

"I doubt that will happen Tracey. I don't think Marie will ever forgive me. How's Ronnie, I'm missing his smile." said Sean. Feeling happier thinking of Ronnie.

"Ronnie is fine, feeding, sleeping and poohing." replied Tracey.

"Good. I'm going to get some lunch somewhere. I'll see if I can get a sandwich here. I'll talk to you later, give Ronnie a kiss from me, love you, bye." said Sean.

"Bye Sean, love you." replied Tracey. They both hung up. Sean sat on the bed for a little while, he had never seen Marie so upset, he could still hear her cry when he was leaving the house. He would never forget that ever. He went down to the bar, it was open and there was a food menu, he ordered himself a tuna panini and a beer. He sat up the bar with his beer, it was quiet, there was only one other couple sitting around the other side of the circular bar. He checked the time it was 3pm, the girls will be finishing school soon. He could have picked them up from school, it was a bit late now, he'd ordered his lunch. His panini arrived with a small salad and some crisps, it looked good. Sean ate it sitting at the bar, he felt lonely on his own.

Hannah and Grace sat next to each other on the school bus.

"How was your day, Grace?" asked Hannah.

"You mean, how many people asked about what happened to Mum?"

replied Grace.

"Yes, it was nonstop wasn't it, all the teachers as well, and Mr Wozniak.

Acting like he cares."

Replied Hannah. She hadn't enjoyed all the attention she had received at

school. Grace on the other hand had, she had felt like a celebrity all day.

"Have you had any messages from Mum or Dad Grace? My phone didn't

charge properly last night, and it's died on me." Hannah asked Grace.

Grace was on her phone talking to one of her new friends,

"No, nothing." she replied. Hannah took that as everything being ok. She

thought that their dad would probably still be over at the hospital when

they got home. The bus dropped them at the usual bus stop and the

sisters walked home. Grace was sending messages while walking along.

"For god's sake Grace, you're going to trip up in a minute, put your bloody

phone away." said Hannah.

"Piss off Hannah, you do it all the time. Just because you forgot to charge

your phone up." replied Grace, nearly walking into a lamp post.

"It isn't my fault. My charger is fucked. I need a new one." replied Hannah. Wishing Grace had walked into the post. As they got near to their house, they could see the car wasn't there.

"Dads at the hospital then." said Hannah. Grace ignored her, still typing away on her phone. Hannah opened the front door, it was quiet. The girls went into the kitchen and threw their bags on the floor. Grace actually put her phone down to open the fridge, she stood there looking into it for a minute then closed it again. Next, she opened the cupboard, she closed that without taking anything out and opened the fridge again.

"For god's sake Grace, what are you looking for?" asked Hannah angrily.

"Food." replied Grace. She took out the jar of peanut butter and sat at the table eating it with her fingers.

"You're gross Grace." said Hannah in disgust. "You should change out of your uniform before eating that crap. I'm going to get changed and look for another phone charge." Grace stuck her middle finger up at Hannah behind her back and picked up her phone again. Hannah walked up the stairs she had to pass her parents' bedroom to get to hers, as she walked past, she saw her Mum lying on the bed. Hannah froze, why was Mum here? Where was Dad? She walked to the door, Marie was facing the other way, Hannah walked around the bed quietly.

"Mum." she whispered, thinking Marie must be asleep. "Mum." she

looked at Maris face, it didn't look right, she touched it. Marie felt cold,

Hannah shook her Mum, but she didn't wake up.

"GRACE, GRACE." shouted Hannah. "GRACE, CALL AN AMBULANCE."

Grace came running up the stairs, she thought Hannah must have hurt

herself.

"What's happened? What have you done?" shouted Grace. She saw

Hannah was in their parents'

bedroom. Grace stopped at the doorway, she could see Marie was on the

bed and Hannah was the other side of it.

"What's Mum doing here?" asked Grace.

"I don't know, phone a fucking ambulance, I can't wake her up." Cried

Hannah. She knew this wasn't right, she looked at the bedside cabinet,

she could see the paracetamol tablets box, and the empty packets, she

counted them, oh my god, has mum taken all these, that's 30 tablets?

That's an overdose. Why? thought Hannah, and where's Dad? Grace was

through to the ambulance service she gave their address and said her

Mum was unconscious in bed. They said an ambulance would be coming.

"Phone Dad Grace, tell him Mum's taken an overdose." said Hannah.

Grace was scared, she started to cry as she phoned Sean.

"Dad." she cried into the phone. "Mums at home, and she's taken an overdose."

"What? Grace, what's happened?" said Sean.

"I don't know, she's in bed she's not waking up, I've called for an ambulance." cried Grace.

"Where's Hannah?" asked Sean. He was already running out of the hotel towards his car.

"She's with Mum. She's trying to wake her up." cried Grace.

"I'm on my way. Tell Hannah to keep trying to wake Mum up." said Sean. He hung up, he was in the car and driving home, as fast as he could without causing an accident. Grace told Hannah to keep trying to wake Marie up.

"Come round here Grace. help me try to wake Mum up." said Hannah. Grace shook her head.

"No. I'm scared." she cried. "I'll go and wait for the ambulance." She ran down the stairs and opened the front door, she walked to the end of the drive, she couldn't hear a siren. She didn't know what to do, she felt helpless and frightened. Is her Mum going to die? After escaping death from being shot. Has she killed herself? why? Thought Grace, why would she do that? Hannah was still talking to Marie.

"Come on Mum, wake up, wake up, what have you done? Why? Has Dad told you about his affair? I'm so sorry. I already knew about it. And that he has a baby son, Ronnie. He is our half-brother. He told you didn't he? He said he would wait until you're better. Why are you home? You shouldn't be here. Please wake up Mum, please wake up, don't leave us. We love you so much. I can't live without you Mum. You are everything to us, please wake up." Grace heard a siren in the distance,

"Please, please be the ambulance." she said. She had her hands together and was praying that the ambulance would arrive soon. The siren got louder and louder until Grace could see the ambulance coming down the road, she jumped out into the road waving her arms.

"Here, here." she shouted. The ambulance stopped and two paramedics jumped out.

"Quick, it's my mum she won't wake up, we think she's taken an overdose." said Grace. rushing back into the house. The Paramedics ran after her up the stairs and into the bedroom, they went round to wear Hannah was sitting on the floor holding Marie's hand.

"Hi, is this your Mum?" asked one of the Paramedics.

"Yes, her name is Marie. She should be in hospital. She was shot on Friday night. I think she's taken all these paracetamols." said Hannah. The

Paramedics asked Hannah to wait outside the bedroom with Grace while they assessed Marie. Hannah and Grace stood in the bedroom doorway watching the Paramedics working on their Mum. They were both praying to God, asking him to make sure their Mum stayed alive. Sean saw they ambulance parked outside the house, he stopped the car in front of it and ran in to the house.

"HANNAH.GRACE." he shouted.

"UP HERE DAD." shouted Hannah. Sean sprinted up the stairs and to the bedroom door.

"What's happened?" he said. Hannah and Grace both started crying. Sean put his arms around them both.

"We came home from school and just found Mum like this. We didn't even know she would be here." cried Hannah.

"But I messaged you Hannah, telling you your mum discharged herself from hospital today." said Sean.

"My phone was dead." cried Hannah. "Did you tell her about Tracey and Ronnie?"

"Yes, I did. I'm so sorry. I wished I hadn't, but I just couldn't lie anymore, oh my god, what has she taken?" asked Sean. He couldn't believe what was happening. He would never have thought Marie would try to kill herself.

"30 paracetamols I think." cried Hannah. "Will that kill her dad?"

"I don't know, oh my god." said Sean. "Is she going to be, ok?" Sean asked the Paramedics. They were putting a line into Marie's arm.

"We can't tell until we get her to the hospital. Is this your wife?" replied one of the paramedics.

"Yes." said Sean.

"I'm sorry I can't tell you anymore, your wife is unresponsive. Your daughter said she was in hospital?" replied the Paramedic.

"Yes. She was shot in the head Friday night. She should be in hospital. She discharged herself earlier today, against the doctor's advice." said Sean.

"Ok. You should follow us to the hospital." replied the Paramedic. They lifted Marie on to a stretcher and carried her down the stairs and into the back of the ambulance. One Paramedic stayed in the back with Marie the other one drove the ambulance to the hospital. Sean and the girls followed the ambulance in the car, both Hannah and Grace cried all the way there. Sean didn't know what to say, he felt this was his fault. He knew if anything happened to Marie, if Marie dies, the girls will never forgive him. He would never forgive himself.

CHAPTER 24

Mollie woke up. She looked at the time, it was 10.30am. She listened to see if she could hear if any of the other girls in the house were up yet. She could hear someone in the kitchen, it sounded like they were emptying the dishwasher. She climbed out of bed quietly, she didn't need to wake Penny up. They were given a pink dressing gown each, she put it on with her fluffy sliders and went down to the kitchen. Zoe was sitting at the table eating breakfast, Ana was unloading the dishwasher. "Morning Mollie, sleep well?" asked Ana.

"Morning. Yes, I did, just not for long enough." replied Mollie.

"Morning." yawned Zoe.

"The kettles just boiled. We make our own breakfast, there's bread and cereal, or fruit. Help yourself Mollie." said Ana. Mollie got a mug from a cupboard and made herself a coffee, she sat down at the table to drink it. She thought she would wait and have breakfast with Penny. Ana was making herself some cereal.

"So, what did you think of last night?" asked Ana.

"It's hard work." replied Mollie. "But I know it could be much worse." she took a sip of her coffee.

"Yes, it is hard work, physically and mentally." said Zoe. Mollie looked at Zoe, it was hard to believe that the sexy woman swaggering around the club last night was the same make up free, woman sitting there up the table wrapped up in her pink dressing gown.

"It's like we're acting in a play, don't you think Mollie?" said Zoe eating her toast. Mollie thought about that for a minute.

"Yes, it is all an act isn't it. It's not real, we just walk around giving the sad bastards what they think we want to give them. Wiggling our hips, licking our lips, it's all total bullshit from us, isn't it? It's worrying that men pay to go into these places. Do they not realize we're acting, let's face it, I mean I hate these sorts of men? I wouldn't spit on them if they were on fire." replied Mollie. Zoe and Ana both sat there nodding in agreement with her.

"Well said, Mollie." said Zoe. "The men that go to these clubs are just sad fuckWits. Let's face it, if they were a good fuck, they would have a happy partner at home. They wouldn't want to come to a club to watch us, would they? these men are losers. Sad fucking losers." said Zoe.

"The stag parties are harmless, they are just silly little boys that have been allowed to run around in a toy shop, and we're the toys." said Ana. "The men I find weird are the ones there on their own. They creep me out, especially the ones that keep their long coats on." Mollie looked at Ana with wide eyes.

"That would freak me out, especially if he had his hands in his coat pockets." said Mollie.

"Yeah, pockets without any lining in them." laughed Zoe. Mollie looked at Zoe and pulled a face.

"Does that actually happen? or are you joking." she asked Zoe and Ana.

"It happens, believe me." said Ana.

"Yep." agreed Zoe. Penny hobbled into the kitchen.

"Morning Penny, feet sore?" asked Zoe.

"Morning, they are killing me." said Penny.

"Morning Penny. Sit down I'll make you a cup of tea." said Mollie. Penny sat down at the table.

"Thank you, Mollie. Morning Ana." said Penny.

"Morning. I've said to Mollie, we all just make our own breakfast, there's toast and cereal, or fruit." replied Ana. Mollie was making Penny some tea.

"Do you want toast Penny? I'm having some." asked Mollie.

"Yes please, thanks Mollie." said Penny. "I'm not sure I will ever be able to wear stiletto shoes like you do Mollie."

"You will Penny, it's just practice, but to be honest I don't normally wear them for that length of time. My feet were hurting by 3am." replied Mollie.

"And mine. About 2 am is my limit. Maybe we should ask if we can change into our fluffy sliders." laughed Ana, the other girls all laughed,

"That would be so much more comfortable, imagine trying to act all sexy in fluffy slippers." laughed Zoe. Mollie brought Penny's tea and their toast to the table, she sat back down to eat her toast. Zoe and Ana left the table they put their dirty plates and mugs into the dishwasher.

"The food shop will arrive soon, we ordered double of everything for this week. Next week you can add things you want yourself to the list. We normally sit down over the weekend and write the shopping list between us." said Ana. Charlotte and Kelly came into the kitchen yawning.

"Morning." chimed the others already there. Ana and Zoe, both went off to get showered and sort their dirty laundry out.

"Are you girls both ok?" Mollie sked Charlotte and Kelly. They were getting mugs out and making toast.

"I'm ok, just shattered. replied Charlotte.

"Same here. How's your feet Penny?" asked Kelly. Penny flexed her feet.

"They are still aching, honestly, how do you wear heels for so long without them hurting? is it just me that finds them so uncomfortable?" asked Penny.

"I think it's only because you're not used to wearing them Penny, you'll get used to them." replied Kelly. "Unlike, getting used to having all those perverts looking at us in the club."

"We were just talking about the sad bastards that go to the clubs." said Mollie. "It could be worse for us though. I wonder how the others are doing. I feel really sorry for them, but I'm glad I'm not in a brothel, and what happened to Michelle?"

"Are we ok talking like this? Are we being listened to?" asked Charlotte. The girls sat down at the table with their tea and toast.

"What are they going to do us? It doesn't matter where we are, we can still talk about things?" said Mollie. She had decided that they probably won't be listening to them, or even watching them 24/7. I mean how bloody boring would that be.

"Yes, I feel sorry for the others too, especially the younger girls. I don't know what happened to Michelle. Maybe we should ask Margo?" said

Kelly. The others all nodded. Mollie said she would ask Margo later. They all finished their breakfasts and cleared up after themselves. Mollie said she was going to wash her hair, and Penny decided to paint her toenails. They looked into the lounge on their way, there was a large book shelve full of paperback books, all fictional novels. The girls started looking through the books, they were pleased to see there was lots of books there they hadn't read. They both chose a book each and took it with them to their room.

CHAPTER 25

After a quick lunch, Brenda, Sue and Karen, went back to visiting the coffee shops. The men went back to the shops and bars. They agreed to meet back at the hotel at 7pm. Have dinner then the men would return to the clubs. They were all feeling wiped out, they were doing a lot of walking, and not much sleeping. Today they were all realizing that it could take a long time to visit every shop, bar and coffee shop in the area. But they couldn't stop, they wouldn't stop. Not until they found their girls. It was raining, Brenda asked the others if they wanted to take a pit stop and sit down in the coffee shop they were in, it was 5pm they had been walking for a couple of hours.

"Yes please." replied Sue and Karen.

"Ok, you two find a table, I'll get the coffees in." said Brenda. She joined the queue. When it was Brenda's turn, she showed the coffee shop staff the photos of Mollie and Penny. They all shook their heads, sorry, they hadn't seen them. Brenda ordered the coffees. She was looking at the girls photos while she was waiting. She was talking to Mollie silently in her head.

"Come on Mollie, where are you? We need to find you." Brenda didn't notice the young man next to her in the queue. He was looking at Penny's photo he knew where she was. He thought about telling the woman that's looking for her, but he knew he could get in big trouble. Everything that goes on in the club is wrong, he knows that, but he wasn't brave enough to speak out. He felt bad. The woman took her coffees and sat down with 2 other women, they all looked tired and sad. Zac ordered his coffee, it was a takeaway coffee. He carried on with his journey, he was due to start his shift at the club.

The shopping arrived at the house at 1 pm, the girls all helped to put it away. There was twice the normal amount, so the cupboards and fridge were both full to the brim.

"What shall we have today for linner?" asked Cherry. "We can have chicken pasta, beef pasta, meatballs?"

"Meatballs." replied Sherry.

"With pasta?" said Zoe "and garlic bread." The others all nodded in agreement.

"We don't mind cooking it today?" said Mollie "do we Penny?" Penny nodded.

"We can both cook. In case you're worried." said Mollie. The other girls laughed.

"Ok, if you fancy doing the cooking today that's ok with me." said Zoe. The other girls were all happy to let Mollie and Penny cook for them.

"Linner will be served at 3pm, is that the right time for linner?" asked Mollie.

"Yes, that's perfecto." replied Ana.

"Can someone show us what to do with our dirty washing? do you share the machine?" asked Penny.

"Yes, come on I'll show you how to use the washing machine, and where we hang the washing. Luckily all our clothes are pink, so nothing runs in the wash." laughed Cherry. She took Mollie and Penny downstairs to the large basement. There was a laundry area with a washing machine, a tumble tryer, 2 long washing lines, an ironing board and a little sink. Then there was a hoover, 2 mops and buckets, and a broom.

"Wow, you have everything for cleaning. No wonder the house is so clean and tidy." said Penny.

"Penny keeps a clean and tidy house." said Mollie. "Even Penny's classroom is clean and tidy."

"Well compared to your classroom it is Mollie." smiled Penny.

"So did you two work together?" asked Cherry.

"Yes, we work together in the same school as primary school teachers." replied Penny.

"I knew you were both teachers, I didn't know you worked at the same school, good friends then?" asked Cherry. Mollie and Penny looked at each other.

"Yes. We are the best of friends." replied Mollie. "Did you work before you came here Cherry?"

"Yes, I worked in a bar in Paris. I enjoyed my work, it was really busy, right near to the Eifel Tower. I had left college 2 years earlier but, hadn't really decided what to do next. I had worked there for 2 years before this happened." replied Cherry sadly.

"How long have you been here Cherry?" asked Mollie. she wasn't sure if she wanted the answer.

"I've been here for 2 years in this house, but I was in an apartment first for 9 months." replied Cherry.

"So, you've been missing for nearly 3 years?" said Penny. Her and Mollie were shocked at this.

"Yes, I try not to think about it too much, this is my life now. This is all our lives now." whispered Cherry.

"But you can't stop hoping that you will be rescued one day, can you?" said Mollie. Cherry looked at Mollie, she looked sad, she shrugged her shoulders.

"I go to bed every night and say my prayers. I pray that tomorrow someone will come into the club that knows me. They will see me and go back and tell my family where I am. That my dad will come and get me and take me home. So yes, I will never stop hoping." replied Cherry. This made Mollie and Penny feel helpless, they knew this could be them in 2 years' time. Still here trapped. It was a sombre thought. Mollie spotted an exercise bike in the corner.

"There's an exercise bike, does anyone use it?" she asked changing the subject.

"It was here when I arrived, I don't think anyone of us have used it. It must have been from one of the previous girls." laughed Cherry. "You two can use it if you think you need to, personally when I get back home, I just want to sleep and rest." Mollie and Penny laughed with her. Mollie wanted to ask Cherry what happened to the previous girls? where are they now? but she thought she'd save that for another time. Cherry left them downstairs to sort out their washing.

"It's all very organised down here, isn't it Mollie." said Penny.

"Everything about this whole situation is organised. I can't imagine being here still in 2 years' time penny." replied Mollie. Penny looked at Mollie and touched her ear, she was still convinced they were being listened too. Mollie didn't believe it, but she changed the subject anyway.

"Ok, let's go and read our books for an hour, before we start on the linner." she said.

"Good idea." said Penny. They both went up to read their books in lounge. Mollie still thinking about where the tenants before them were. Penny dreading having to go to the club later.

CHAPTER 26

Sean, Hannah and Grace followed the ambulance to the hospital. Sean parked the car in the nearest empty parking space, they jumped out of the car and run over to the ambulance just as Marie was being taken from it into the emergency entrance of the hospital. They followed Marie inside. There were nurses and a doctor waiting for her, they rushed her into a cubicle, one of the nurses stopped Sean and the girls from going into the cubicle.

"Sorry, you will need to wait outside." she said. And closed the curtains around Marie's bed, Sean and the girls all looked at each other.

"I hope Mum will be ok." said Grace crying. Sean put his arm around her.

"She will be ok Grace. The doctors and nurses know what to do." replied Sean. trying to sound positive.

"Where was you dad?" asked Hannah. Wanting to know why he wasn't at home. Sean looked at Hannah he could see she was still angry with him.

"I told Mum about everything. She was very upset with me, and she told me to leave. I didn't want to go, but she wouldn't let me stay with her. So, I went to the Marriott Hotel, I've booked a room there for a few days." explained Sean.

"I knew Mum would be really angry and upset." said Hannah." So that's why she has taken an overdose because of what you've done?" Sean looked at Hannah he felt so ashamed of what he has done to Marie.

"Yes, it's my fault Mums here now I should have waited until she was home from hospital." said Sean.

"Or maybe, you shouldn't have done what you did in the first place, what are you going to do now Dad now that Mum knows?" asked Hannah. Sean looked at Hannah, he couldn't tell her that as soon as Marie was better and back home, he would be going back to the UK, back to live with

Tracey and Ronnie for good, so he said nothing. A nurse came along the corridor.

"Come and sit in here, it's the family room." she said taking them to a little room with blue sofas, a coffee machine and a table with leaflets and magazines on it. "I'll find out what's going on." She went off towards Marie's cubicle. Sean and the girls sat down, Sean picked up the top leaflet it was counselling for relatives after a death, he put it at the bottom of the pile that wasn't something he wanted to read about now. The nurse came back quickly.

"Hi, Marie is stable now, but she isn't awake yet. once she wakes up the doctor will do some more tests, to check there isn't any lasting damage from the overdose then Marie will be moved up to a ward. But she will probably be asleep for a few hours." said the nurse.

"But she will be, ok?" asked Sean.

"The doctor will do more tests once she has woken up, but at the moment Marie is ok, its normal after taking an overdose to sleep for a few hours." replied the nurse. Sean looked at the girls

"I think I should drive you two home, and then I'll come back and sit with Mum." said Sean. The girls shook their heads in disagreement with Sean.

"No. I want to stay here. I want to see mum when she wakes up." said Hannah.

"So do I." added Grace. The nurse looked at the two girls still in their school uniforms and their faces red and blotchy from crying.

"Why don't you all go home and decide there who comes back, Marie will be sleeping for a while yet. We will phone you if she wakes up earlier." said the nurse. Sean nodded his head.

"Come on girls let's go home, you need to change out of your uniforms, if Mum sees you in them, she won't be happy." said Sean. Hannah looked at her dad she was still angry with him.

"Mum isn't happy full stop dad." said Hannah. But she got up and said to Grace "Let's go home and get changed Grace." Grace nodded at Hannah. Sean got up and thanked the nurse for her help.

"What ward will Marie be going to?" asked Sean.

"She will be back in the room she was in this morning." replied the nurse. Sean thanked her again and left the hospital with the girls. They began the short drive home. Sean remembered he still hadn't done any shopping,

"I haven't been food shopping yet. Do you want a takeaway for dinner?" he asked the girls.

"Ok." They both replied.

"McDonald's? Burger King?" asked Sean.

"KFC?" added Grace.

I don't mind, I'm not that hungry." said Hannah.

"KFC then please Dad." said Grace. Sean drove to the nearest KFC restaurant he parked the car, and they went inside it wasn't too busy. Sean looked at the time it had just gone 6pm. They ordered their meals and sat down at a table.

"I think you two should stay at home. I'll go back to the hospital to be with Mum, she is going to feel tired and not very well when she wakes up. You can both see her tomorrow." said Sean.

"But Mum needs us to be there when she wakes up." said Hannah.

"I think it will be best for Mum Hannah, let her wake up and get her head together. She knows how much you two love her she wasn't thinking straight today. So, let's give Mum tonight to recover and you will see her tomorrow." replied Sean. He knew he needed to talk to Marie without the girls there.

"Ok, but we're coming to the hospital in the morning." agreed Hannah. The food arrived, it was a means to an end, I will have to go food shopping tomorrow thought Sean. They finished their chicken dinners and went home. Sean checked the girls had everything they needed, picked up

Marie's bag that she had brought back with her earlier, and returned to the hospital. He knew he would be home late and told the girls to go to bed, but they both said no, they wanted to wait up for him. He left them both laying on the sofa watching TV. Sean drove back to the hospital. So much was going around in his head. So many what ifs. What if he hadn't met Tracey, what if he had told Marie earlier, what if Marie doesn't wake up.

When he arrived at the hospital, he went up to the room Marie was in before she discharged herself. Marie was asleep, she looked peaceful and calm. Sean crept quietly into the room, he sat down on a chair next to the bed and picked up Marie's hand, it was so soft, Marie always has soft hands, he kissed Marie's cheek.

"I'm sorry Marie, I'm so sorry, if I could turn back time, I would have told you about Tracey earlier, I hope you will forgive one day. I'll always love you. You're the mother of my girls, you're the best Mum, they are so lucky, I've been so lucky." He was whispering to Marie, he hoped she could hear him. She didn't respond, he stayed there holding Marie's hand, thinking about what had happened in the last few days. Marie being shot, the two teachers taken, and still missing as far as he knew, then Hannah reading Tracy's message on his phone, Sean telling Marie about Tracey and Ronnie, Marie discharging herself from hospital, then telling him to leave the house. The girls finding Marie Unconscious, and now sitting here back in the hospital waiting for Marie to wake up from an overdose. It has been a nightmare. His phone beeped it was a message from Tracey, asking for an update she wanted to know if he was he ok? He hadn't told her about Marie taking the overdose, he messaged Tracey back telling her what had happened. That the girls had found Marie and now he was sitting next to Marie's bed waiting for her to wake up. Tracey was shocked when she read Sean's message, like Sean, she felt responsible for Marie taking the overdose. It was a horrible feeling she felt helpless not being there to comfort Sean. She wished Ronnie had a passport. She would have jumped on a plane to be with Sean, she knew he needed her, and she needed him. Tracey messaged back telling Sean how much she loved him. Sean sat holding Marie's hand while reading Tracey's message, he messaged her back telling her he loved her too.

It was past 11pm when Marie opened her eyes, it was dark and quiet in the room. She felt someone holding her hand, she turned her head and saw it was Sean. He was asleep and his head was laying on the bed. Marie laid in bed looking at him. Her Sean. Then she remembered everything that had happened he wasn't her Sean anymore. He loved someone else.

He had a new life, and she wasn't part of it. Why was he here? Maybe he has changed his mind? Maybe he has decided he still loves her? She didn't move she didn't want to wake him up. She knew taking the overdose was a stupid thing to do, she didn't want to die. She thought about the girls where are the girls? She decided they must be at home. Did they know what she had done? Sean moved he sat up and looked at Marie.

"Marie, hello." smiled Sean. Marie smiled back she loved him so much.

"Hello Sean." she whispered her throat was sore and her voice was barely a whisper. "I'm sorry." she whispered. Sean leant over the bed and put his arms around Marie. He began to cry.

"I'm so sorry Marie, I'm so sorry." He didn't want to cry but he was so relieved to see Marie awake. Marie hugged him back she run her fingers through his hair. She loved him so much her heart was hurting.

"It's ok Sean. I'm sorry it was such a stupid thing to do. I didn't mean it. I was so upset I'm so sorry." whispered Marie, she didn't want to let Sean go, she knew this was going to be the last time she would be able to hold him like this, to run her fingers through his hair, to feel him laying on her, they stayed like that for a while, just cuddling, like they did before they were married. Back then they would just lay together for hours, talking about what they would be doing in 30 years time, when they were both old and grey together. They had decided that their children would be a boy and a girl. They would have grown up and left home. That they would be the best grandparents ever, they would take their grandchildren to the zoo and the fair together and they would spoil them rotten. They planned to travel around the world on fab holidays. They would grow old together. Stay together until the end.

"I remember doing this. Do you remember when we used to lay together for hours like this, planning our future?" asked Marie.

"Yes. I am sorry it's all changed Marie. I didn't want it to change I was happy with you and the girls and our life it just happened. I'm sorry I've hurt you." replied Sean. Marie knew then that she had to accept that Sean was leaving her that he hadn't changed his mind she had lost him. Tracey had taken Sean from her. Marie started to cry.

"Sorry." she sobbed. Sean sat up he held Marie's hand again. "I know we're finished Sean. I will let you go but it's so hard. I love you so much. I can't imagine my life without you." sobbed Marie.

"I will still be here a part of your life, if you'll let me." whispered Sean. Marie knew that would be heart-breaking for her but that she would sooner have him in her life as the girls dad than not at all.

"I will always love you, Sean." whispered Marie. Sean began crying again he knew he still loved Marie. He felt guilty and ashamed of the hurt he had caused her.

"Let us stay friends Marie. I will always love you." whispered Sean. "We will find a way through this we need to for Hannah and Grace."

"Are the girls at home? do they know what I did?" asked Marie hoping they didn't know.

"Hannah found you Marie." said Sean gently he knew this would upset Marie. She put her hands over her face.

"Oh no what happened? is she ok?" sobbed Marie. She felt terrible her daughter shouldn't have seen her like that.

"I was at the hotel. I messaged Hannah to let her know you was at home, but her phone had died. She didn't get the message. Hannah and Grace went home after school they didn't know you was there, and Hannah found you, Grace was downstairs. Hannah was great she saved your life. She told Grace to call for the ambulance and to call me. They are ok Marie don't worry about them they wanted to be here. I had to buy them a KFC to convince them to stay at home. I've said I would bring them in to see you in the morning." Said Sean. Marie was wiping her eyes with a tissue.

"I feel so stupid. I hope they are both ok. Will you move back home to look after them just until I'm out of here?" asked Marie. Sean nodded.

"Of course, I will. I'll have to pop to the hotel and pick my things up. I'll do that tomorrow. I've brought your bag back." said Sean. Marie smiled at him.

"Thankyou. I don't suppose you took the dirty washing out?" she said smiling.

"No sorry I didn't think to, I'll take it home now. Do you want me to bring anything back?" asked Sean.

"Some clean underwear please." whispered Marie. She knew once he walked out of this door, he would no longer be her Sean he would just be the girl's dad. But she knew she had to let him go. But she loved him so much. She could feel her heart actually breaking.

"You should go Sean just in case the girls are still up waiting for you to get home." whispered Marie.

"I'll be back in the morning with Hannah and Grace." Replied Sean. He bent down and kissed Marie on the head.

"Bye Sean drive carefully. I'll see you in the morning." Whispered Marie.

"Bye Marie." Said Sean. He picked up Marie's dirty washing and left the room. He stopped at the nurses station and told them Marie was awake and that he would be back in the morning.

Marie waited until she was sure Sean had left and then she cried. She cried for the life that she has lost. Her whole adult life has been centred around Sean. She hates it when he is in the UK working, she counts down the days to when he is back with her. She doesn't know how she is going to find the strength to carry on without him. She knows he will be phoning her to talk about the girls but that's not what Marie wants. She wants Sean. She hates Tracey, she has taken Sean away from her. She doesn't know Tracey. But she hates her more than she has ever hated anyone in her whole life.

CHAPTER 27

"This is really good thanks Mollie and Penny. You two can cook linner again." said Ana eating the meatballs and pasta the girls had cooked for linner. The other girls all nodded in agreement.

"You are good cooks well done." agreed Zoe.

"You're welcome." replied Mollie. "Actually, it was Penny that did most of the cooking she is a proper domestic Goddess." smiled Mollie. Pennie smiled at Mollie.

"That's what my Mum always calls me whenever I cook for her." said Penny.

"Ahhh sorry Penny I didn't know that." said Mollie looking sadly at her friend.

"Don't be sorry I like hearing things like that." replied Penny. Mollie looked at the other girls they all looked lost in their own thoughts.

"We all miss our families don't we it's only been a few days for us but for some of you it's been years, it must be sad for you some days." said Mollie. She wanted to know how they all cope in this situation.

"We miss our friends and families everyday Mollie. But we must get on with things. We have no other choice, so this is our little family here, this is where we live, and we look after each other. You've only been here for a couple of days but already you're part of our family. It's the only way to keep going." said Ana. Zoe, Cherry and Sherry all agreed with her. Mollie looked at these 4 strong beautiful women she admired them, the way they managed to carry on everyday living this life, being kept prisoners. Being forced to work in a strip club and thinking they're lucky because it's not a brothel. She felt like they were part of this family now. Part of a family unit, supporting each other, feeding each other, and caring for each other. Penny started to clear the plates.

"Mollie did make the dessert it's a Mollie special fruit salad. There's no cooking involved." smiled Penny lightening the mood. Mollie gave a shocked and surprised look to Penny and the other girls all laughed. "But there is ice cream." added Penny "Thank the Lord for Ice cream."

Once the fruit salad and ice cream had been eaten all the girls helped clear up the kitchen.

"Ok we'd better get our skates on; the minibus will be here soon." said Ana they all left the kitchen at the same time to get ready for tonight's shift at the club.

Zac was at the club he was re stocking the bar. He could not stop thinking about seeing Penny's photo earlier in the coffee shop. He was sure one of the three women sitting at the table must have been Penny's Mum. They were here looking for her and Mollie he should have said something. He wished he had. But he knows he would be in serious trouble if he is seen helping Penny and Mollie. He has been working at the club for 4 years now. He is the head bar man. Margot trusted him. He knows what goes on he knows the girls aren't working here through choice like he was, but he always told himself that the girls that working in this club were ok. They are looked after and protected from the customers. He has even convinced himself some of the girls enjoyed working there. But seeing the women today in the coffee shop with the photos of Penny and Mollie reminded him that these girls are taken against their will and then sold on to the highest bidder. They are forced to walk around half naked or dance naked on a stage in front of groups of leering men. He knows there's worst clubs to work in than this one, in a way the girls were lucky they didn't have to have sex with the men. Zac knew that wasn't right the girls weren't lucky at all. He felt guilty to be part of this club that takes girls and forces them to work against their will and keeps them prisoners unable to leave the club or their house to ask for help.

"Hi Zac. How was everything last night after I left?" asked Margot.

"Hi Margot, everything was fine. It quietened down by 3am you know what it's like at the start of the week." replied Zac. He liked Margot. Even though she was part of everything that's wrong with this club. He still liked her, and he knew she did care about the girls.

"How did the new girls get on?" asked Margot. Zac knew she would ask him that question.

"They all did great Margot. No problems at all." replied Zac. He wanted to ask Margo what she knew about Penny, but he knew not to. In the past if any of the security or bar staff show any interest in a girl the girl would disappear. He didn't want that to happen. It wasn't long and the girls started to come into the club all dressed in stiletto heels and sparkly miniskirts or hot pants and all topless. They greet each other as friends do and then get on with the job. He looked for Penny He could see her. She was with Mollie they came up to the bar to get a tray each.

"Hi girls how's it going?" asked Zac. Mollie and Penny both smiled at him.

"We're ok, thanks for asking Zac." replied Mollie. Zac looked at Penny she didn't look ok, he moved closer to her.

"Are you really ok Penny?" he asked her quietly. Penny looked at Zac, he was a good-looking man. In her normal life she would fancy him. She could see the kindness in his dark eyes. They looked at each other for a second too long. Penny blushed and put the tray in front of her breasts.

Mollie had seen the look they had shared together. Zac moved away from Penny he had never felt this way about anyone before he knew he had to save her. He wished he had said something in the coffee shop. The customers started to come into the club and Zac began to get busy. He kept his eye on Penny as much as he could, he needed to wait until Margot had left before he could talk to Penny. Penny couldn't keep away from Zac. She served as many customers as she could so that she could go back to the bar with the orders. Zac didn't get to serve her every time but when he did, she could feel the electrifying connection between them. Penny had had a couple of boyfriends nothing serious, she would call herself choosy when it came to men but there was something about Zac. She felt as though she knew him like they had met before, she knew that wasn't likely. She had found out from him that he was a Parisian and that he was 31 years old. She knew that when she wasn't looking at him, he was looking at her and when their eyes did meet it was like a bomb going off. Penny looked around the club had anyone else felt it. Margo left at 2am. The customers were slowly leaving. Zac was praying that there wouldn't be a large crowd coming in. He knew he had to be careful without the customers to watch the security men would be watching the girls. He waited until Penny was back up at the bar on her own.

"Hi penny. When is your next break?" he asked quietly.

"At 2.30 why?" asked Penny she hoped she hadn't got Zac wrong and that he just wanted to try it on with her. Zac moved closer.

"Is it with Mollie?" he asked. He knew they met each other for breaks.

"Yes why?" asked Penny.

"I need to talk to you. It is important but no one can see us, apart from Mollie. I will come to your dressing room at 2.15. Open the door if it's just you and Mollie in there Mollie will have to keep watch while I'm in there though, ok?" explained Zac.

"But why? What do you want to talk to me about?" asked Penny.

"I want to help you." whispered Zac. Penny nodded and walked away she thought she had already been talking to Zac for too long she didn't want anyone to get suspicious. At 2.30 am Penny went to the dressing room Mollie was already in there. Penny went and looked in the bathroom it was empty she came back to Mollie.

"Listen Mollie Zac is going to come in here in a minute. He needs you to wait outside and check no one else comes in." said Penny. Mollie looked at Penny in surprise.

"Wow, Penny I spotted the attraction between you two, but this is a bit quick?" said Mollie.

"No, he said he wants to tell me something he wants to help us, Mollie." explained Penny.

"You need to go outside and watch that no one else comes in here." said Penny. Mollie got up.

"Ok Penny be careful we don't know Zac. What about the cameras?" asked Mollie.

"I don't know maybe he knows something we don't about them." replied Penny. Mollie opened the door she couldn't see anyone outside or in hallway, she stood there for a minute then she saw Zac he was walking along quickly with a mop and bucket and was wearing rubber gloves. He came up to Mollie.

"Ok, you said the shower is flooded. I'll look and see if I can sort it out." he said. Mollie played along she pointed into the dressing room.

"Yes, there's water everywhere." she said, waving her arms about dramatically. Zac told her to stay at the door and to look like she was waiting for him to sort it out. He went into the dressing room he nodded hello at Penny and then went to the bathroom and wedged the door open with a chair. Penny realised what he was doing and what his cover was. If anyone was watching they would just think Zac was clearing up a mess in the showers. He had actually done this before, and Margot was thankful to him then. Penny knew she needed to get closer to the bathroom so they could talk, she walked over to the large wardrobe, opened it and started to look through the outfits, looking like she was picking one for tomorrow night.

"Hello." she said quietly whilst looking through the clothes.

"I was in a coffee shop earlier today and there was 3 women with photos of you and Mollie. They were searching for you." said Zac quietly mopping the floor in the showers. Penny froze what did Zac just say? Three women looking for her and Mollie? She felt her heart thumping so fast it scared her.

"Did you tell them where we are?" asked Penny.

"I'm so sorry Penny, no I didn't, I wish I had of. But they are here in St Petersburg looking for you. Can you give me a mobile number of someone that I can phone and then these women can come and find you?" asked Zac. At first Penny didn't understand why Zac hadn't told the women where her and Mollie were, but she realised that if Zac had and he was seen then he would be in great danger. What he was doing now was dangerous. Penny couldn't think of a phone number no one dialled numbers these days everyone was just saved in her mobile under their name.

"Hang on." she said, she went to the door Mollie was standing guard outside.

"Can you remember a phone number from your contact list Mollie?" she whispered.

"No why?" asked Mollie.

"Zac saw 3 women with our photos they are here in St. Petersburg Mollie they are looking for us, Zac couldn't be seen talking to them earlier but if we can give him a phone number, he will phone someone, and they can tell them where we are." explained Penny. She was excited and scared at the same time.

"I can't think of a bloody number Penny. Ask Zac to google the school it will have a phone number, he can tell whoever answers the phone where we are tell him google the bloody school." said Mollie.

Penny went back into the dressing room and over to the wardrobe.

"Zac can you google The Elizabeth School in Javea? that will have a phone number It's where we work, we're both teachers." Zac listened to Penny, The Elizabeth School Javea, he could remember that easily. He finished what he was doing and walked out of the bathroom he nodded at Penny and waited at the door, Mollie could see him she nodded at him to say it was safe he came out and pointed into the dressing room.

"All sorted." he said to Mollie.

"Thank you, Zac." said Mollie, and she really meant it. Mollie went back into the dressing room. Penny was sitting down she sat next to her.

"Oh my god, Penny." she whispered.

"There's 3 women looking for us I wonder who it is?" whispered Penny.

"We need to get back into the club don't say anything about this to anyone else." whispered Mollie. The girls went back into the club. Zac was back behind the bar the girls collected their trays. There was a receipt on Penny's tray she picked it up she didn't remember leaving anything on her tray, she looked at it and on the reverse of the receipt were the words "I love you P. Will you marry me? Z" Penny read it three times she knew it was from Zac, she looked across the bar at him he was watching her she nodded to him. She knew she was looking at her future husband. Once all the customers had left the club the girls all went to their dressing rooms. They took off their costumes and heels. Some of them had showers, they all put on their matching jogging suits. Penny and Mollie were buzzing they couldn't wait to get back to the house so they could talk about what Zac was going to do for them. Penny couldn't wait to tell Mollie she was going to marry Zac. Back at the house Mollie and Penny acted normal made a cup of tea and then said good night to the other girls. When they got into their bedroom, they put their cups down and then both went in to the en suite, Mollie run the shower to make some noise. Penny told Mollie about the note on the receipt.

"No way? Wow I could see he likes you Penny. So, what is he going to come back to Javea with us?" asked Mollie.

"Yes, he will have to leave the club, if they find out he is helping us he will be in danger Mollie you saw what they did to Marie and what's happened to Michelle?" whispered Penny.

"We will need to see what he tells us tomorrow night, I hope its good news." said Mollie. They went back into the bedroom got undressed and climbed in to bed. Neither of them wanted the tea instead they both just laid in the dark praying that Zac would remember the name of the school. Zac knew that tonight would be the last time he would be in the club. If he helped Penny and Mollie, it wouldn't be safe for him to go back there. He went home and googled The Elizabeth School Javea on his laptop. It came up straight away he added the schools phone number into his phone. He decided to go to bed for a few hours, the school would be open at 9am.

Mollie and Penny couldn't sleep their minds were buzzing, they felt so excited just knowing people were here looking for them. it was the best news ever. They knew that they couldn't tell anyone else in the house. If they were rescued, they would come back and rescue the other girls. One way or another they would make sure the police knew what was going on in these clubs. They got up at 9-30. No one else was awake yet, they made a fresh cup of tea and sat at the kitchen table, they didn't dare speak about it. It was a relief when the other girls got up. Mollie and Penny didn't say much they were too excited, Penny couldn't wait to see Zac later, she was totally in love with him he was her hero.

Zac couldn't sleep either he was checking the clock every 10 minutes until it was 9am, he phoned the number for the school.

"Good morning The Elizabeth School, can I help you?" said a woman's voice.

"Hi, you don't know me. But I know where Penny and Mollie are. I need someone to tell the 3 women that are looking for them in St. Petersburg where they are. Can you help me?" asked Zac. The phone line was silent for a few seconds, then the woman spoke again.

"Hang on, I will get the headmaster for you, hang on, don't hang up." she said, he could hear people shouting, calling out for Rick. A man's voice came on to the phone.

"Hello, I'm the headmaster Rick Wozniak, how can I help you?" asked Rick.

"Hi, I know where Penny and Mollie are, can you pass my phone number on to the women that are looking for them in St. Petersburg? They can phone me, I'm in St. Petersburg. Penny told me to ring the school, can you help?" asked Zac.

"Yes, of course I can, is it this mobile number that you're calling from that you want me to pass on?" asked Rick.

"Yes, it is, can you do it now? The girls need to be rescued." replied Zac.

"Are they alright?" asked Rick. "Should I call the police?"

"No, don't call the police not yet, if you do that the people that have the girls might find out and move them." said Zac. "Look, they are working in a club against their will. You can't give my number to anyone else just the women that are looking for the girls, ok?"

"Yes, I won't give your number to anyone else. I know who it is in St. Petersburg." replied Rick.

"Who is it?" asked Zac.

"It's their parents, and Mollies Aunt and Uncle and Mollies boyfriend." replied Rick.

"Ok, can you give them my number now, I'll be waiting for them to call me." said Zac.

"I will do it now. Thank you for calling." replied Rick. The phone line went dead. Zac hoped he was doing the right thing.

Rick quickly wrote down Zac's phone number then phoned Brenda.

Brenda and the others were sitting in the hotel restaurant, they had just finished breakfast when Brenda's phone started to ring.

"Hello" said Brenda.

"Hello, Brenda, Its Rick Wozniak, listen, someone has just phoned the school they have given me a number for you to ring, this person says he knows where the girls are, he knows you are looking for them." said Rick.

"What? Someone knows where the girls are. Where are they?" asked Brenda, the rest of the group sat like statues looking at Brenda.

"He said they are alright they are working in a club in St. Petersburg, he is there in St. Petersburg. Listen he said don't call the police, whoever has the girls might find out and move them, ok. He wants you to phone him, I'm going to text you his number, he said phone him now." said Rick.

"Oh my god, I can't believe it, what is his name?" asked Brenda,

"He didn't say, phone him now Brenda, good luck, bye." said Rick.

"Bye" replied Brenda. Immediately Zac's phone number came through in a text to Brenda's phone.

"Who was that? What's happened?" asked Sue.

"Mr Wozniak, the headmaster, he has just spoken to someone. They phoned the school, they said to pass their number on to us. They know where the girls are, they are here working in a club." said Brenda "I've got to ring it now."

"Should we tell the police?" asked Bill.

"No, he said no police, the people who have the girls might find out and move them." replied Brenda.

"Phone the number now Brenda." said Karen. Brenda phoned Zac.

"Hello" said Zac.

"Hello, I've been given your number, you know where Mollie and Penny are?" said Brenda.

"Yes, they are ok. Look can I meet you somewhere private?" asked Zac. Brenda looked at the others.

"He wants to meet somewhere private?" said Brenda, they all looked at each other.

"Here, tell him to come here. We can meet in my room." said Artiom.

"Ok, can you come to our hotel?" asked Brenda.

"Yes, that's a good idea where are you?" replied Zac.

"It's the St. Peters Hotel, do you know it?" asked Brenda.

"Yes, I'll be there in 15 minutes, look, I have got to be careful, so please be quiet when I arrive, I will message you to tell you I'm there ok?" said Zac.

"Yes, don't worry, I will meet you at the door and then we can talk in a hotel room ok." replied Brenda.

"Yes, that is good, see you soon." said Zac and he hung up.

"Oh my god, this is unbelievable. He knows where the girls are, he said they are ok, but yes they are working in a club, we will find them now." said Brenda she started to cry.

"This is fantastic news, let's hope we find them today." said Artiom. Sue and Karen were crying as well. The men sat there thinking of the girls working in one of the clubs they'd been in. It wasn't a nice thought. Artiom looked at their faces he knew what they were thinking.

"Listen, we are going to find them and get them out of whatever situation they are in, focus on that now, ok? Why don't you all go and wait in my room? Give me your phone Brenda I'll wait for him and bring him upstairs." said Artiom. He felt he would be the best person to meet this informant.

"Yes, ok that sounds like a good idea, he will be here in a minute." replied Ant. Artiom gave him his room key card.

"I'll bring him straight up to my room ok." said Artiom. The others all left the table and went up to Artioms hotel room. Artiom left the hotel he stood against the hotel wall near to the entrance. He wasn't there very long when he saw a good-looking man walking towards the hotel, he was carrying a large holdall. He stopped suddenly and sent a message on his phone, Brenda's phone pinged.

"I'm Here," said the message. Artiom let him walk to the door then he walked forward.

"Hi" he showed Zac his message on Brenda's phone. "I'm Mollies boyfriend."

"Hi, Mollie and Penny are alright, can we go inside." replied Zac. He was expecting to meet Mollies boyfriend, but he didn't think he would be Russian, he was a bit worried at that point. Artiom walked into the hotel and up the stairs, he didn't talk to Zac. Zac followed him up the stairs, he was hoping he hadn't been found out that he was helping the girls, and this was a trap. Artiom opened his hotel room door. Zac could see the three women he saw in the coffee shop, he breathed a sigh of relief and walked into the room. Artiom closed the door.

"Hello, you know where Mollie and Penny are?" said Steve. Zac looked at the faces of the people standing in front of him, they looked scared and tired with big eyes he felt them moving closer to him they wanted answers.

"Hi, ok my name is Zac, I work or worked, because I can never go back now, in fact I will have to leave Russia after this. I worked as a barman in The Pink Kitten Club, that's where Penny and Mollie are working." said Zac.

"What sort of club is it?" asked Sue. They needed to know just what their girls where being forced to do.

"It's a strip club, the girls are topless, but the customers are not allowed to touch them, there is a lot of security men protecting the girls. I know this might sound strange but it's not one of the bad clubs to work in." There was a sigh of relief after what Zac said.

"So, are they ok?" asked Karen. "I'm Penny's Mum." Zac could see the resemblance.

"They are ok, please stop thinking the worst, like I said its one of the best clubs here, I know that sounds strange. What we need to do now is make a plan to get the girls out of there." said Zac.

"What do you think Zac? Have you got any ideas?" asked Artiom.

"I think the only way to get the girls out is to phone the police once you're in the club and you have the girls with you, it would be good if the women could be there too. Are you Mollies mum?" Artiom asked Sue.

"Yes, I am, and this is her Dad Bill." replied Sue she pointed to Bill.

"I'm Steve, Penny's dad." said Steve. Brenda introduced herself and Ant.

"I've asked Penny to marry me." said Zac. Everybody's jaws dropped.

"What? Why?" asked Steve.

"I can't explain it, but something magical happened when we met, and therefore why I'm doing this. I need to save Penny so I can marry her." replied Zac. Karen looked at Zac, she could see why Penny liked him, if she did like him. They only had Zac's word about that.

"So, you will come to Spain with us then?" asked Artiom.

"I hope so. The club will open at 6pm, I won't be there. I'm going to phone in sick so that I can come back to Spain with Penny. If I try to leave the club with you and the girls, I think I will be shot. The police will protect the girls they won't protect me." said Zac.

"What's the best time to go to the club?" asked Artiom.

"I think you should get there before it's too busy, go in find the girls, they know you are here looking for them, tell Penny that I'm here waiting for her, she will wonder where I am. Then phone the police, the police will have to help you, there won't be any time for a corrupt officer to tip the club off." replied Zac.

"So, you think the women should come with us?" asked Steve.

"Yes, the police will be more helpful if Penny and Mollies Mums are there. The person in charge of the girls is Margot." said Zac.

"A woman?" asked Brenda.

"Yes, you will see her, she is the only woman fully dressed in the club, she will try to make the girls go to the dressing room, don't let the girls out of your sight, take a couple of shirts for them to wear, hold on to the girls all the time." said Zac.

"Thank you for helping us Zac. Where are the girls now?" asked Karen.

"I don't know where they are, the girls that work in the clubs all live in houses together, I don't know where these houses are sorry." replied Zac.

"And they are locked in?" asked Steve.

"Yes, they are locked in, and there's cameras watching them all the time. The same in the club, there's cameras and the security men all watching the girls, to make sure they don't get away." replied Zac. The others realised that they might have to fight for their girls later, but they knew they will fight if they have too.

"I take it you won't be going back to your flat or house any more Zac?" asked Artiom looking at Zac's large holdall.

"No, I will need to stay out of sight now." replied Zac.

"You can stay here, we will see what Penny says about your marriage proposal." said Steve."

"Can we stay here tonight? or should we leave straight away once we've got the girls?" asked Karen.

"I think we should leave tonight. We should have everything ready so we can get straight on the road." replied Zac.

"Just one problem there, we only have two cars, will we fit three more people in?" said Brenda.

"Yes, just about, two can get in my car and one in your car Ant." said Artiom.

"We have three seats in the back of our car it might be a squeeze." said Brenda "But who cares let's just get our girls home."

"We can stay at my grandparents home tonight, they live about an hour away, then tomorrow morning we can start the drive back to Spain." said Artiom.

"Will your grandparents mind? There's a lot of us." replied Sue.

"No, they will be happy to see me and to meet Penny. They have a couple of spare bedrooms. I'll call them and let them know we are coming." said Artiom. He went outside to call his grandparents.

"So, we will need to drive to the club, where will we park?" asked Ant.

"There is a layby nearby, I will come to the club with you, but I'll stay in the car. I'll show Artiom where to park." replied Zac.

They knew they had to wait all day until they could go to the club and rescue Mollie and Penny, so they started to pack up their things slowly. Artiom and Zac got to know each other.

CHAPTER 28

Sean, Hannah and Grace were at the hospital at 10am, the girls couldn't wait to see their Mum. Marie was sitting up in bed, she had changed into clean pyjamas and tidied up her face and the hair she could get to, she knew she looked a mess. She decided that once she was out of hospital, she was going to lose some weight. She thought Sean might want to come back to her if she was thinner. She decided she would get her hair cut shorter, she always looks younger with shorter hair, everyone tells her that.

Marie had decided that this Tracey was just a blip, and if she loses weight and takes more care of herself, she could win Sean back.

Sean and the girls got to Marie's room they stopped outside, Marie saw them.

"Come in then, I can't hug you from there." Marie called out in a cheerful whisper. Hannah and Grace rushed in, and both flung their arms around Marie.

"Oh Mum, we were so worried, please don't ever do that again." said Hannah.

"I won't Hannah. I'm so sorry you found me." replied Marie.

"I thought you were dead." said Grace.

"Grace! Don't say that." said Hannah, sometimes she couldn't believe what comes out of Graces mouth. Marie smiled.

"You won't get rid of me that easily. I'm not planning on going anywhere anytime soon Grace." said Marie.

"Good, because I don't want to lose you Mum." replied Grace. Sean came in and kissed Marie on the cheek.

"Hi Marie, how are you feeling?" he asked. Marie looked at him, he looked terrible, like he hasn't slept for a year.

"I'm ok Sean." replied Marie. "Have you been to the hotel yet?"

"No, not yet." said Sean.

"Why don't you pop there now, the girls can stay here with me." suggested Marie.

"Ok, if you're all ok here without me, I will be as quick as I can." replied Sean. Once he had left Marie looked at Hannah and Grace.

"Ok, so you know about Tracey." said Marie. Both girls nodded.

"I saw a message from her on dads' phone." replied Hannah.

"Dad has shown us photos of her and Ronnie." said Grace "Have you seen him?"

"Yes, he looks a bit like you two when you were babies." replied Marie.

"So is dad leaving us?" asked Hannah.

"Yes, he is. Once I'm back home he will fly back to live in the UK." replied Marie. Grace started to cry Marie rubbed Graces back.

"But you two will see dad all the time. You can both go and stay with him in the school holidays." said Marie.

"But I don't want to stay with Tracey." said Grace "I hate her she's taken dad away from us."

"I don't want to stay with this Tracey woman either, if dad wants to see us, he will have to come here." said Hannah. Marie was secretly pleased her girls thought Tracey was a bitch. She wasn't going to try to talk them in to liking her. No. Tracey is a bitch.

Hannah's phone pinged, she read the message.

"No way!" she shouted. Marie and Grace looked at her waiting to hear what the message was.

"It's from Katie, guess what?" said Hannah beaming.

"No idea Hannah tell us." said Marie.

"They know where your friends are mum." replied Hannah.

"What? who knows? Where are they?" asked Marie, she couldn't believe what Hannah had just said.

"A man phoned the school this morning, he said he knows where the teachers are." said Hannah she was still reading the message.

"They are working in a club in St. Petersburg, against their will. That's horrible." said Hannah her smile had turned in to a frown.

"How can people do that, just take women off the street and make them work in a sex club?" asked Hannah. Marie was still taking in what Hannah had said.

"How does Katie know about this Hannah?" asked Marie.

"Everyone knows about it Mum, it's true." replied Hannah. Marie picked up her phone, she googled for the school's phone number, it came up, she pressed the call button. Laura Wozniak answered.

"Hello The Elizabeth School. Can I help you?" said Laura.

"Hi Laura, its Marie Cole here." Marie tried to speak as loudly as her sore and croaky throat would allow. Laura was surprised that it was Marie phoning.

"Marie! How are you?" asked Laura.

"I'm getting there Laura, is it true Mollie and Penny have been found?" asked Marie.

"Yes. It seems that way, I don't have all the details, but it looks like they have." replied Laura.

"Oh my god! That's great news." croaked Marie, she still couldn't believe it.

"Are you still in hospital?" asked Laura, she was just being nosey so she could pass the gossip on.

"Yes, I will be home soon hopefully." replied Marie.

"If you need anything, let me know." said Laura, she didn't really mean it but it's what people say.

"Actually, would it be ok if Sean picks up my overnight bag, it's at the apartment." asked Marie, she really wanted her make-up bag, it's got her expensive anti-wrinkle eye cream in it.

"I can bring it in to you?" offered Laura. She thought she could take the opportunity to question Marie about Mollie and Rick.

"That would be really kind of you Laura, I'm on ward 7." replied Marie. She would have preferred Sean collecting it for her, but she didn't mind Laura. They have something in common now as well.

"I will pop in after work, about 4pm?" said Laura.

"I'm not going anywhere, see you later Laura." replied Marie.

"See you later Marie." said Laura she put the phone down, she liked Marie, she wasn't a threat to her unlike Mollie. Laura opened her desk drawer she took out the little envelope with the gold hoop earring in it, she did put it in the bin, but something made her take it out and put it

back in her drawer. She wasn't as happy as everyone else that Mollie had

been found, but she was pleased about Penny. Laura thought she would

pop to the apartment in her lunch hour and pick Marie's bag up. How will

she know which bag is Marie's? She decided she will have to look inside

all the bags to find out. Marie put her phone down.

"I can't believe it; its true Mollie and Penny have been found. I'm so

happy, I hope they are ok." whispered Marie still in a mixture of shock and

surprise.

"It's really good news. I wonder what they went through?" said Hannah,

she was old enough to know that working in a club in St. Petersburg

against your will wasn't going to be good. Grace didn't really understand

all of what had happened, but she was pleased the teachers had been

found.

"Laura is popping in later with my overnight bag, it's got my make-up bag

in it, and my nice pyjamas." said Marie.

"She is probably coming in to find out something to gossip about at

school." said Hannah.

"Yes. Probably. I don't want anyone to know about what I did so don't tell anyone. I'm talking to you as well Grace, I don't want anyone to know." said Marie. Both girls nodded.

"We won't tell anyone, will we Grace?" said Hannah.

"No, I won't say anything to anyone." replied Grace. Unfortunately, it was too late, Grace had messaged a few of her "best friends" and updated them with all the news about Marie taking an overdose. She regretted doing that now. She did tell them not to say anything to anyone else. Fingers crossed.

When Sean got the hotel, he went straight to the reception and explained the situation, they were helpful and cancelled his reservation for the rest of his booking, just charging him for the 1 night. He went to his room and collected his things. Once he was back in the car he phoned Tracey, he had already messaged her to tell her about Marie's overdose.

"Hello." said Sean.

"Hello Sean, how's everything?" asked Tracey.

"Well, I've just picked up my things from the hotel, I'm staying in the house with the girls until Marie is out of hospital." replied Sean.

"When will Marie be home?" asked Tracey, she was missing Sean.

"I'm not sure, she needs to stay there until at least next week. We had a long talk about everything, I think she has accepted that our marriage is over. I felt terrible Tracey, seeing Marie so upset, I never wanted to do this to her." said Sean still feeling guilty and to blame for Marie taking an overdose.

"I know Sean, but now Marie is going to be ok now." replied Tracey, trying to lift Sean's mood.

"I hope so. How's Ronnie? I miss seeing his happy little face each day." said Sean, thinking about Ronnie made him smile.

"Ronnie is fine, he misses seeing his dad every day. So do I." replied Tracey. Sean missed Tracey and Ronnie. Being in the UK with them is where he wanted to be.

"Once Marie is home, I will be on the first flight back. I promise." said Sean.

"I hope so. I love you so much." said Tracey.

"I love you too. I'll phone you tonight. Bye Tracey." said Sean.

"Bye Sean. Love You." replied Tracey. She put her phone down on the kitchen table and looked baby Ronnie sleeping in her arms.

"Daddy will be back home soon Ronnie, and this time it will be forever." she whispered. Ronnie smiled in his sleep. He has his Daddy's smile, thought Tracey.

Sean drove to the hospital. He was surprised to see Marie looking happy.

"Guess what Dad?" said Hannah excitedly as he entered Marie's room.

"What? I don't know?" replied Sean, wondering what has happened to make them all so happy.

"Mums two friends have been found!" said Hannah.

"Really? That's fantastic news. Who found them?" asked Sean.

"We don't know all the details yet, but they were in Russia. Working in a sex club against their will." said Hannah.

"Oh, that's not good, I hope they are, ok?" replied Sean. He was happy they had been found for Marie's sake more than anything, he knew she blamed herself for not being able to help them more when they were taken.

"Laura Wozniak is coming to see me at 4 o'clock, she is bringing in my overnight bag, the one I left at the apartment." said Marie "I'll see if I can find out any more information about the girls. I'm just so relieved they have been found alive."

"I could have got your bag Marie." said Sean.

"It's ok, I phoned the school because Hannah had seen the news about the girls on Facebook, I wanted to find out if it was true. Laura answered the phone she asked if I needed anything, so I said yes, my bag, and she offered to bring it in, probably just wants to be nosey. I've told Hannah and Grace I don't want anyone to know about what I did yesterday." said Marie. Sean nodded.

"No, we will keep it between us. Don't tell any of your friends." Sean said to Hannah and Grace.

"We wouldn't anyway dad, it's private." replied Hannah. Grace didn't say anything.

"We will need to get some food shopping today girls." said Sean. The girls both made a sad face at him. "We can't keep eating fast food."

"Yes, we can." replied Grace. Marie smiled. This is her family, grown up Hannah, cheeky Grace and Sean, she wanted it to stay like this forever.

"You should go and get the shopping done now, all of you can go. I'm fine here. Laura is coming later, I can read the magazines." said Marie, she felt happy knowing Mollie and Penny were safe. She wanted to google some diet plans and look at ideas for her new hair style. She thought Sean and the girls are probably bored sitting here, the girls are on their phones the whole time anyway, and Sean could be doing things at home, instead of sitting on a chair in a hospital room. Sean looked at Marie would she be ok without us here?

"Are you sure you'll be ok here on your own?" asked Sean.

"I'm really on my own, am I? there's about 2000 other people in the hospital as well." smiled Marie.

"You know what I mean. Or I could go and do the shopping and leave the girls here to keep you company?" suggested Sean. The girls looked at their dad.

"I would sooner come shopping." said Grace.

"I think we both should go with dad. He doesn't really know what to buy." said Hannah to Marie.

"Yes, I think so too. Can you buy me a nice shower gel and bring it in tomorrow?" asked Marie.

"I was planning on coming back later about 6ish?" said Sean.

"Oh, ok I'll see you later. You two don't have to come back and you can go to school tomorrow." replied Marie. They all needed to get back to normal. Like they were this time last week. Sean and the girls kissed Marie goodbye, Sean said he would be back later. Once they had gone Marie closed her eyes, she was still feeling tired after the overdose of paracetamol it wasn't long before she was asleep.

CHAPTER 29

Laura drove to the apartment in her lunch hour. She spotted Mollies car

parked outside. Bitch. She thought to herself. Once inside the apartment

she had a look around, she hadn't been there for a while, she knew they

had bookings confirmed from June through to September, she would have

to get a cleaner in to give it a good clean and get it ready for the first lot of

holiday makers. Fucking Rick, letting any old slag stay in it for free. The

thought of Rick meeting Mollie and who knows who else here for sex

made he feel so angry. You are a bastard Rick she thought to herself. She

went into the bedrooms. There were three bags next to each other on the

double bed in the main bedroom. She knew which one was Marie's bag

straight away, it was the first bag she looked in, the knickers gave it away,

clean, ironed M&S cotton briefs. She zipped the bag up and put it on the

floor. She didn't have to look inside the other two bags, but she thought

as she was there, she might as well. She unzipped the second bag and

looked through it, could it be Mollies? she wasn't sure, the knickers were

black cotton, not skimpy but not as big as Marie's, could be Penny's bag?

Laura opened the third bag. This was Mollies bag, inside was two thongs,

one was a red satin thong the other one was a black lace thong, there was a black lacy see-through negligee as well. Slut thought Laura. She zipped

the bag back up picked up Marie's bag and walked out of the room. She

got to the front door and stopped, she knew this was wrong, but she

couldn't help herself she went back to the bedroom opened Mollies bag

and took out the thong, she put it in to her handbag and left the

apartment. Back at school she made sure no one was watching her and

put Mollies red thong into her drawer with the earring. She could feel her

heart beating fast. All afternoon when she was sure no one was in the

office she opened the drawer and looked at Mollies thong. She hated

Mollie. She was a slag. She wasn't feeling happy that mollie has been

found.

Laura arrived at the hospital at 4 o'clock. She took the lift to Marie's ward

and asked at the nurse's station where Marie was. She could see Marie

through the window of her room she was sitting up in bed, she had a large

bandage around her head, and she looked rough.

"Hello Marie, how are you?" gushed Laura as she breezed into Marie's

room. Marie was pleased to see her.

"Hi Laura, I'm feeling so much better today. Come and sit down." replied

Marie pointing to a chair next to the bed. Laura put Marie's bag on the floor and sat herself down, she gave Marie a shopping carrier size pink gift bag.

"From everyone at school. You are missed Marie." said Laura. Marie was nicely surprised she hadn't expected anything, it brought a tear to her eyes.

"Oh, thank you. I wasn't expecting a gift." said Marie tearfully. Laura looked at Marie's face she could see she was totally surprised and emotional. She liked Marie.

"Open it then. The children have been working hard all day." said Laura. What actually happened was, Laura told Rick Marie had rung the school to ask if it was true that Mollie and Penny had been found. Then she asked if Sean could collect her bag from the apartment, so Laura offered to take it to Marie at the hospital. Rick thought that was a lovely thing for Laura to do. He asked if Laura had organised a gift and a card from all the pupils yet? Laura hadn't even thought about it. It hadn't crossed her mind. So, Rick quickly asked one of the teachers to arrange a giant card to be made and everyone sign it and he went out and bought Marie some perfume and chocolates. Laura thought it was a shame he never run out and bought her gifts. He better not of bought Mollie the slut perfume in the past.

Marie opened the bag and took out the giant card it was drawing of Marie with a big smile on her face holding a bunch of flowers.

"Ahhhh, that's lovely. I don't look like that at the moment, we need to add a big white bandage to my head." she gave a little smile. Then Marie opened the card and saw that every member of staff and every pupil in the school had signed the card, some had added kisses or little hearts. It was too much for Marie, she couldn't stop the tears.

"I'm sorry." she sobbed. She was looking for a tissue. Laura saw the box of tissues and gave them to Marie.

"Oh Marie, don't get upset, everyone loves you at the school, they all just want you to get better and come back to work." said Laura feeling slightly emotional herself. Only slightly.

"It's been an emotional day, Laura. When I heard the girls have been found I was so relieved and so happy." sniffed Marie.

"Well, someone phoned to say he knows where they are." replied Laura.

"Oh, so they haven't been found yet then?" asked Marie feeling confused.

"You know their families are there in Russia looking for them?" replied Laura.

"Yes, and Artiom, that's Mollies boyfriend." said Marie. Laura looked at Marie confused.

"Mollie has a boyfriend?" said Laura. How come she didn't know this, or did she? Why is she messing about with Rick if she has a boyfriend? And does he know his girlfriend has been sleeping with my husband? The slag.

"Yes Artiom. He is a dish, big strong good looking and Russian." replied Marie. Laura carried on.

"Well, the person that phoned is in Russia as well, and he asked Rick to give the girls families his phone number so he could tell them where the girls are." explained Laura. She was still taking in mollie has a boyfriend and a dishy one at that. Why was she messing about with Rick then?

"But he knows where they are definitely?" asked Marie.

"He said he did, he said they are working in a club." replied Laura.

"A sex club?" asked Marie.

"Most likely I would have thought." replied Laura.

"I hope we hear that they have been found and are on their way home, that would be such good news, wouldn't it?" said Marie. Laura forced herself to agree. Marie opened the perfume and chocolates.

"Thank you all so much, I feel so lucky and loved." said Marie.

"You are welcome Marie." replied Laura "so is Mollie in a serious relationship with her boyfriend?"

"Well, I think Artiom is more serious than Mollie, you know what Mollie is like." replied Marie.

"I don't really know Mollie that well myself, my husband on the other hand knows Mollie very well." said Laura. Marie started to feel uncomfortable, did Laura know about Mollie and her husband?

"Well, I mean Mollie is just a young one isn't she, she's a bit of a flirt, but she's a lovely girl, just lively." said Marie.

"She is definitely a flirt Marie. I think she's been sleeping with Rick." said Laura. She was surprised she had said that to Marie.

"Oh." replied Marie, she didn't know what to say, she felt sorry for Laura, she knows exactly what it feels like to find out your husband is shagging someone else. "I'm sorry Laura, what I can tell you is that it wasn't anything serious and Mollie was going to end it all." said Marie.

"Really? Oh, that makes it all ok then. Do you know what it feels like knowing your husband is shagging another woman? A younger woman." replied Laura angrily. Marie knew exactly how to answer that.

"Yes, I do know how it feels, I've just found out Sean has been having an affair for 18 months with a younger woman in the UK they have a baby boy between them. So yes, I do know how it feels." replied Marie. She didn't know why she told Laura all that, it just came out. Laura looked at Marie in surprise.

"What? Your Sean has been having an affair for 18months? and has a baby with the woman? Wow, I'm sorry Marie, what are you going to do?" asked Laura.

"Nothing. Sean is going to live with Tracey and the baby." replied Marie.

"Is that her name? Tracey" asked Laura.

"Yes, and the baby is called Ronnie. Sean always wanted a boy." replied Marie. Laura sat there looking at Marie, how is she so calm? If I was Marie, I'd be going mental. This puts a few secret shags with a little slag into perspective. Carrying on for 18 months and having a baby together. Wow, wait until everyone at school hears about this. And Sean he is the last person anyone would have expected to have an affair. He is about as exciting as a wet dishcloth. Laura felt sorry for Marie.

"Do you know what Marie? You need to carry on without Sean. You are still young. You will find someone new, a toy boy maybe. Don't let Sean and Tracey the slag ruin your life." said Laura, thinking her words of wisdom were helpful.

"I've already decided to go on a diet and get my hair cut and restyled." replied Marie. She didn't say she was doing it to win Sean back.

"Good for you Marie." said Laura meaning it.

"What are you going to do about Mollie?" asked Marie.

"Rick doesn't know that I know about him and Mollie. I'm not going to do anything yet." replied Laura.

"Well, I don't think Mollie is going to meet him anymore anyway." said Marie reassuringly. Laura smiled and said she'd better go. The boys will be wanting some dinner. She wished Marie a speedy recovery and they said goodbye. Laura left the hospital with more knowledge than she had hoped for. Marie looked at the card again, how lovely she thought to herself. She looked at the big box of chocolates, normally she would have already eaten half of them. She put them unopened back into the gift bag, she would let Hannah and Grace eat them.

Sean and the girls did the shopping. Both girls adding extras to the shopping trolley. An eye liner for Hannah and a tub of Ben & Jerrys ice cream for Grace. Sean knew Marie wouldn't have bought these items, but he let the girls have them. They'd decided on pizzas for dinner today, not a big improvement on a takeaway but easy to cook. They nearly forgot Marie's shower gel, Hannah picked a nice one with a coconut fragrant. Sean was relieved they didn't bump into any nosey neighbours today. They finished doing the shopping, popping into the Iceland's supermarket quickly on the way home so the girls could choose their goodies for their packed lunches. Once home Sean put the shopping away. He decided to cut the grass before he put the pizzas in for dinner. Hannah and Grace both sat at the kitchen table to do some homework. They were eating crisps and sweets, to help them concentrate explained Grace.

CHAPTER 30

Mollie and Penny were wishing the hours away. It had been a long day. Finally, they were sitting in the minibus on their way to the club for tonight's shift. It had been hard not being able to share with the other girls in the house, their news, that their families were here looking for them, and Zac was helping them to escape. They wanted to tell them that they will be back to help them too, they had found out enough information from each girl to be able to let the police know where they were. And hopefully they too will be reunited with their families. But first Mollie and Penny needed to be found and rescued. Penny was excited to see Zac again, she had been thinking about him all day. He is her knight in shining armour. Her hero. When they arrived at the club, they acted normal. They got dressed and then went into the club and to the bar to collect a tray. Penny looked for Zac, she couldn't see him, maybe he was out the back.

"Where's Zac?" Mollie whispered in Penny's ear.

"I don't know Penny, I hope he is ok." whispered Penny. Both girls felt worried. They started work acting as normal as they could. Zac wasn't in the club, they were sure of that. Penny was worried, she knew Zac wouldn't let them down. But where was he? Mollie decided to ask one of the other barmen.

"Hi where's Zac tonight?" she asked casually.

"Zac phoned in sick, so you have my ugly mug to look at." replied the barman smiling.

"I think your mug is pretty good actually." replied Mollie. Penny was listening. So, Zac has phoned in sick? That must be part of the plan, thought Penny. Mollie picked up her tray of drinks.

"What do you think Penny?" she whispered in Penny's ear.

"I think it's part of the plan. Zac won't let us down." Penny whispered back.

At the hotel Zac and the others were getting their belongings together. They were all feeling a mixture of excitement and nerves, excited at the thought they would be finding the girls but nervous about what might happen. They booked out of the hotel and got into their cars. They were ready to do this. To save their girls. Zac was in the back of Artioms car, he gave Artiom directions to the Pink Kitten Club. Both cars parked in the layby nearby. Zac put his hoodie up.

"Go in and look for Penny and Mollie, they will most likely be together. Once you find them phone the police and tell them you need them to come to the club quickly, the girls know you're coming to find them. Don't let them out of your sight. Good luck." said Zac. He really wanted to go in with Artiom and help to rescue the girls, but he knew that would be dangerous for him. He watched the others get out of the cars and walk towards the club.

"Ok. Brenda, Sue and Karen, you three go in first, it will look strange if we all go in together." said Artiom. They knew it was going to look strange anyway three middle aged women going into a strip club. They walked to the door and smiled at the two burley looking door men, the men didn't batter an eyelid just greeted the women and opened the door. Well, that was easy thought Brenda. They walked to the kiosk to pay the entrance fee, the young woman in the kiosk smiled at them.

"Good evening ladies, you do know what sort of club this is?" she asked them in broken English.

"Hello, yes we know, thank you." replied Sue. The young women smiled again took their money and pointed to the double door that led into the club. The three women walked towards the doors.

"This is it ladies. Deep breath. Let's go and get our girls." said Sue. The three women didn't feel nervous anymore, their nerves had been replaced with bravery, they were prepared to fight if they had to, they knew they wasn't leaving without Mollie and Penny. Both Sue and Karen were wearing an extra shirt over the top of their clothes ready to give to their daughters to cover their nudity. The doors opened. The sight that greeted Brenda, Sue and Karen was a shock, they knew the young women working there would be topless and that some would be naked dancing on the stages and wrapping themselves around poles. The music was loud, the lights were bright and flashing, the smell of men hit them all in the face like a strong wind.

"God, it stinks in here." said Sue. They started to walk slowly around the club. Even though they had been told what to expect they were all shocked. The sight of men watching young women dancing and walking around either topless or naked was very unnerving. It made the 3 women feel physically sick.

"This is so wrong." said Sue "What year is it? 2021? These men make me so angry. They are disgusting wanting to come in these clubs to watch young women being exploited like this."

"Some of these men are old enough to be Mollies Grandad. It's wrong." agreed Brenda. Karen nodded in agreement. She was disgusted at every man in the club. They got near to bar area when Mollie spotted her mum, she stopped dead on the spot. Sue saw Mollie standing there in front of her wearing a black mini skirt and high heels nothing else. They both looked at each other, Mollie realised she had to stay calm, then she saw Auntie Brenda and who she guessed was Penny's mum. She smiled at them and nodded, then she turned round and looked for Penny, she was still at the bar. Mollie walked back to Penny.

"Our mums are here. Don't make a scene Penny, Let's just walk over to them and talk to them, no one knows they're our mums." whispered Mollie. The two girls walked over to their mums and Brenda.

"Hi, we won't cuddle you yet, what's the plan?" asked Mollie smiling the same as she would be with a customer. The older women were so happy to see Mollie and Penny looked ok, apart from being topless.

"Are you both ok?" asked Karen. Penny looked at her mum, she just wanted to hug her.

"Yes, we are both fine, wish we had some clothes to put on." replied Penny.

"You can put these shirts on once Artiom, Bill and your dads get in here." said Brenda. Mollie and Penny both put the trays up over their breasts, they didn't want their dads, Ant or Artiom to see them topless.

"Did Zac phone you?" asked Penny.

"Yes, he is waiting outside in Artioms car, he didn't want to risk coming back here. So, you're going to marry Zac?" said Karen.

"Thank god he is ok." replied Penny. Feeling relieved knowing Zac was safe. Artiom, Bill, Steve and Ant were walking around the club looking for the women and the girls, Mollie spotted Artiom.

"There's Artiom can you give us the shirts to put on please." she said pointing in Artioms direction. Karen and Sue took the spare shirts they were wearing off and helped the girls put them on. Artiom had seen Mollie he run over to her. Steve, Bill and Ant were following Artiom. They had created a large group now and a couple of the security men had noticed what was happening.

Artiom had his phone out and had called the local police. He had his arm around Mollie.

"Artiom, thank you for finding us." said Mollie she cuddled up to Artiom she never wanted him to let go of her ever again. Penny's dad put his arm around Penny.

"Stay with me Penny, don't go anywhere." He said to Penny. Penny cuddled up to her dad.

"I love you dad, thank you for coming to find me." she said.

Margot saw what was going on and came rushing over to them.

"Take your hands off my girls." she shouted at Steve and Artiom. Karen and Sue both flew at her.

"They are our daughters you are a disgusting excuse for a woman." shouted Karen into Margot's face. Margot took a step backwards.

"How dare you make these girls work here. You are a terrible person. You must have something wrong with you." shouted Sue she pushed Margot over to the floor and jumped on top of her, she had managed to get two good punches into Margot face before the security men got there and started to pull Sue off Margot. Brenda saw this as her chance to give Margot a slap, so as Margot stood up with blood on her face from her busted nose Brenda gave her the biggest punch she could and knocked Margot off her feet. Margot was out cold on the floor. By now the other security men had gathered round to see what was going on, a couple of them had their phones out. Artiom had hold of Mollie and wasn't letting go, Penny was flanked either side of her by her parents they both had their arms tightly linked around Penny. Some of the other girls from the house were watching the goings on, Mollie saw them.

"We won't forget you." she said to them. She knew she couldn't shout out they were going to help them because they would be moved to another club. They all started to move towards the front exit of the club. Margot was sitting up on the floor she had a bloody nose and a large cut over one eye. The security men were trying to get the other girls back to work, they didn't want a mutiny on their hands. As they were passing the customers in the club Mollie and Penny were telling anyone that could hear them that they had been taken from the street and was kept prisoners in a house and were forced to work in the club against their will. They were telling the men all the girls were being forced to work there. Some men left the club, but others just shrugged their shoulders. The local police arrived inside the club as Mollie and the rest of the group were leaving. "What's going on." asked one officer. Mollie looked at his face she recognised him. He had been in the club as a customer.

"These girls are our daughters. They were taken, abducted from a street in Spain and brought here to this disgusting club. They have been kept imprisoned and made to work in this shit hole. They are coming home with us." said Sue and she pushed him out of the way. The police weren't really that bothered about the girls being rescued. They already knew what was going on inside the club.

Once outside they all ran to the layby, Zac was in the car, he was looking out for them, it felt like they had been gone ages and he was getting worried, he couldn't even phone anyone to see what was happening because he had deliberately dropped his phone down a drain outside the hotel so he couldn't be traced. Then he spotted Penny and he couldn't stay in Artioms car any longer he opened the door and got out, Penny saw him and ran to him, she fell into Zac's arms.

"Thank you, Zac, thank you so much." said Penny. Zac put his face down to Penny's face and kissed her on the lips. It was their first kiss. Fireworks went off in Penny's head. She pulled away.

"I love you Zac." whispered Penny.

"I love you too." replied Zac. The others were at the cars now.

"Come on get in let's get out of here." said Artiom.

"Where are we going?" asked Mollie.

"We are going to drive to my grandparents house. Replied Artiom. It's about 1 hour away. We can stay there tonight and then start our drive home in the morning. Penny, Zac, Karen, and Steve all got into Artioms car.

"I will see you soon Mollie. I love You." Artiom said to Mollie as she climbed into her uncle Ants car with her Auntie Brenda and her mum and dad. Mollie sat on the back seat in between her mum and Brenda they were both holding Mollies hands. They drove in silence for 10 minutes.

Mollie was just so relived to be sitting in her Uncle Ants car with her mum and Auntie Brenda either side of her and her dad in the front seat. She could not believe just how lucky her, and Penny were. Some of the other girls at the club had been there for a couple of years, their families must have tried to find them. She wondered what had made her family come to Russia.

"Why did you come to look for us in Russia, and in St. Petersburg, how did you know that's where we were?" asked Mollie.

"Marie told the police the men that took you were Russian, and Artiom did some detective work and found out the names of the men." replied Mollies mum. Mollie looked at her mum.

"Hang on you just said Marie told the police. How did she do that? Is Marie not dead then?" asked Mollie confused.

"No love. Marie isn't dead, she was very lucky, the bullet got wedged in her skull, she is in hospital, but she is ok. Artiom has been in to see her." said her mum. Mollie sat there in shock and surprise. She could not believe Marie was alive, she started to cry. Her mum put her arms around her.

"Oh my god, you thought Marie was dead?" said Brenda "You poor things, on top of everything else you were going through."

"I need to tell Penny Marie is alive. We saw one of the men shoot Marie in the head and then Marie fell to the ground. She looked dead." said Mollie

"I'm so happy Marie is alive. Penny will be too. Oh my god, I can't believe it." Mollie sat there smiling, it was fantastic news.

"So, Marie told the police the men were Russian?" said Mollie.

"Yes, she remembered everything that happened. Artiom found out the names of the three Russian men, they are part of a Sex trafficking gang. He told the Spanish police their names and they showed Marie their e-fit photos and she said they were the same men that abducted you and Penny and shot Marie. Then Artiom heard that they trafficked girls to St. Petersburg, and he said he was going there to look for you, so we all decided to come with him. He really loves you." said Sue. Mollie was still taking in the news that Marie was alive. She was impressed with Artiom the way he had turned detective and worked out where her and Penny were. He must love me so much thought Mollie. She felt guilty suddenly, and worried. What if he finds out about her and Rick? She wondered if he already knew. He had been to see Marie, would Marie of told him? Mollie felt sick. She had realised just how much Artiom means to her on that Friday night. She was going to tell Rick she did not want to see him anymore. She was worried now. If Artiom didn't already know he would probably find out once they get back to Javea. She wondered if she should

tell him herself. Before he hears it from someone else.

Penny was sitting in between her mum and Zac in the back of Artioms car.

She was holding Zac's hand. She closed her eyes and silently thanked god

for saving her. When she opened her eyes again, she could feel Zac

watching her.

"Hi, how are you feeling?" asked Zac. Penny looked at his face. He was so

handsome. She realised they knew nothing about each other, not even

how old they each was.

"Hi. I'm just so happy we have been found. Thankyou Zac." replied Penny

smiling, then her smile disappeared.

"What's the matter you look sad?" asked Zac.

"I was just thinking about our friend Marie, she was with us the night we

were taken. They shot her in the head. We watched her fall to the ground

dead. She would have loved you. She was always telling me to find myself

a boyfriend." replied Penny sadly. Artiom looked at Penny in the rear

mirror.

"No Penny, Marie is alive. She didn't die. The bullet got stuck in her skull,

she's in the hospital I went to see her." said Artiom. Penny looked at

Artiom she couldn't speak for a minute.

"Marie is alive? Really?" she said shocked.

"Yes really, I went to see her in hospital. She is very sore, but she is going to be ok. She was more concerned about you and Mollie than herself." replied Artiom. Penny put her hand together closed her eyes thanked God for saving Marie.

"Are you religious?" asked Zac.

"No not really, but I've been asking god for a lot recently." replied Penny.

"Well, he has been listening to you Penny." replied Zac.

"Are you religious Zac? There's so much we don't know about each other." said Penny.

"No. I'm not religious. But I do believe in positive thinking and fate." replied Zac "We have all the time in the world to get to know each other better." Zac kissed Penny on the lips.

"Can you two waits until we get to my grandparents house, please." laughed Artiom. Penny's parents both laughed with him.

"Where do your grandparents live Artiom?" asked Steve.

"We are about 20 minutes away now, it's a bit out in the sticks, I'm going to turn off the motorway in a minute. They own a farm." replied Artiom.

"A farm? What sort of farm one with animals?" asked Karen.

"It has cattle, quite a lot of cattle. They have dogs and a cat as well."

replied Artiom. Steve and Karen were intrigued by Artioms grandparents

farm. He wasn't giving much away.

CHAPTER 31

Artiom turned off the motorway he checked in his mirror that Ant was still following him.

They travelled for 15 minutes along a narrow lane with fields either side of it. There weren't any houses or any other cars, all they saw was cattle. Finally, Artiom slowed down as they passed a huge house it was bigger than a house it looked like a mansion.

"We are here, that's my grandparents house." said Artiom. They were all looking at the mansion.

"What? that mansion is your grandparents house?" asked Steve.

"Yes, it is, I forget how big it is." replied Artiom in a matter-of-fact way. He drove through two enormous black metal gates that were already open and down an exceptionally long driveway. Both sides of the driveway there was trees and flowerbeds, there was a huge water fountain in the middle of a large, pebbled driveway. Artiom stopped outside the mansion Ant pulled up behind him. The big front door of the mansion opened, and an elderly man and woman came out and walked down the steps towards Artiom.

"Hello Darling Artiom. How are you? We were so pleased when you phoned to say you were coming to see us." Artioms grandparents both hugged and kissed Artiom, he returned the hugs and kisses.

"Hello nan hello gramps." he replied.

"And who are your friends?" asked Artioms nan.

"My girlfriend and her friend were abducted by a Russian gang in Spain and taken to St. Petersburg. I went there with their parents and family to rescue them, it's a long story, we will tell you all about indoors." replied Artiom. His grandparents looked at everyone as they climbed out of the two cars. Mollie and Penny hugged each other.

"Oh, Penny I can't believe it Marie is alive." said Mollie.

"I know it's the best news ever isn't it Mollie, I can't wait to see her again." replied Penny.

"Come in, come in, we have some food ready for you all." said Artioms nan. She waved them all into the mansion eager to hear the rest of the story. Once inside they were met by a housekeeper.

"Can I take your coats?" she asked them all. The men were wearing jackets they gave them to the middle-aged Russian housekeeper.

"Thank you, Olga. We will be going straight to the dining room. I think these lovely people must be needing something to eat." said Artioms grandad to Olga.

"Ok Sir. I'll let the cook know." replied Olga and she walked off towards the kitchen. Mollie and the others were all standing in the very large hall just looking around. They were all surprised at the size of Artioms grandparents' home, it was huge. Mollie couldn't believe where she was, that this was owned by Artioms grandparents. How rich were they? This is a millionaire's house without a doubt. All the furniture was big and lavish, you couldn't buy this furniture from Ikea. Artioms nan introduced herself to the group.

"I'm Irina and my husband is Andrei. Please follow us to the dining room." Irina turned and opened a door that led into a large room, it had lots of sofas in it and little tables. Mollie counted six sofas. The furniture was all big, there were glass display all around the walls with colourful pottery in them. The fireplace was the size of a double doorway, there was a fire alight in it even though it was summer. The ceiling was tall and there were four large crystal chandeliers hanging from it. Irina walked through the middle of the room until she came to some large double doors, she opened the door and walked into the dining room, everyone else apart from Artiom and his grandad, who were chatting to each other in Russian, stopped at the doorway. The room was like something they had seen on TV, Penny thought of Downton Abbey, she couldn't believe she was going to sit in this magnificent room and eat dinner. Irina looked at them all standing in the doorway.

"Please come in, come and sit down you must be hungry." said Irina.

Artiom looked back at them all standing in the doorway, he smiled.

"Sorry guys, sorry Mollie, I suppose I should have told you how big my grandparents home is, but I didn't want to spoil the surprise, come on sit down, cook always makes really good food, especially her desserts. Mollie come and sit next to me." said Artiom. Mollie walked into the dining room, it was a long room with a table that sat twenty-four people, it was long. The table was set for dinner up one end it even had a candelabra on it with lit candles. What the fuck is this all about. Thought Mollie, this is serious money. I wonder where his parents live. She sat down in between Artiom and his grandad.

"It's lovely to finally meet you, Mollie." said Andrei "Artiom has told us all about you, you're a teacher?"

"Yes, I'm a primary school teacher in Spain. Artiom hasn't told me all about you. Well not that you live in such a big house, he told me you are a farmer." replied Mollie giving Artiom a wide eye look, Andrei and Artiom laughed.

"Well, it's not something that I like to tell people, some people think you're bragging or showing off if you tell them about your family and where they live, so I keep quiet about it." replied Artiom. "And my grandparents are farmers, that is true."

"Artiom, do your parents live in a house this big as well?" asked Mollie.

"Yes, they do actually, but its six hours away in the other direction." replied Artiom.

"So, you grew up in a mansion?" said Mollie.

"Yes, I did, why does it matter where I grew up?" replied Artiom.

"It doesn't matter, I don't know any of this about you that's all." said Mollie. Artiom held Mollies hand under the table.

"Well, perhaps it's time for you to know all about me then, but not here, I'll tell you my life story later." replied Artiom. Mollie nodded, she was still in shock at the size of this house and now it sounds like Artiom comes from a very rich family, she felt excited and worried at the same time, what would he think of her if she told him about Rick? Olga came in with a large food trolley carrying roast potatoes, carrots, cabbage, parsnips, peas, mash potato, roast lamb, gravy and mint sauce. She laid it all on the table, the food was all presented in silver dishes.

"Would you like me to serve dinner?" asked Olga.

"No not tonight Olga, thank you." replied Irina "Please everyone serve yourselves to dinner, come on Artiom you start." Artiom nodded at his nan and served himself some lamb then passed the platter to Mollie. He carried on serving himself with the reast of the food and then passing the dish to Mollie and she passed it on to Andrei, so the food was passed around the table, soon everyone had served themselves with the roast dinner and following Artioms lead they all began eating. The food was delicious, and along with a few glasses of very nice wine they all felt like they were eating like royalty in a palace. Irina and Andrei were very talkative, and the conversation didn't stop. Brenda explained to them what had happened to Mollie, Penny and Marie last Friday night, and how Artiom had turned detective to find out where the girls were, then how lucky they were that Zac had fell in love with Penny, had seen them in a coffee shop with a photo of the girls and decided to help them rescue Penny and Mollie. Artioms nan and grandad asked Artiom if his parents knew what had been happening.

"No, I haven't spoken to mum or dad this week, I will tell them everything when I get back to Javea." said Artiom "I didn't want to worry them."

"Your mum will be phoning me tomorrow, can I say that I've seen you?" Irina asked Artiom.

"Yes, you can tell her everything nan, save me doing it." laughed Artiom.

Mollie watched the exchange of conversation between Artiom and his nan, apart from sitting around probably the biggest table she's ever seen in a huge dining room, inside a house the size of a palace it was just a normal conversation between a nan and her grandson. Who was Artiom really? wondered Mollie. Was he a rich Russian Prince? She was looking forward to hearing him tell her about himself later, she realized she didn't know much about him at all.

Once dinner had been eaten Olga came back and cleared the table, she put all the dishes and plates back on to the food trolley and left the room.

"I wonder what dessert is going to be?" said Artiom.

"Your favourite of course." replied Andrei "When we told cook you were coming for dinner tonight, she started rushing around the kitchen like a mad woman, she loves it when you come to visit."

"So do you Andrei." laughed Irani "Cook isn't allowed to make desserts every day, only weekends and special occasions like when Artiom comes to visit." Olga came back with the food trolley full of desserts, every one's eyes lit up at the sight of the desserts, there was a large trifle, a black cherry gateau, strawberry cheesecake and Artioms favourite large meringues topped with banana, strawberry nuts and hot chocolate sauce.

"Wow" said Bill "I think you might be having dessert for the rest of the week Andrei. Andrei laughed.

"I hope so." he Replied. Mollie looked at all the different desserts.

"So Artiom, which one is your favourite?" she asked.

"Have a guess?" replied Artiom. Mollie had already guessed it must be the meringue dish, she knew Artiom liked meringues.

"I think it must be the meringues, I know you love them." replied Mollie.

"Yes, this is my favourite dessert and Cook has been making this for me all my life." replied Artiom. He picked up a meringue it didn't even go on to his plate, he took a big bite from it.

"Mmmm these are so good." He said with a big mouthful of meringue. Everyone laughed at him and started helping themselves to dessert.

Coffee followed the dessert then it was time for bed. Irani and Andrei wished everyone a good night's sleep and Olga showed them all to their rooms for the night. Each room had a huge four poster bed in it and a large en suite bathroom.

"Wow, this is unreal, how come Mollie didn't know Artioms grandparents live in a house this big?" said Sue.

"Maybe, like he said he doesn't like to tell people, I mean why would he tell anyone anyway?" replied Bill. Climbing up into the huge bed.

"Do you think this means Artiom is actually really rich? He does drive a nice car?" said Sue.

"Yes, he has got a nice car, I think he must be fairly well off, let's hope Mollie keeps hold of him, she could do a lot worse." replied Bill. Sue got in to bed she began imagining what sort of wedding Mollie and Artiom would have, it would be big she was sure of that, and would he buy Mollie a big villa in Spain? She fell to sleep thinking of what sort of outfit she would wear to Mollies and Artioms wedding.

Zac closed the bedroom door, Penny was sitting on the bed, her feet didn't touch the floor.

"This bed is so big I had to climb up to get on it." laughed Penny, she was feeling nervous and excited at the same time, this was the first time her and Zac had been alone together. Zac could feel Penny's nerves he went over to her and sat next to her on the huge bed.

"Look Penny, we don't have to do anything tonight, let's just get in bed and cuddle up, we have got the rest of our lives together, let's take it slow, we have only just met, I wouldn't ordinarily sleep in the same bed with a girl this quickly." he said To Penny. But Penny wasn't thinking like that she wanted to get in bed with Zac and make love to him, she knew he was the one for her, he was the man she had been saving herself for.

"Zac, I am nervous because I haven't ever been in bed with a man before to sleep or anything else, but I want to with you. I don't want to wait. Look at this room, look at this bed, it's the most romantic room I've ever seen. Let's get in bed and see what happens." Zac reached over and kissed Penny, when Zac kissed her, she felt tingles from her lips to her toes, she kissed him back.

Mollie came out of the bathroom to see Artiom sitting up in bed.

"Ok Mollie, let me tell you about myself." said Artiom. Mollie climbed into the king size bed next to Artiom.

"Is this your room?" asked Mollie.

"Yes, it's my room, when I was little it was filled with my toys, I think they are in the attic now." replied Artiom. "My family are rich, they own a lot of land, farms and businesses in Russia, I am lucky I know that. I don't have to work, but I enjoy being a personal trainer, I am going to open my own gym in Javea soon., I just haven't found the right premises. I'm sorry I didn't tell you about myself when we first met, it's just I want people to like me for me." Mollie understood Artioms reasons for keeping his wealth a secret. There is a lot of people that would just see him as a cash machine if they knew.

"Why do you live in Spain? Why did you choose Javea?" asked Mollie.

"I visited Javea with my friends when I was younger, I felt at home there." replied Artiom.

"Just like me." said Mollie. Artiom nodded.

"Does it change anything about us? Do you still like me as much?" asked Artiom. Mollie didn't just like Artiom she loved him.

"Artiom, I love you. I would still love you if you're a millionaire or only had 5 cents to your name." replied Mollie, she kissed him hard on the lips.

"I love you too Mollie. But there's something I need to ask you." said Artiom. Mollie felt sick she knew what he was going to say, should she admit it or deny it?

"What is it?" asked Mollie she wished she could turn the clock back.

"A friend of mine told me that you have been having a thing with your boss?" said Artiom "I told him you wouldn't do that to me, but then I've been thinking about it and why did he always let you stay in his apartment?" asked Artiom. Mollie looked at the man she wanted to spend her whole life with, she felt sick, she knew she should tell him the truth, but she also knew if he found out about her and Rick, he would end their relationship.

"What? Who said that? No way would I do that to you Artiom, especially not with Mr Wozniak. I mean I do flirt a bit with him, you know just joking, that's all, my god some people are just troublemakers. I love you Artiom, you must know that I would never actually sleep with someone else, you are the only man for me." lied Mollie. She decided that she would risk denying the fling with Rick, I mean Rick isn't going to admit to it so unless someone has photos or video evidence, she will deny everything. Artiom pulled Mollie into his arms he wasn't sure whether she was going to admit to sleeping with Rick or not. He had been sent an anonymous message telling him about Mollie and Ricks fling, so he had paid someone to follow her, and he had seen the photos of Mollie and Rick entering and leaving the apartment on the same days within 10 minutes of each other, they were inside the apartment for an hour each time, unless she was cleaning the apartment it was obvious what they were up to. But Artiom still loved Mollie and didn't want to lose her.

"I love you Artiom, you do believe me, don't you?" said Mollie.

"Yes, I believe you Mollie, and I love you too." replied Artiom. He switched off the light.

The next morning, they all had a hearty breakfast in the dining room, there was bacon, eggs, sausages, mushrooms, toast plus fruit and croissants all freshly baked.

"This has got to be the breakfast I've ever eaten." said Zac "And these croissants are as good as any baked in France."

"Where abouts in France are you from Zac?" asked Steve they hadn't really found much out about Zac yet.

"Paris. I was born in Paris, and I lived there until I was 12." replied Zac.

"What made you leave Paris?" asked Steve.

"My parents both died within a year of each other, I was sent to London to live with my mother's cousin." replied Zac. The room went quiet everyone was listening to Zac story. "But things didn't go too well. He was a bully, he would hit me with a stick that he kept next to his chair. He was an old man, but he could still hit me hard." Penny had tears in her eyes listening to Zac tell his story, it was the first time she had heard Zac talk about himself. "One day I had had enough, I decided that I couldn't live with him anymore, I was 17 by then, I had learned to speak English and I was working in a café in Covent Garden. I had made friends with a guy that worked in a restaurant next door to the café and he offered me his sofa until I found myself a room somewhere, then luckily his flat mate moved out to move in with his girlfriend so I took over his room, anyway I

worked myself up to be the manager of the café, I met a Russian girl, we

became a couple and then she wanted to move back to Russia. I got the

job in the club by chance, Margot's niece was a friend of my then Russian

girlfriend, we didn't last very long together in Russia." said Zac sadly.

"Why what happened? asked Penny.

"She didn't like me working at the club, even though she had helped me

get the job, we drifted apart, you can't have a relationship if one of you

doesn't trust the other one, it doesn't work. So, she moved out and I

never saw her again. The End." said Zac and he helped himself to some

more bacon.

"Wow" said Penny "and here you are now on your way to a new life in

Spain with me." Zac looked at Penny and smiled.

"Yes, and I feel like I'm the luckiest man alive." replied Zac. Penny

blushed, not at what Zac had just said but at the memory of what they did

last night. She was still tingling at breakfast. The conversation went on to

their journey home, they decided to drive to Narbonne and stay in the

same Ibis hotel as they stayed in on Sunday night and then be back home

in Javea by Thursday night. Once they had all finished breakfast, they

packed their bags and thanked Irina and Andrei for their hospitality and their kindness. Artiom hugged his grandparents and promised to visit again soon. They got back in the cars and Bill followed Artiom down the long driveway and out of the large black metal gates. They drove back down the long narrow lane without passing any other cars and turned back on to the motorway.

CHAPTER 32

Sean went back over the hospital to see Marie, the girls decided to stay at home, they were watching the TV and painting their nails. Marie was sitting up in bed reading a magazine when Sean arrived.

"Hi Marie, you look better." said Sean he kissed Marie on the cheek.

"Do I? I feel much better than I did this morning, did you do the shopping ok?" asked Marie, she had put some make up on after Laura had left and it made her feel more like herself.

"Yes, shopping all done. I think Hannah and Grace are pulling a fast one though, an eyeliner went in the trolley today." smiled Sean. Marie rolled her eyes.

"You need to watch them two, they try it with me every week." smiled Marie. Sean gave Marie the coconut shower gel.

"That's lovely, thanks Sean, I'm going to have the bandages off tomorrow, I can't wash my hair yet, but I will be able to shower." Marie put the shower gel on her table and showed Sean the giant get well card and gifts that Laura had brought in with her.

"That's nice of them, was Laura, ok?" asked Sean.

"Yes, Laura was fine, we just talked about how good it is that someone knows where Mollie and Penny are." replied Marie, she didn't want to tell Sean she has told Laura about him cheating on her for 18 months, living a double life in the UK with this woman and their baby. Marie wished she hadn't said anything to Laura she knows Laura will tell everyone. She shouldn't have told her.

"What did you have for dinner?" asked Sean.

"It was chicken and chips, I ate the chicken but not the chips." replied Marie.

"Why what was wrong with the chips?" asked Sean, he knows Marie loves Chips.

"Nothing, but I'm on a diet, I know I've put weight on, it's down to eating crap food all the time. I'm going to lose a few stone. I hate being so fat." said Marie.

"You're not fat Marie." said Sean. He had noticed that Marie had put on weight over the last couple of years. She doesn't eat that much food but the sort of food she does eat is fattening, chips and white bread, crisps and chocolate. Tracey has a much healthier diet. She only eats brown bread and loads of fruit and vegetables. Sean had lost weight since he had been with Tracey, because her cooking is a lot healthier, but he wouldn't tell Marie this, he had hurt her enough already.

"Well, I feel fat and old, so I'm going to change my eating habits." replied Marie.

"Has the doctor said when you will be able to go home yet?" asked Sean. Marie looked at him she thought he probably wants to go back to the UK to his new little family.

"No, he hasn't said anything yet, I'll ask him tomorrow, when I get home will you be able to stay on a few more days just to help me get back on my feet?" asked Marie. She wasn't going to let go of him just yet. Sean didn't really want to stay any longer than he had to, but he had already planned to be in Spain for 2 weeks.

"Yes, I'm sure I can, as long as I'm back in the UK for work like planned." replied Sean. More like Tracey the slag wants you back as soon as possible. Marie wondered what Sean had told Tracey, she probably thinks Marie is a nut case. Sean stayed for a couple of hours. They chatted about Hannah and grace, about when they were little girls all the funny things they used to do. Marie gave Sean the box of chocolates Laura had brought in.

"Give these to the girls, they can open them tomorrow after school, tell them to go to bed when you get home otherwise, they will stay up until midnight." said Marie.

Sean kissed Marie good night and headed home. Marie watched him go, she couldn't imagine not seeing him every few weeks, she wasn't ready to let him go yet.

When Sean arrived home the girls had showered and were watching TV in their pyjamas.

"Hi dad, how's mum?" asked Hannah.

"Mum's ok, she looked more like her old self." replied Sean "She said to tell you two to go to bed when I got home, so goodnight."

"What? We don't up to bed yet!" said Grace "We go up at 11."

"No, you don't Grace, you go up at 10, so off you go." replied Sean. He wanted the girls in bed so he could phone Tracey from downstairs.

"Ok, night dad." said Hannah, she went over and kissed Sean goodnight.

"Night dad." Said Grace, she kissed Sean goodnight too. Then the girls went up to bed. Sean got a beer from the fridge and sat on the sofa he phoned Tracey.

"Hi, it's me." said Sean.

"Hi Sean, how's things?" replied Tracey.

"I've just got back from the hospital, Marie is a lot better, she didn't take the overdose to kill herself, she was just really upset." replied Sean.

"That's good, she won't do it again then?" asked Tracey.

"No, she knows it was a stupid thing to do, she is talking about losing weight and stuff, so I think she is looking toward a future without me in it." said Sean.

"That's good to hear Sean." replied Tracey.

"I'm going to stay here for the 2 weeks like I planned anyway. I'll help Marie settle back in at home then come back to the UK." said Sean.

Tracey didn't really want Sean to stay in the house with Marie, but she didn't tell him that.

"Ok, no worries, Ronnie is missing you." said Tracey.

"I'm missing him too, and I'm missing you, Tracey." replied Sean. They carried on talking about Ronnie and made plans for a little holiday in Cornwall for when Sean got back. Sean finished the phone call. Grace crept back up the stairs she had come down to get a drink of water but had heard Sean talking on the phone, so she sat on the stairs and listened to him talking to Tracey. When the call was finished Grace crept back up to bed. She felt sad knowing her dad loved Tracey and Ronnie so much. It wasn't fair thought Grace. He was our dad first.

CHAPTER 34

Laura couldn't wait to get to work, she had some gossip that was going to blow the socks of everyone. She had already told Rick the gossip yesterday when she'd got home after visiting Marie.

"How is Marie?" asked Rick.

"Marie is ok considering." replied Laura.

"Considering?" asked Rick.

"Considering Sean has been having an affair for 18 months with some tart he met in the UK." replied Laura. Rick looked wide eyed at Laura.

"Did Marie tell you that?" asked Rick.

"Yes, she told me everything, basically Sean has been living a double life over there, he even has a baby boy with this tart." replied Laura.

"Wow, I can't believe it. Sean would be the last person I would expect to be unfaithful, he is so nice." Said Rick, in shock. Laura looked at Rick with the urge to pick up a kitchen knife from the draining board and stab him with it. Now she knew for definite Rick had been shagging Mollie the slag she hated Rick, she really hated him.

"Did you know Mollie has a boyfriend?" asked Laura casually. Rick did

know, yes. Why was Laura saying this? What has Marie told her.

"Yes, he is Russian I think." said Rick, he turned his back on Laura and

started on chopping the vegetables for dinner. Laura wasn't finished with

the conversation.

"He's named Artiom, and he is a personal trainer. Marie says he really

loves Mollie. He obviously doesn't know she is a two-timing little slag."

spat Laura. She was winding herself up. Rick started to feel uncomfortable

he feared Laura when she starts ranting.

"Well, you don't actually know she is two timing him, do you?" said Rick.

Which was the wrong thing to say. Laura saw red, she picked up the large

kitchen knife from the side and pointed it at Ricks face.

"Marie has told me you and Mollie have been shagging in our apartment

Rick. So, stop fucking lying. She also said Mollie the slag was going to

finish with you. So, there you go, you've been dumped by your bit on the

side. I wonder if Artiom knows about you and Mollie? He might just have

to find out. I hate you, Rick. I really hate you. I could stab you right now I

hate you that much. But I won't because I'm not going to prison. But if

you cheat on me once more, I'm going to divorce you and tell everyone what a horrible sleazy piece of shit you really are." Laura put the knife

down, she was shaking with rage.

"I'm sorry Laura. I promise I won't do it again. I didn't mean to, but she

wouldn't leave me alone. She started it all. I'm glad it's finished I was

going to tell Mollie it was over to leave me alone, honestly I was." said

Rick squirming. Laura didn't believe him. She would never believe

anything Rick says again.

Laura looked around the office she was on her own. She opened her

drawer and put her hand inside she could feel the silky fabric of Mollies

skimpy knickers. She wanted to wear them herself. She took them out and

put them in to her handbag then went to the ladies toilets, she was

sweating with excitement. Laura went into a cubicle and took the red silky

thong out of her handbag, her heart was racing fast, she lifted her skirt

and took off her own white cotton mummy knickers and slipped on

Mollies thong. Laura felt the silky fabric against her skin, she felt sexy. She

decided to keep them on. Laura folded up her own knickers and put them

in her bag then she left the cubicle. She was alone in the toilets, she

wanted to see what the thong looked like on her, so she lifted her skirt

and looked at her reflection in the mirror. The Image of herself wearing

Mollies thong sent tingles through her body, she felt a rush of excitement, she felt sexy. So, this is what Rick likes to look at. Laura put her skirt down before someone came in and saw her looking at herself in a sexy red thong with her skirt up around her neck. Laura went back to the school office and sat back at her desk. It wasn't long before the teachers started to arrive. They came into the school office to sign in for the day.

"Hi Laura, how was Marie?" asked one of the teachers.

"Hi, Marie is doing really well, she looks battered and bruised but she will recover from that, it's what Sean has done to her that will take her longer to recover from." said Laura. This got the attention of the teachers in the office. They all turned to look at Laura.

"What has Sean done?" asked one of the teachers.

"Well, Marie told me yesterday that Sean has been living a double life back in the UK." replied Laura. She was enjoying the look of shock on the teachers faces. If only they knew she was wearing Mollies knickers as well.

"A double life? What with another woman?" asked another teacher.

"Yes. Her name is Tracey, and they have a baby boy together." replied Laura.

"No Way!" came the replies "Poor Marie!"

"You just never know what is going on in a marriage do you?" replied Laura. She was feeling quite important sitting there at her desk gossiping about Marie wearing Mollies knickers. The teachers were all shaking their heads, calling Sean a bastard and making plans to visit Marie once she was home. The children started to arrive on the school buses and the teachers all went to the classes ready to start the days teaching. Everyone that came into the school office stopped for a little gossip with Laura about Marie and Sean. Everyone felt sorry for Marie, Sean was the bad guy. Laura wondered what they would say if they knew Rick and Mollie had been shagging each other behind Laura's back? Would they all feel sorry for Laura? Laura hoped no one else would find out. Not now their sordid little affair was over. Rick came into the office.

"Hi Laura, everyone is talking about Sean having an affair? Did you tell anyone?" asked Rick. Laura looked at her husband, she still fancied him.

"No, they didn't hear it from me. I wouldn't gossip about something like that." replied Laura.

"Good, it's not a nice thing to be gossiping about. I'm going to be in my office looking through some paperwork, in case anyone wants me." said Rick. Laura watched him walk out of the office. She wasn't ready to give up on her marriage. She waited until Clara arrived, she oversaw the uniform shop and when Laura was out of the office Clara would answer the phone and deal with visitors. 10 Minutes later Clara arrived, Laura filled her in on the gossip about Marie and Sean, Clara like everyone else was gob smacked.

"Do you think you could cover for me Clara? I just need to pop this paperwork down to Ricks office." asked Laura.

"Yes, no problem." Replied Clara. Laura picked up some paperwork and walked down to Ricks office, she knocked on the door.

"Come in." replied Rick. Laura went in, Rick looked up.

"Laura, what's up?" he said. Laura closed the door then locked it.

"What are you locking the door for?" asked Rick feeling confused. Laura didn't answer him, she walked around to Ricks side of the desk and lifted her skirt, Ricks eyes nearly popped out of his head when he saw the thong Laura was wearing. Laura bent down and kissed Rick on the lips, Rick couldn't believe this happening he kissed Laura back.

Clara was on the phone when Laura came back to the office.

"Hang on, Laura is here now, I'll pass you over." said Clara. She handed the phone to Laura, she thought Laura looked a bit flushed and her hair was messy, I wonder what has she been up to with Rick in his office? Clara thought smiling to herself. A few minutes later Rick was in the office, Clara noticed he too was flushed, and his shirt looked creased up not its normal ironed to an inch of its life look. Rick bent down and kissed Laura.

Well, that confirms things, decided Clara, they have definitely just been shagging in his office, wait until I tell everyone. She didn't have long to wait. Rick and Laura both left the school at lunchtime, together. Something they had to do at home apparently. Clara told just about every member of the staff during the lunch break about the flushed faces of Mr and Mrs Wozniak following a meeting between them in Ricks office and the kiss he gave Laura before they both left school together on urgent business at home. So much gossip going around The Elizabeth College today.

Rick and Laura didn't go home, they went to their holiday apartment. Once inside Laura told Rick to go into the lounge and wait for her, she had another surprise for him. Laura went into the bedroom with Mollies overnight bag in it, she took out a black lacey thong and the see through black lacey negligee. She was getting a hot flush just touching Mollies underwear. Laura went into the bathroom and changed into Mollies black thong and negligee. She looked at herself in the mirror, she liked what she saw, she still had a good body, probably thanks to all the sport she used to play when she was younger, she'd never worn sexy underwear before, she didn't know this was Ricks thing. She was feeling excited at seeing his reaction. Rick didn't know what he had done for his luck to change twice in one day, Laura walked into the lounge in Mollies thong and negligee,

Rick knew they belonged to Mollie but, that just made him feel more

excited. Laura couldn't wait any longer she pulled Rick into the bedroom.

Clara was smiling at Rick and Laura when they arrived back at school. Rick

went down to his office and Laura sat back down at her desk.

"All ok at home?" asked Clara grinning.

"Yes, fine thanks, all ok here?" replied Laura wondering what Clara was

grinning at her for.

"All fine here, nothing to report. So, what did you go home for? Or is it

private?" asked Clara still grinning. Laura realised Clara had guessed what

they had been up to. She felt herself blushing.

"We just needed to do a couple of things at home." said Laura, trying to

look busy on her computer.

"Urgent, was they? You couldn't have waited until later?" asked Clara.

"Actually, no it couldn't have waited." replied Laura she wasn't going to

tell Clara they had been for sex in their apartment while she was wearing

Mollies underwear. She was still wearing the black lacey thong, she took it

off, but Rick told her to keep it on, he wanted to think about her wearing

in the school office. Laura changed the subject, but Clara knew what they

had been up to. If only you really knew, thought Laura smiling.

CHAPTER 35

Artiom pulled off the motorway and into the Ibis Hotel in Norborne

France. Ant pulled in and parked beside Artiom. They all got out of the

cars and stretched their legs. Brenda had made the booking, so she went

into the hotel first and up to the reception, the man behind the desk was

the same man as before. He remembered the group and welcomed them

all back so soon. Brenda explained they had booked one extra room this

time and it will only be for one night again. Once they had all received

their room keys, they went to the restaurant to see if they could book a

table for ten. The restaurant was quiet, and the waiter said the table will

be ready in 15 minutes.

"Just enough time to use the loo then." said Brenda. They all agreed and

said they would all meet down in the restaurant in 15 minutes.

They all arrived back in the restaurant 15 minutes later all feeling hungry

and in need of an alcoholic drink. They sat at the table set for ten and

looked at the menu it was the same meal of the day as before, the waiter

came and they all agreed to order 4 bottles of wine 2 red and 2 white, when the waiter came back with the wine, they were all ready to order

their food. Ant and Bill poured out the wine into everyone's glass.

"Let's do a little toast to us for going to Russia and getting our girls back."

said Bill. They all raised their glasses in a toast.

"To us on getting our girls back" they all sang. Then Karen rose her glass in

the air.

"A toast to Brenda and Sue for punching that bitch Margot on the nose

and knocking her out." said Karen.

"To Benda and Sue for knocking that bitch Margot out." they all toasted

Brenda and Sue.

"Well, she deserved it." said Sue defending their attack on Margot.

"Yes, she absolutely did bloody deserve it." agreed Karen "although I'm

never going to piss you two off." Everyone laughed and Artiom started so

hum the theme tune to Rocky.

"Oh, stop it Artiom. Or Brenda will punch you on the nose." laughed Sue.

The food arrived and they all enjoyed a relaxing dinner, talk was about the

past few days, Mollie and Penny told the stories of everything that had

happened to them, and Mollie said she was determined to help the girls

that are still trapped in the clubs and brothels. She didn't know how she

was going to get them help, but she was going to. She had promised them she wouldn't forget about them. Soon the food had been eaten and the wine finished.

"We're off to bed." said Penny holding Zac's hand. She kissed everyone goodnight and agreed to meet at 8am for breakfast then they went up to their room. Penny and Artiom wasn't far behind them. The oldies watched them go.

"Well, what a week we've all had." said Brenda. The others all nodded in agreement.

"Shall we have a brandy to end it on a good note?" suggested Ant.

"That's the best thing you've said all day." replied Brenda. They called the waiter over and ordered the brandies. The waiter told them to go into the bar he would bring them in. They did what they were told. The bar was empty apart from one couple sitting up the bar. They sat at a table and the waiter brought the brandies over to them.

"Enjoy." he said as he put the tray of brandies on their table.

"We will, thank you." replied Ant. They all took a glass Bill raised his in the air.

"Thank you, god, for giving us our girls back." he said. The others all repeated him. Once they had finished their brandies, they all retired up to bed. It was gone midnight now and they had to be down at breakfast at 8am.

They all slept well, the wine and then the brandies probably helped. Artiom and Mollie were first down for breakfast they sat down at the table they had sat at last night, everyone else arrived together and sat down. The waiter came over and told them to help themselves to the breakfast buffet, he would bring tea and coffee to the table. The buffet was good, and they all managed to eat a hearty breakfast. Once they had finished at breakfast and packed up their bags, they gave in their hotel room keys and went out to the carpark. This last bit of the journey was homeward bound back to Javea. Artiom said he would drop Penny's parents off at Penny's house and then come over to Brenda and Ants house to pick up Mollie. Penny and Mollie had arranged to go and visit Marie in hospital before they did anything else. The drive back to Javea was straight forward and they arrived back in Javea by 6pm. Artiom dropped Steve and Karen at the end of Penny's Road.

"Thank you Artiom for everything you've done, you are a wonderful young man, Mollie is very lucky." said Karen and she hugged Artiom. Steve shook Artioms hand.

"Thanks, Artiom. For everything." said Steve. Penny hugged her parents.

"We won't be long. We just need to see Marie." said Penny.

"See you in a little while." waved Zac.

"See you both soon. Give Marie our best wishes." said Steve. Artiom drove off and Karen and Steve walked along the path to Penny's little house. Mollie was waiting for Artiom to pull into the drive, the others were inside the house. She jumped into the back of Artioms car and sat next to Penny, Zac had moved into the front seat.

"Ok, let's go and see Marie. I can't wait to see her." said Penny.

"I hope it's not too much of a surprise, us just turning up." said Mollie.

"I think Marie will be really happy to see you both." said Artiom as he drove towards the hospital.

CHAPTER 36

Marie started the day with fruit for breakfast, she likes fruit, so it wasn't too much hard work swapping it for her normal toast and jam. Then Doctor Dura came in and took her bandages of her head. Marie was dreading seeing how much hair was shaved off, but it was only a 1inch square bald patch on her head and it was towards the back of the top of her head so if she kept her chin upwards no one would see it anyway. The stiches were healing nicely. Marie asked if she could wash her hair and Doctor Dura asked a nurse to take Marie to the bathroom and wash it for her, so the stitches didn't get too wet or damaged. Marie had a shower then Nurse Helen washed her hair for her.

"Thank you, Helen, I feel so much better for that." said Marie. Nurse Helen dried Marie's hair with a hairdryer very gently.

"You could be a hairdresser if you get fed up with being a nurse." laughed Marie.

"I think I'll stick at nursing." replied Helen laughing. Marie put her nice pyjamas on once she was back in bed, she put some make-up on. She gave herself a quick spray of her new perfume then looked in her hand mirror, she liked what she saw, she felt so much better about everything today, she was hoping to hear some news about Mollie and Penny, if she hasn't heard anything by tonight, she had decided she will ring Artiom.

Sean came in to see her after lunch, she told him she was having a shower in the morning so not to come in early.

"Hi Marie, wow you look so much better today, how are you feeling?" asked Sean.

"I'm feeling so much better too, I'm so glad I've had the bandages off and I've had a shower and nurse Helen washed my hair and she blow dried it, I'm hoping Doctor Dura tells me I can go home on Monday. He won't let me go home today, so I've got to stay here over the weekend." said Marie.

"Why won't they let you out over the weekend?" asked Sean.

"I'm not sure exactly, but nurse Helen told me it won't be until Monday now. It's ok Sean, I know the girls are ok with you at home, I'll just take it easy until Monday." replied Marie.

"Yes, if the doctor thinks you should stay here the weekend, then you should. I'm going to cut the hedge tomorrow and wash the car." said Sean.

"That's good it's looking like a jungle out there, I nearly got lost putting the washing out." laughed Marie. Sean laughed at Marie he was happy to see her happy again. He held her hand.

"We will always be friends Marie. I can't imagine us not being friends, not just for the girls, but for each other." said Sean. Marie didn't say anything she didn't want to just be friends with Sean she wanted to stay married to him. They sat there in a comfortable silence for a few minutes. Then Marie spoke.

"I love you Sean, I can't just stop loving you."

"I love you too Marie." replied Sean.

"No. I love you the same as I did when we first met, nothing has changed for me. I will forgive you Sean, if you change your mind and come back to me, I will forgive you. I love you that much. I will never stop loving you. I don't want anyone else." said Marie "but I know you don't feel the same about me anymore, you say you love me but it's not the same love, is it?"

"No, it's a different love, but I do love you, Marie. I'll always love you." replied Sean. He had a single tear run down his cheek, Marie saw it and wiped it away. She had done all her crying. She didn't have any more tears left.

"Once I'm home you can go back to the UK. Go back to your new family. Spend this weekend with Hannah and Grace, tell them about baby Ronnie, why don't you Facetime him with them. I know I can't make you stay here with me. I love you too much to try to make you stay. I'm letting you go Sean." said Marie. Sean looked at Marie and for a moment he wanted to change his mind, he wanted to tell her that he didn't want to go to the UK he would tell Tracey he was staying here with Marie. With his wife. But he knew that wasn't what he really wanted. He really wanted to be with Tracey. He touched Marie's face.

"Thank you, Marie." he replied. They sat there talking about Hannah and Grace, Marie even asked to see a photo of baby Ronnie again. After a while Marie suggested Sean should leave. Go home and cut the hedge today so that he could spend the weekend with the girls having fun. They said goodbye to each other, Sean taking Marie's dirty washing with him.

"I'll come in tomorrow with Hannah and Grace." said Sean.

"Ok, not for long though. Take them out for lunch, they will enjoy that." replied Marie. She watched Sean walk out of her room. So that's that then she said to herself, you've let him go. She picked up a magazine and carried on reading an article on "Life after your husband leaves you for

another woman" Step number one: You have got to let him go. Well, that'
step one done. Thought Marie.

Marie's dinner of ham salad with coleslaw arrived, Marie enjoyed it and
decided she would be eating salads every day when she got home. She
thought she would be feeling a lot sadder than she was, she had accepted
that her and Sean's marriage was over. She thought about Mollie and
Penny again, she looked at the time it was 6:30pm I wonder where Artiom
is? She decided to ring him. She picked up her phone and scrolled down to
Artioms number but just as she pressed the call button she looked up and
saw Mollie and Penny standing in the doorway of her room. Marie
couldn't believe what she was seeing she dropped her phone and climbed
out of bed Mollie and Penny came running in to Marie they all hugged
each other. Marie felt her tears running down her face, but these were
tears of joy not sadness. Mollie and Penny let go of Marie.

"Oh, Marie, we thought you were dead, we couldn't believe it when we
heard you were alive." said Penny crying.

"How did you survive being shot in the head Marie?" asked Mollie with
tears streaming down her face.

"Apparently I have a thick skull." laughed Marie. Mollie and Penny wiped their tears away and laughed with her. Artiom and Zac were standing in the doorway.

"Come in Artiom, who's this?" asked Marie looking at Zac.

"This is Zac, my future husband. Zac meet Marie my other best friend." smiled Penny. Zac came over and double kissed Marie.

"Hello Marie, I'm really pleased to meet you, I've heard so much about you." said Zac. Marie sat there dumbstruck, she looked at Penny.

"Your future husband? well then congratulations to both of you. I think you two guys better pull up a chair because we have got some serious catching up to do." smiled Marie. They all sat around Marie's bed. Mollie and Penny told Marie everything that had happened to them and how they were going to find a way to help the other girls and young women that they left behind in Russia being forced to work in the strip clubs, the sex clubs and the brothels. Then Marie told them about Sean, living a double life in the UK with Tracey and Baby Ronnie for 18 months. Mollie and Penny were shocked.

"What are you going to do Marie?" asked Penny.

"I've let Sean go. I've told him he should go and live with his new family in the UK. We will always be friends. We still love each other but Sean's love is a different one to mine. My love for Sean will never change. He is my one and only." replied Marie. Mollie and Penny looked at their brave friend they both reached out to her and held a hand each.

"We will help you through this Marie. We are here for you." said Penny.

"You know you can phone us any time, day or night." said Mollie.

"Thanks. I'm just so glad you're back." smiled Marie.

"Thank fuck its Friday!" said Mollie "It's been a very long week."

COMING SOON!

SECRETS

FOLLOWING ON FROM TAKEN

ALL IS NOT WHAT IT SEEMS. LIES,

SECRETS AND A MYSTERIOUS

DEATH!

MORE GOSSIP, REVELATIONS

AND SCANDALS IN JAVEA.

Printed in Poland
by Amazon Fulfillment
Poland Sp. z o.o., Wrocław

79916511R00210